THE OFFICIAL MOVIE NOVELIZATION

Also available from Titan Books:

THE CABIN IN THE WOODS

The Official Visual Companion

THE OFFICIAL MOVIE NOVELIZATION

TIM LEBBON

BASED ON THE SCREENPLAY

WRITTEN BY JOSS WHEDON & DREW GODDARD

TITAN BOOKS

The Cabin in the Woods
The Official Movie Novelization
Print edition ISBN: 9781848565265
E-book edition ISBN: 9780857689702

Published by Titan Books
A division of Titan Publishing Group Ltd
144 Southwark St, London SE1 0UP

First edition April 2012
1 3 5 7 9 10 8 6 4 2

A CIP catalogue record for this title is available from the British Library.

Printed and bound in the United States.

THE
CABIN
IN THE WOODS
THE OFFICIAL MOVIE NOVELIZATION

ONE

Never did understand the whole kid thing, Gary Sitterson thought. *Mess your house up, drain your resources, and make you grow prematurely old.*

He held his mug beneath the coffee dispenser, setting on "strong." He'd have used "nuclear" strength if it existed; it was going to be a long day, and he was tired. Beside him Steve Hadley sighed, and Sitterson smiled to himself.

Besides, it's obvious for all to see: women are mad.

It had been brought to his attention more than once that this attitude made his job far easier.

"It's hormonal," Hadley said, continuing the rant which, if anything, was more of an expression of bemusement. "I mean, I don't usually fall back on, you know, 'It's women's issues'..."

"But child-proofed how?" Sitterson asked. Hadley, married and still childless, had been bemoaning the fact that his wife was preparing their home for the arrival of a child not yet conceived, though one for which they had been practicing for some time. "Gates and stuff?"

"No, no, dude," Hadley said. Bemusement was turning rapidly into exasperation. "She *bought* gates, they're stacked up in the hallway. She did the *drawers*! We're not even sure this fertility thing is gonna work and she screwed all these little jobbies where you can't open the drawers."

"At all?" Sitterson asked, holding his coffee mug halfway to his mouth. *What the fuck?* There was mad, and there was plain crazy-batshit. He'd met Hadley's wife briefly and, patently insane though she was, he'd not thought she was any higher on the scale than most women. But screwing all the kitchen drawers closed? What, to stop Hadley getting at the food so he'd go to bed and screw her instead?

"They open, like, an inch," Hadley said, illustrating with thumb and forefinger and shaking his head. His own coffee cup had overflowed once already, but he pressed the serve button again. Dude was definitely somewhere else today; that wasn't good. "Then you gotta dig your fingers in and fiddle with this plastic thing, a catch, lock, like a sorta..." He shook his head and grabbed his cup, spilling half of it. "It's a nightmare!"

"Well, I guess sooner or later—"

"Later!" Hadley spat. He shoved past Sitterson and started pumping dollar coins into the vending machine. Chocolate bars and bags of chips tumbled, and Sitterson thought, *He really* can't *get into his kitchen cabinets*.

"What I mean is—"

"She did the upper cabinets as well, man! Kid won't be able to reach those 'til he's thirty! Assuming, you know: *kid*. Hell, *she* can't even reach them—has to stand on a stool or call for me!" He looked into some depressing distance for a few seconds, then mused, "Wonder how the hell she got up there to drill."

"She chosen the kid's college yet?"

Hadley paused in tearing open a chip bag, staring at Sitterson as if, for a moment, he was going to rip open his own friend's throat.

"This isn't a fucking joke, Gary," he said.

"I know," Sitterson said, mock-stern. But he couldn't keep a straight face, and as his lips twitched and his eyes started watering with restrained mirth, Hadley shoved the food into his pockets and hefted the bundle of files under one arm. Coffee cup gripped in the other hand—still spilling, though almost empty by now—he pushed past Sitterson and left the room.

Still laughing, trying to calm himself, Sitterson picked up the white cooler box at his feet and went after him.

"Hold up!" he called. Hadley had started along the plain concrete corridor, starkly painted white walls echoing his offended footsteps. "Hey, Steve." Hadley paused and glanced back, a defeated smile softening his own features.

"Shithead," he said.

"Yeah, I know." Sitterson took a swig of coffee. "It's a talisman. It's an offering."

"Don't even—!" He shook his head. "Man, *you* have women's issues."

"Please," Sitterson said softly, feeling a little sad for his friend now. He knew how long Steve and his wife had been trying, and maybe he should try to empathize a little more. "You of all people—"

"Me of *no* people. It's a *jinx*! Guarantees we won't get pregnant, and it takes me twenty minutes to get a fucking beer."

"Look out," Sitterson whispered, spying movement along the corridor past Hadley. "Here comes trouble."

Trouble in this case was a tall, severe-looking woman in a white lab coat. Six feet tall even without the two-inch heels she wore, Wendy Lin was one of the few women ever to make Sitterson feel uncomfortable.

No wonder he'd always wanted to get into her panties.

She might have been beautiful if she wasn't so tense, and she mightn't have been so tense if she didn't choose to tie her hair back so tightly. Sometimes Sitterson thought that Lin must employ the aid of some arcane preening device to pull her hair back so far each morning. And just to make him more firmly convinced of his generalizations, she was quite patently mad.

"Stockholm went south," Lin said. No greeting, no preamble. And with news like that, it was hardly a surprise.

"Seriously?" Sitterson gasped. "I thought they were looking good."

"What cracked?" Hadley asked.

"I haven't seen the footage," she replied. "Word's just going around." Sitterson felt a chill at the news, but it was mostly one of excitement. With Stockholm gone, it made them that much more important.

"That scenario's never been stable," Hadley said. "You can't trust... what do you call people from Stockholm?"

"Stockerholders?" Sitterson grinned at Lin, knowing how she hated flippancy. She was as serious as her hairdo, and probably twice as tight.

"Ha!" Hadley coughed, making a gun with his fingers and shooting Sitterson for such a bad, sharp, quick joke.

"That means there's just Japan," Lin said, pointedly ignoring them both. "Japan and us."

"Not the first time it's come down to that," Hadley said. He chewed on a Snickers to cover his nervousness, but Sitterson could see the way his friend's eyes were shifting.

He's thinking about his kid that's not yet conceived, he thought. *And who can blame him?*

"Japan has a perfect record," Sitterson said, stating what they all knew anyway. And he admitted to himself that, yeah, okay, he felt a little nervous at the news as well. Even well-oiled machines fell victim to gremlins on occasion.

"And we're number two, so we try harder," Hadley said. He hated being beaten by anyone, but especially the Japs. If Sitterson was sexist—something he was aware of, and comfortable with—then Hadley's main fault was his casual racism. Sitterson had never brought him up on it, because it was just too uncomfortable. Too damn serious. And the only way he got by was by ignoring anything serious unless he had no choice but to confront it.

"It's cutting it close," Lin said.

The three of them started walking, passing beneath steadily glaring fluorescents and moving along the featureless corridor. The floor was power-floated concrete sealed against dust, the walls were unadorned and unbroken, and the ceiling hid a network of pipes and wires above its suspended panels. There wasn't a single nod to aesthetics. Identical doors were spaced at equal distances along one side, and behind the other wall was something else. Something that didn't have doors.

Their footsteps echoed dully, and around the corner sat three golf carts, their "charged" lights blinking green. The wider corridor before them was just as bare and featureless, its far end swallowed by perspective. Sitterson had walked it a few times. But why walk when there were wheels?

As usual, Hadley took control of the cart, with Lin and Sitterson sitting in the back.

"Yeah, cutting it close," Hadley said, dropping his vending machine haul onto the seat beside him. "And that's why it's in the hands of professionals."

"They hired professionals?" Sitterson asked, grinning at Lin's sour face. "What happens to us?"

"You guys better not be messing around in there," Lin said.

"Does this mean you're not in the betting pool this year?" he asked, raising an eyebrow and smiling. He liked to think that was his finest feature, a mischievous look that women found irresistible.

Statistics had yet to prove him right.

"I'm just saying that it's a key scenario." Damn, she really was the Ice Queen. Sitterson wondered idly whether her face would slide off her skull if he were to surreptitiously sever her hair band and relieve the pressure.

"I know what you're saying," Hadley said, pushing the electronic ignition. The cart started to purr beneath them. "But remember '98? That was the Chem department's fault. And where do you work again, Lin? Wait, it's coming back to me..." He accelerated away, and Sitterson half-stood to avoid spilling his coffee.

"Gonna be a long weekend if everybody's that puckered up," Hadley continued, quietly. Then he seemed to liven up, weaving the cart back and forth across the corridor, narrowly avoiding striking both walls several times.

"Damn it!" Sitterson said as he lost the battle and spilled coffee on his sharp-creased trousers. Wiping it with a napkin, he rolled his eyes at Lin, who regarded him coolly. He glanced down at the front of her lab coat. She always wore it large and loose, and he always wondered...

But when he glanced up again, her expression forbore any wondering. He rolled his eyes again. She blinked slowly and looked away.

Later, he thought. *When all this is over and the celebrations are starting, maybe—*

"Hey, you want to come over Monday night?" Hadley called back to him. "I'm gonna pick up a couple of power drills and liberate my cabinets." He laughed like a banshee, and barely slowed the cart to take the first ninety-degree corner.

Sitterson gave up and tipped the rest of his coffee out of the cart.

Monday, he thought. *This'll all be over by then.*

"Sure," he said.

◇ ◇ ◇

Dana Polk loved to rock and roll. Most girls her age were into some of the softer, safer, middle-of-the-road rock music that the new millennium had brought. She could listen to Coldplay if she had to, but for her they lacked edge. She could put up with Nickelback, if they were forced on her. But her preference as a thoughtful—some would say sexy, though she still had trouble applying that word to herself—sophomore, was music with... well, balls.

She loved to rock out, feeling the music driving her blood and increasing her heartbeat, and sometimes she thought that was part of the reason she stayed so fit. The best workouts she'd ever had—well, the *second* best—were in the mosh-pits at rock concerts.

And so what better music to pack to than the Foo Fighters.

Dave Grohl... now there was a man. Her friend Jules would issue an *Ewww* whenever Dana mentioned him. *He's too old for you by far, and too... hairy*. But he was a guy with edge. He had, as Dana's mother liked to say, "The Grrr Factor." He was also happily married, but that never stopped Dana's mind from wandering his way now and then.

She bopped and skipped as she packed, shirt flapping around her bare thighs, swinging an invisible microphone stand in front of her and launching into a chorus just when a guitar solo burst in. *Whoops*, she thought, feeling a blush of embarrassment even though she was on her own. Perhaps for now she should concentrate just on filling her weekend bag.

Dana glanced around her room, wondering what else she should take. She'd miss this place. The room was neat and restrained; books stacked mostly in alphabetical order, CDs stored in tidy piles. Unlike some students, she'd quickly imprinted her personality on the place, displayed most prominently in the several sketches and watercolors about which she'd been confident enough to frame and hang.

Most of them were portraits, or pictures of imaginary people, but a few were more abstract landscapes which Jules said she sometimes found spooky. Forest scenes with ambiguous shapes suspended in high branches. Fields of corn with shadows where there should be none. Dana thought they were just offbeat, but she supposed someone who wasn't living in her mind could justifiably see them as weird.

She ran her fingers along the bookshelves and pulled out a few political science textbooks. No harm in taking some reading, in case things were quiet this weekend. She threw in some art supplies, as well—stuff she never traveled anywhere without, including pencils and charcoals. Picking up her sketchpad, she started flipping through the pages.

Like any naturally artistic person she was eternally self-critical, but she could also remove herself to a distance and view the work objectively. And she knew that some of what she did wasn't at all bad. Sure, she could find something to criticize in *everything* she sketched, but that was the curse of a true artist. She flipped the pages, musing more upon her passion for art than the pictures themselves, until—

There he was. The son-of-a-bitch.

Gorgeous. Longish hair, glasses... the very epitome of a college lecturer. Damn it, if only she hadn't been so fucking stupid. But he was so handsome. Bastard.

She sighed, thought about finding a pair of jeans, and—

"What a piece of shit!"

Dana gasped, letting out a little shriek. She hadn't even heard Jules approaching.

"I rushed it," Dana said, recovering quickly and not taking her eyes from the picture.

"You know what I mean." Jules's voice was low and sultry, a natural attribute which she put to great use. "Why haven't you stuck that asshole's picture on the dartboard yet?"

"It's not that simp—" Dana began, but as she turned around, shock cut her off. For a second confusion overwhelmed her.

"Oh my God, your *hair*!" she gasped.

Jules struck a pose that would have made lesser men weep, and even strong men quake in their boots.

"Very fabulous, no?"

"I can't believe you did it!" Her friend certainly did look very fabulous. She'd been talking about going blonde for months now, but Dana had never believed she'd actually go through with it. Brunette had served her well, but Jules was nothing if not experimental. She sometimes called Dana "rock chick," but she was far from the stereotype that usually went with that term. Rock yes, chick no. Out of the two of them, it was Jules who wore that badge with pride.

"But very fabulous, right?" she asked again, scowling a false frown. "Hurry up with the very fabulous, I'm getting insecure about it."

"Oh God, no," Dana said, "it's awesome! It looks really natural, and it's great with your skin. I just didn't think you were ever gonna—"

"Impulse," Jules said. "I woke up this morning and thought, *I want to have more fun. Who is it that has more fun?*" Still posing, she ruffled up her hair and pouted. "Marilyn, dahling."

"Manson?"

"Monroe! Imbecile."

"Curt's gonna lose it," Dana laughed.

"He'll have more fun too," Jules said. "And so will

you..." She snatched the sketch pad from Dana and stared at it, scowling at the image. "...while we are burning this picture."

Dana grabbed the pad back, her good humor slipping just a little. She understood that Jules was being protective of her, and angry at the man who'd hurt her. But really, it was only Dana who knew everything that had gone on.

"I'm not ready to," she said. "And seriously, this isn't all his fault."

"What's not his fault?" Jules asked. Her posing and pouting was over now, and she stalked Dana's room like a cat looking for a mouse. "Being thirty-eight and married, fucking his student, or breaking up with her by email?"

"I knew what I was getting into," Dana said, looking at the picture and silently acknowledging how much crap that was. She hadn't known at all. In retrospect she'd come to understand it all, but that was what learning by mistakes was all about.

"Right," Jules said. "Dana Polk, homewrecker. Puh-*leeze*." She moved to the dresser, and started rifling shamelessly through Dana's open drawers. Dana loved Jules as a best friend, but sometimes she was so damn... *close*.

"You know what I—" she began.

"You know what you're getting into this weekend?" Jules asked, her mood brightening again. She was holding up Dana's little wine-colored bikini. "This. And if Holden's as cute as Curt says he is, possibly out of it as well."

"That's the *last* thing—" Dana said, then she saw the truth behind Jules's smile. "If you guys treat this like a set-up, I'm gonna have no fun at all."

"I'm not pushing," Jules said, doing exactly the opposite. She crossed to Dana's bed, flipped up her suitcase's lid and ran her hands over the surface of the stuff she'd already packed. "Hmm. But we *are* packing the bikini. Which means..." She pulled the textbooks out and dropped them on the bed, one, two, three. "...we *definitely* won't have room for these."

"Oh, come on, what if I'm bored?"

Jules gasped and looked at her, and Dana closed her eyes, realizing just how lame that sounded.

"These'll *help*?" Jules said. "*Soviet Economic Structures*? *Aftermath of the Cultural...*?" She tossed one of the books theatrically across the bed, not even blinking when it bounced onto the floor.

If that cover is broken, the library will charge me, Dana thought.

"No!" Jules cried, grasping the remaining two books to her chest. "We have a lake! And a keg! We are girls on the verge of going wild— Just look at my hair, woman!"

Dana looked, and nodded, and she had to admit to herself, *Yeah, this has the feel of being an epic weekend.*

"It *is* great," she said, and she was about to add more when a voice called from the doorway—

◇ ◇ ◇

"Think fast!"

Curt had only been listening for a few seconds—well, maybe thirty... okay, perhaps a minute—and while the idea of snooping for longer on his girlfriend and her hot friend had its attractions, he couldn't bring himself to do it. He thought of himself as a decent guy, and decent guys didn't do things like that.

Besides, there was the risk he'd hear something he didn't want to. And he'd been timing himself.

So swinging around the corner into the room and throwing the football had seemed a suitable way to overcome his slight embarrassment. Perhaps he should have thought to check on whether both girls were dressed.

One of them let out a surprised yelp, though he didn't know which one. As the ball sailed between them and directly through the open window, he had an instant to register two facts about the view: one, his girlfriend's hair had changed color; and two, Dana was only wearing a shirt and panties.

It took him only a heartbeat to confirm that he liked both things.

"Well, faster than *that*," he said, grinning.

"Curt!" Jules snapped, but he was already darting into the room. He shoved them toward the window, and all three of them looked out to see what had become of the ball.

It was a nice street, with close-built three-story town houses, mostly given over to student accommodations, and a variety of vehicles parked along the curbside.

Some students had new cars bought for them when they came to college, others had to buy their own—gleam sat next to rust, but both seemed very much at home here. The whole place exuded a good vibe, and that's why Curt liked it so much.

Also out on the street was a guy dropping his duffle bag and rushing sideways into the road, hand reaching, arms stretching, feet leaving the road surface as he leapt. And the thrown football landed in his hands as if drawn by some invisible force.

The squeal of brakes was only slight—a perturbed gasp rather than an upset screech—and the car that touched his leg seemed to do so almost tenderly.

"Yes!" the guy said, holding the ball up in one hand. Then he became more contrite, backing out of the road and half-bending so he could look in at the car's driver. "Sorry," Curt heard him say. "Sorry. Move along."

"Niiice!" Curt breathed. Damn, the guy could catch. He detected disapproval battering him from both sides, so he remained looking out into the street. The guy saw him and waved up.

"Is that Holden?" Dana asked.

"Come on up!" Curt called, and he thought, *Is that interest I hear in her sweet little voice?* He took a step back so he could look from Jules to Dana, speaking to both of them. "Just transferred from State," he confirmed. "Best hands on the team. He's a sweet guy."

"And he's good with his hands," Jules said, looking pointedly at Dana.

Curt laughed out loud, then let his laughter fade away

as his expression dropped into one of embarrassment.

"Um, hi," he said to Jules. "I'm sort of seeing this girl, but, uh, you're way blonder than she is, and I was thinking we could..." He glimpsed the book she was holding to her chest, and abandoned the play. *Time for another angle.* "What is this?" He snatched the books from her, tugging lightly when she tried to resist. She growled, but he knew when her eyes were smiling.

"What are these?" he demanded. "What are you doing with these?"

"Okay," Dana said, "I get it, I'll—"

"Where did you *get* these?" Curt asked Jules, stretching the joke. "*Who taught you about these*?"

"I learned it from *you*, okay?" Jules gushed, holding one hand up to her forehead, feigning tears and storming breezily out of the room.

Curt was enjoying himself. He felt Dana's slight discomfort, but he was also enjoying denying her the opportunity to pull on her pants. His girlfriend sure chose some cute friends, that he *could* say. He leaned close to Dana, struggling to keep his eyes on her face and not those long, smooth legs.

"Seriously?" he said, voice anything but. "Professor Bennett covers this whole book in his lectures. Read the Gurovsky; it's way more interesting and Bennett doesn't know it by heart, so he'll think you're insightful.

"And you have no pants."

He smiled, threw the books on the bed and shouted out into the living room, "Holden! Crazy mad skills of catching!"

Behind him he heard Dana's small gasp of panic, and he glanced back to see her hauling her jeans up over her thighs and shapely behind.

Damn, he thought, *eyes off, Curt. Eyes off.*

As he left the bedroom Dana followed him out. He hoped he hadn't upset her. It was set to be a momentous weekend; the great outdoors, beer, and sex. But probably not in that order, and in far from equal quantities.

◇ ◇ ◇

Jerk, Dana thought, but it was with intense affection. Jules and Curt had been an item for over a year now, and she was really fond of her friend's boyfriend. He was hot, too, but not really her type. A little too... *jock* for her liking. Though she'd never say that to him, or even to Jules. She wouldn't want to hurt their feelings.

As she followed him out into the living room Jules was already opening the front door, and Dana had time to think, *Damn it, didn't brush my hair, are my jeans done up, did I button my shirt up because dammit I'm not wearing a bra yet and—*

Holden stood framed in the doorway. Dana caught her breath.

"You laid it in my hands, I did but hold them out," he said, smiling at Curt. He was even better looking close up than he'd seemed out in the street. Dark, strong, short hair—way shorter than any jock would choose to wear—and he had an easy smile that was completely unforced.

"There was the small matter of almost being hit by a car," Curt said.

"It's never a great catch unless there's a challenge attached." Holden tossed the ball to Curt, and grabbed a bag from beside his feet.

"Hey, I'm Jules," Jules said, holding out her hand.

"Hi," Holden said, eyes widening slightly. "Man, Curt did not exaggerate."

"That's a first," Jules said, but Dana could see how flattered she was. She was surprised her friend didn't start giggling and hiding her face against her shoulder like a coy little girl. The compliment had sounded pure and honest, though—if it hadn't been, Holden surely would have come out with something smoother.

And then…

"Dude, this is Dana," Curt said.

"Hey," Dana said. *Hey?* Hey? *Couldn't she think of anything…?* But they locked eyes then, and Holden dropped his bag and walked past Curt to where Dana stood, making a point of closing the distance between them. Nevertheless, his three steps seemed to go on forever.

He shook her hand, his grip strong but gentle.

"I'm Holden," he said. "Really nice to meet you." He held her hand for just a little too long, then grinned and looked around at the others. "And thank you guys for letting me crash your weekend. I'll just put a disclaimer up front: you don't have to explain any of your in-jokes. I'll probably be drunk and think they're funny anyway." A soft frown. "Should I have left out the part about being drunk?"

"With hindsight, yeah," Curt quipped.

"Damn." Holden looked past Dana at her bedroom door. "Can I help anybody carry anything?"

"Thanks, but I'd better finish packing first," Dana said. She turned smartly and entered her bedroom again, looking at the open suitcase and the books spilled onto her bed, and the red wine-colored bikini Jules had insisted that she take. Her sketch pad still lay open on the bed beside the books, and her ex-lover's eyes stared at her, rendered with Dana's expert hand while they had still been together. Back then, she'd drawn him with love in his eyes. After what he'd done to her, even though she could not deny the feelings she still had for him, she didn't think she could ever draw him again. Not that she would ever want to.

She dropped the bikini into the case. Maybe there *would* be some swimming in the lake this weekend, after all.

◊ ◊ ◊

Jules had many fond memories of Curt's family Rambler. The recreational vehicle slept six at a push, but the three times she and Curt had used it, it had just been the two of them. And they'd made full use of all the space inside. One time, when they'd been parked up in the mountains, sun setting behind the peaks and bleeding orange down the mountainside, she'd sat on his lap in the driver's seat. Then, in neutral, he'd revved the engine. *Damn*, those vibrations. They'd used half a tank of fuel that night without going anywhere.

Now here it was, about to take them away again, and she was certain the memories she'd bring back from this weekend would be of somewhere else entirely.

Jules was glad to see the quiet, tentative communication going on between Holden and Dana. That scumbag lecturer had done a real job on her friend, and she hated it when Dana said, *I'm not ready to let it go yet*. It wasn't that she was weak or feeble, it was just that... well, maybe Dana thought about things too much. And with what he'd done, it didn't even need thinking about. He was a shithead, and she was better off without him.

You need someone to romance you, take your mind off him, she'd said, and Dana had replied, *No, not that*.

Well then, maybe you need a good screw, she'd said, and Dana had denied she needed that, either.

Maybe Holden's the one to give her whatever the hell it is she needs, she thought.

Dana was inside the Rambler storing their stuff, and Jules watched as Holden passed up her own suitcase, then the polite smile that passed between them. Was that a brief touch of hands on the suitcase handle? She couldn't tell from where she stood on the sidewalk, but—

Stop it! she scolded herself. It was up to the two of them now. She and Curt had done their bit. It was time for nature could take its course.

"That pretty much it?" Holden asked, turning around and looking at her. He had a film of sweat on his forehead. Well, maybe three suitcases *was* a little excessive for just one weekend.

"Fuckin' better be!" Curt said. "Jules, it's a weekend, not an evacuation."

Jules took a step closer to her boyfriend and prodded him in the chest.

"Trust me when I say there is *nothing* in those cases you won't be glad I brought."

"I'm shuttin' right up," Curt said. He raised one eyebrow, but Jules just smiled enigmatically and turned away. He loved it when she dressed up, and she wasn't about to reveal any of the surprises she had in store.

"Oh my *God*!" Dana said. She was standing in the Rambler's doorway looking along the street, and when Jules followed her gaze it took a moment for it to register.

Martin Mikalski. Marty.

◇ ◇ ◇

He'd been part of their close circle for a couple of years, and to outsiders it might have looked like a strange combination. But whereas Curt was the wildman jock, Dana the sweet young thing with a fiery centre, and Jules the opinionated blonde type—today, *literally*, Marty was the most unaffected of them all.

There were no airs and graces with Marty. He called it as he saw it, was totally comfortable with himself, and seemed to want for nothing. He cherished his friends, Jules knew—he'd told her enough times, stoned and relaxed—and he seemed completely unselfconscious. And he was funny.

If Jules had been born a guy, she'd told herself many times, she would have wanted to be Marty.

But as soon as she saw him and what he was doing, Jules snorted in disbelief. It was almost a laugh, she supposed. But not quite.

Marty had parked his car and was still smoking a huge bong while climbing out. It was an awkward maneuver, but he concentrated hard to maintain his balance and avoid knocking the bong against the doorframe. It looked to Jules as if he'd done this many times before.

They all glanced around to see who was watching, who might see, and whether there were any cops in the area. The police often cruised by at regular intervals, and sometimes if they were bored they'd park up and watch for any students they could hassle for something. It didn't happen much... but for them, something like this would have been pure gold.

"Marty..." she muttered, not quite knowing what to say.

"Fuck is wrong with you, bro?" Curt said, a little louder.

Marty took the bong away from his mouth and slammed the car door behind him. He blinked slowly.

"People in this town drive in a very counterintuitive manner, and that's what I have to say."

"Do you *want* to spend the weekend in jail?" Curt asked. "'Cause we'd all like to check out my cousin's country home, and not get boned in the ass by a huge skinhead."

Speak for yourself, Jules thought of quipping, but Curt sounded serious. And pissed.

"Marty, honey, that's not okay," she said instead.

"Statistical fact," Marty said. "Cops will never pull over a man with a huge bong in his car. Why?" And damn if he didn't take one more hit before continuing. "They fear this man. They know he sees further than they and he will bind them with ancient logics." He smiled, wide and honest, and then the faintest frown creased his forehead as he focused on Jules and asked, "Have you gone gray?"

"You're not bringing that thing in the Rambler," Curt said.

"A giant bong, in your father's van?" Marty asked as if the very suggestion was mad. Jules was trying not to smile, but it was hurting her face. She glanced sidelong at Curt and saw his simmering anger, but then she heard a muffled giggle from behind her. She couldn't tell whether it was Dana or Holden, or maybe both of them.

She was going to look down at her feet, but then Marty suddenly became more animated. He emptied the bong's water, removed the bowl, placed it into a recess inside the tube and pushed the entire length closed. Then he plucked a lid from the bottom and fitted it neatly on top, and the bong had become a silver thermos flask.

"What are you?" he asked Curt, maneuver complete. "Stoned?"

Curt broke. His tension went and he walked forward, clapping Marty on the shoulder. As they passed her by Marty gave Jules a quick wink. She rolled her eyes.

Dana and Holden got into the Rambler, and Marty leapt in after them.

"It's going to be a fun weekend," she said, probing to see whether Curt was okay. He held her tight, grabbed her around the hips and planted a quick, passionate kiss on the lips.

"Damn right it is," he said, and Jules smiled inside.

From inside the Rambler they heard Marty speak up.

"Dana, you fetching minx. Do you have any food?"

He's got the munchies already, Jules thought. And then she thought of the keg sitting in the RV and, notwithstanding that it was barely in the p.m., she thought that a drink might be a good way to commence their vacation.

She climbed in after Marty, Curt behind her, and when he slammed the door it felt as if their weekend had finally begun. She sat up front with him, and they grinned at each other, remembering their last weekend in this vehicle. He shook a little in his seat, and she giggled.

"Everybody ready?" Curt called, and there came a cheerful chorus of assent.

"Wagons ho!" Marty called.

"Go, dude!" Holden said.

"Let's burn daylight!" Dana whooped.

Curt laughed.

"Then let's get this show on the road!" He turned the key, Jules sighed as the Rambler vibrated beneath her, and then they were on their way.

◇ ◇ ◇

Free will is a precious commodity. It's relished as much as political freedom, and most people believe it is a central part of their existence, whether this conviction is a tenet of their religious beliefs or born of a more secular outlook. All five people in the Rambler considered it to different degrees, and believed that they oversaw their own destinies. Perhaps Marty thought about it more than most, but then he always had been a thinker rather than a doer.

In his early teens it had been conspiracy theories and fear of the Big Brother society, but his thinking now usually went deeper. Most people didn't see that in him at all—even the friends he had around him now—because for them, the drugs dulled his personality as much as they believe they dulled his senses.

But for all of them, belief in free will stemmed largely from not being aware of what was occurring all around them. Senses and perception only stretch so far, even if fueled—perhaps augmented—by a gentle drug intake, and a willingness to believe.

Further than those senses, and that awareness, was the *real* world.

◇ ◇ ◇

On the rooftop of the townhouse that had just been vacated, six figures watched the Rambler drive along the street and disappear into the distance. They observed for a couple more minutes after the vehicle had vanished, in case of a sudden return for something one of the kids had forgotten.

The six figures were made androgynous by their apparel: they wore clean-suits, full body outfits of an opaque material that hooded their heads, stretched down to gloved hands, then all the way down their legs to enclose their booted feet. The material around their boots was triple thickness and heavily bound by elastic around their ankles, and their gloves were similarly reinforced. Only their faces were exposed, though their mouths were covered with soft white masks, and the exposed skin of their cheeks and chins glistened with a gel that prevented the shedding of any dead skin cells or hair.

One of the figures—there was no way of telling whether he or she was the leader, because they were all identically dressed, and no body language at all distinguished one from another—pressed a hand to its ear, then spoke into a microphone. All had similar devices poking from the necks of their suits.

"Nest is empty, we are right on time." There was no telling from the voice whether it was a man or woman; flat, monotonous. The shape then tilted its head—as did all the others—listening to a voice from even further away, issuing orders that no one else could hear, of which no one else would ever be aware.

For the first time, a small element of superiority distinguished this shape from the rest of the group. Its hand rose and circled its index finger in the air, three times precisely. Every movement the shape performed was precise. There was no energy wasted.

"Go for clean-up," it said. "Go, go, go."

The six shapes walked to the rooftop door, opened it, and disappeared inside.

Clean-up began.

TWO

Haven't seen this one before, Gary Sitterson thought. *I wonder if he has any fucking idea what to expect?*

The thick metal door had just wheezed open as he and Steve Hadley approached, a soft breath of air wafting out around them as pressures equalized. The control room was always kept slightly pressurized, though he'd never been given a believable reason as to why. Some said it was to preclude the risk of chemical or biological attack, but that idea was countered by the fact that there were no air locks for entry or exit. And besides, who could attack them when no one knew they existed?

Others suggested that it was because people worked better and became less tired at slightly higher air pressure. Sitterson wasn't sure about that one, either. He guessed it was just a design aspect of the facility. Maybe a fuck-up with the ventilation system.

He held his breath until the soft gasp had passed,

then smiled at the slightly nervous soldier who was standing upright in front of them.

"Identification, please," the soldier said stiffly, holding out a handheld card reader.

Sitterson and Hadley plucked their ID cards from chains around their necks and passed them to the soldier, who bent slightly and swiped them over the reader. Soft beeps and a gentle green glow marked them as safe and known. Sitterson had always wondered what noise and color the reader would emit should a card not be recognized. *Probably a loud siren and a blast of red.*

And then the bullets would come.

"Mister Sitterson, Mister Hadley, thank you." The soldier stood straight again, and for a stunned moment Sitterson thought he might actually be about to salute. But perhaps he saw the look on Sitterson's face because, after a pause, he said simply, "Please come in."

They entered the control room, known generally, and unimaginatively, as Control. The soft whirr of machinery and air conditioning welcomed them, along with the occasional blip or beep from one of the many computers it housed. Where they stood, down in the room's lower level, there were two large tables with built-in monitors and phones, several closed files placed neatly on each surface. The chairs were identical, and tucked beneath the desks.

To their right as they entered, the upper level resembled a scaled-down version of a Houston control room, with banks of computers, flashing lights, switches and dials. Two large desks contained a riot of communication equipment and computer monitors, and two other desks housed a swathe of smaller computer screens, wires and cables snaking out of sight like a strange sea-creature's tentacles. Two comfortable wheeled chairs sat side by side not far from the doorway, ready for Sitterson and Hadley to occupy. They, too, were of identical design, but Sitterson could already tell that the one on the left was his. He'd sat in it enough to know it by sight.

On the far wall at the other end of the lower space, three huge screens hung side by side, with digital time displays and blank flat screens above, each empty at the moment, glowing a faint silver as they awaited the power surge and the images that would tell their story for today.

Hadley led the way up the short curving staircase, Sitterson behind him carrying a small cooler. The soldier followed them, obeying regulations to the letter. He had to see them sat down and plugged in before he would be permitted to return to the door.

He even *walked* stiffly, Sitterson noticed.

Maybe it's time to start fucking with him, he thought, but Hadley beat him to it.

"What's your name, soldier?"

"Daniel Truman, Sir."

"Well, this isn't the army, Truman, so you can drop the 'sir' shit. But Sitterson likes to be called 'ma'am.'"

They'd reached the top of the stairs, and Sitterson slid the small cooler beneath one of the communications desks.

"Or 'Honey Toes,'" he said.

"Yes, he will also answer to Honey Toes." Hadley wheeled Sitterson's chair over to him and took his own across to the other sizeable desk. He fiddled with the height lever and back regulator, as always, and returned them to the exact same position they'd been in when he first touched them. As always. "Are you clear on what's gonna be happening here?" he continued.

"I've been prepped extensively," Truman said. Still very formal, still very military. *This'll be an easy one to crack*, Sitterson thought.

"And did they tell you that being prepped is not the same as being prepared?" Hadley asked, not looking at the solider. He tapped a touchpad and lights flashed on his panel.

"They told me," Truman said. "I'll hold my post Mister Hadley. I'll see it through."

"Not much else you gotta do," Hadley said. "Stand watch, check IDs, shouldn't be a lot more than that. And you have to get us coffee."

There was a pause for a couple of seconds, and Sitterson couldn't help but glance back at the soldier standing behind them. He was smiling uncertainly.

"They also told me you would try and make me get you coffee," Truman said.

"Balls," Hadley said. Sitterson giggled, attracting his friend's attention. Hadley pointed at him then, speaking from one side of his mouth back over his shoulder, asked the soldier, "Can you make *him* get us coffee? With your gun?"

"*And* that you would try to make me do that," Truman said, his tone remaining unchanged.

Well I'll be damned, Sitterson thought. *He's not as uptight as he looks.* "It wasn't funny last time, either," he said aloud.

Hadley moved over to a bank of electronics, flicking switches all across the face, seemingly at random. The hum in the control room rose in volume and tone, becoming something like a soft moan, and the click and beep of electronic activity erupted around them.

Sitterson tapped away at his computer, the familiar tingle of excitement blossoming into a vague burning sensation that coursed through his body. It was all about to begin, and here at his fingertips sat the heart of everything that was to come. He accessed his internal emails, and confirmed that the clean-up had already been done. That was step one complete.

Glancing across at Hadley, he nodded once so that his companion—his friend—knew to initiate his own systems. In this room where so much was computerized, mechanized, and recorded, it was often the understanding between these two men which ensured that everything ran smoothly from beginning to end. Any monkey could press buttons, but it took someone special to understand the implications of each pressing.

Sitterson pushed away from his desk and swung around as he went, landing perfectly against one of the rear control panels. He felt Truman's eyes on him, and flushed with a flicker of pride. He shoved that down quickly.

This is nothing to be proud of, he thought, and he frowned, not sure where that had come from.

Screw it.

He lifted the cover from a row of three buttons and rested his thumb against the first.

"Let's light this candle up, boys," he said. "Up is go on your command." He flicked the buttons.

The three screens across the room came to life. Pale gray at first, and then a glaring white that lit the room to uncomfortable levels. Then they settled, each of them showing the initial image they'd been programmed to show: approach, outside, inside. This was the default setting.

"Lovely," Hadley said.

Sitterson wheeled back to his desk and thought about that coffee.

Soon, it would begin.

◇ ◇ ◇

She was taking things slowly, but it felt like they were moving faster than that. The air between them sizzled. She'd caught him looking at her a couple of times now, but not in the way most guys looked at her. It never hurt to be given a compliment, even though sometimes those compliments were silent and communicated through glances and smiles.

She suspected that he'd spotted her looking at him as well. That was why the game was so thrilling.

With Holden, though, he was looking at her with

a combination of interest and... what, bemusement? It must have been that; a tiny frown, eyes open in perpetual surprise. She'd only just met him, so she couldn't claim to read him just yet, but she hoped he was feeling the same as her. Interest, and surprise at how deep that interest already was.

Just another ploy to fuck you, Jules would say. *He'll act interested and deep, but in the end he just wants you to hold his dick. But hey, look at him—why not?*

"It's different," Dana whispered, and Marty looked up from rolling a selection of elegant joints.

"Huh?"

"Nothing, Marty," she said, and she nodded toward the objects of his labors. "They're nice. Anyone who didn't know you would think you're a dope fiend."

He grinned, ran his tongue along another paper and added another to the selection. They were all the same length and thickness, and she couldn't help but be a little bit impressed.

Curt was still driving, nodding his head lightly to the middle-of-the-road rock station they'd found on the radio. Dana had offered to bring along a handful of CDs, but Jules's wrinkled nose had persuaded Curt to decline. Jules was still riding shotgun, her attention flicking back and forth between the GPS and an open map book on her lap. An empty plastic cup was propped between her legs, and Holden was in the bathroom filling four more cups from the keg.

Dana found it fascinating watching him. He didn't spill a drop, even though the Rambler was now bouncing along an old road wounded with potholes and last maintained, she guessed, just after the Civil War. When the vehicle jumped he'd follow the motion of the jog with his hand, cup of beer rising or drifting left or right, foamy head licking at the lip but never quite slipping over. It was quite a talent.

He caught her watching him and smiled.

"Like steering into a skid," he said, offering her a cup.

Dana chuckled softly and took the drink, their fingers touching briefly. The Rambler bounced, Dana grimaced, and beer splashed onto her jeans.

"Shit."

"I hope this is the right road," Jules said. "'Cause right now it looks like the *only* road."

"What about that road-like thing we crossed back there?" Curt asked.

"Doesn't even show up on the GPS. It's unworthy of global positioning."

"It must feel horrible," Dana said distractedly, dabbing her jeans with a cloth.

"That's the whole point!" Marty shouted, startling them all. "Get off the grid! No cell phone reception, no markers, no traffic cameras… Go somewhere for the goddamn weekend where they *can't* globally position my ass. This is the whole issue."

"Is society crumbling, Marty?" Jules asked without looking up from the map. She was teasing him and, Dana thought, mocking him a little. Marty was too kind or too obsessed to notice.

"Society is *binding*. It's filling in the cracks with concrete. No cracks to slip through anymore. Everything is recorded, filed, blogged, chips in our kids so they don't get lost... What's the use of free will when nothing you do is your own anymore? Society *needs* to crumble. We're all too chicken-shit to let it."

"I've missed your rants," Jules said. Dana was pleased to see her throw Marty a smile. He grinned back and held up a beautifully rolled joint for her perusal.

"You will come to see things my way," he said.

"I can't wait," she said. "Is that the secret stash?"

"The secret *secret* stash." I haven't told my other stash about it because it would become jealous."

"A sign," Dana said, suddenly excited. "Up there!"

Jules turned to look back through the windscreen, then examined the map again quickly.

"Yes. And... okay, left. Bear left."

"You sure?" Curt asked.

"Not even a little bit."

Holden edged forward with more beers, taking Dana's half-cup and replacing it with a full one. She smiled her thanks, but didn't catch his eye.

It was Jules's voice in her head, though: *Make him work*.

◇ ◇ ◇

Holden drank most of his cup of beer in one swig. He'd already had two when he was filling the others, and was feeling a pleasant buzz. He didn't usually drink so quickly. It was weird. But then again, so was what he felt happening here.

He had never, *ever* been so attracted to a girl whom he didn't want to instantly fuck.

Oh, he *did* want to, at some stage. Without a doubt. Dana was gorgeous—beautiful brunette hair he could get lost in, blue eyes, soft skin, and a scintillating, gentle smile that didn't say, *Look at how beautiful I am*. She was nothing like the girls he usually went for, and she was suddenly everything he wanted. So there *was* the sex thing, yes... but there was also something else. There was a need to know her, unlike anything he had ever felt before.

And they were off together for a weekend in the wilds.

"So what is this place exactly?" he asked.

"Country home my cousin bought," Curt said. "He's crazy for real estate, found this place in the middle of nowhere, it's like Civil War era, really. Said it was such a good deal he couldn't let it pass."

"There's a lake, and woods everywhere," Jules said. "We saw some beautiful pictures." She turned in her seat and looked at Dana. "You will be doing some serious drawing. No portraits of pedophiles..."

Holden glanced at Dana just in time to see the end of the "shut up" frown she'd given Jules. He'd heard a bit about her from Curt, about how some slimy bastard shithead had used and dumped her. He didn't understand how someone could do that to a girl like this. Taking a chance, heart thumping, he sat down on the seat next to her, holding his breath just a little when their legs pressed against each other. A silence fell then, not intentional but awkward nonetheless.

Across the table the guy they called Marty hummed some nameless tune as he packed his rolled joints. Curt and Jules looked ahead along the tree-lined road. Holden wondered whether he was the only one who could feel the atmosphere thickening, though he wasn't quite sure what it carried.

"You're an art major?" he asked, breaking the silence and using the question as an excuse to turn to Dana.

"Art and political science," she said. *Those eyes…*

"Oooh, triple threat," he muttered.

A frown, a smile. He liked both.

"That's only two things," she said quizzically.

"Yes, a double... threat. That sounds weird. Let's just say I find you threatening."

"I thought you were dropping art?" Curt asked.

"Uh, no, never mind…" Jules said, slapping Curt's thigh and glaring at him.

"I'm switching a few courses," Dana said coolly.

"How come?" Holden asked, and then he twigged it. *Oh, so slimy bastard shithead had been a lecturer?*

"For no reason!" Curt blurted. "For very good reasons that don't exist." Then he pointed. " Hey look, trees!"

"We have patterns," Marty said, and Holden felt the pressure lift. He'd only known him for a couple of hours, but he liked Marty already. A chilled dude. "Societally. The beautimous Dana fell into one of the oldest patterns and we are here to burn it away and pour ash into the grooves it has etched in her brain. Cover the tracks and set her feet on new ground."

Holden leaned sideways in his seat until his and Dana's shoulders were touching, and he felt her hair on his cheek and neck. "Is it okay if I don't follow that?"

And she actually *leaned back into* him before saying, "I'd take it as a favor."

"Gas!" Curt shouted. Through the windscreen, Holden caught sight of a ramshackle building beside the road. "Gas," Curt repeated, quieter, "and maybe someone who knows where we actually are."

The five friends fell silent as he brought them to a standstill beside two ancient fuel pumps. The red, rusting hulks stood on a crumbling concrete pedestal, a bucket of sand sitting between them, a rickety-looking tin sheet canopy above supported by weathered timber posts. It looked as if the slightest breeze would knock the whole thing over, and Holden thought vibrations from the Rambler might just do the job.

"Does anyone have a banjo I can borrow?" Marty asked. "In fact, I see one bald kid, and I'm outta here."

"It's just a bit run down," Holden said, but his observation was so far off the mark that no one even challenged him. "A bit run down" might mean something that needed a lick of paint, or a bit of reorganizing, or the attention of someone used to calmness and order. This place—the pumps, the building beyond them, and the surrounding area—looked as if it had been blown up and put back together again by a blind man. With no tools. Or hands.

"Shit," he whispered to himself.

Beyond the pumps, the main building appeared to have been assembled from the tumbled remains of several others. Timber boarding didn't quite meet flush, no corner was quite ninety degrees, and the patterns of fading the sun had left on the wall were uneven and haphazard. Many of the boards had nail holes where there were no longer nails, and in some places the bent, rusted remains of a nail still protruded, as if someone had tried to fix the boards from within. The corrugated roof covering was uneven and rusting, holes punched in two places for small chimneys.

Windows were out of true, dusty glass hiding any view of the inside. Even in several panes where the glass had been smashed out there was nothing to be seen. Holden thought perhaps the building had been plucked from the ground by a tornado and dumped here from several miles away, and ever since it had been preparing for collapse.

Scattered around the building, like the detritus of that same tornado strike, were all manner of objects, whole and in parts. Oil or gasoline barrels, rubber pipes twisted like long snakes in the grass, a chopping block with piles of splintered timber and a rusted axe buried in its top surface, an old cement mixer, and the carcasses of furniture now devoid of upholstery, their springs and metal bracing joining the rest of the surroundings in rot.

"Well," Curt said, stretching in his driver's seat. "We still need gas. And directions."

"And I need to take a leak," Jules said. She opened the door and stepped out, glancing back nervously as she did so.

Holden looked at Dana and smiled, pleased to see that her nervousness lifted as she smiled back.

"Maybe they'll sell home-made jerky," Holden said, and propelled by groans of disgust he followed Jules outside.

They stood close to the fuel pumps. The smell of fuel was almost reassuring, because it meant that they were still working even though they looked like they hadn't been used in years. Holden scraped the dusty ground and shifted aside sand that had been scattered on places where fuel had spilled. Despite all appearances to the contrary, he thought perhaps this was actually a working fuel stop.

He just wondered what the insides of the building contained.

"Billa bing, bing-bing, bing-bing, bing-*bing*," Marty said, playing an imaginary banjo.

"I'm thinking this place won't take credit cards," Curt said, touching a pump delicately as if afraid it would fall apart.

"I don't think it knows about *money*," Marty said. "I think it's *barter* gas."

Curt leaned left and right, stretching up on his toes, trying to see if anyone was around.

"Well, I need to pee," Jules said again, heading around the side of the building.

"I'll see if anyone's home," Holden said, looking

across at Curt. His friend nodded, then glanced back at the Rambler. *I'll keep watch*, his look said, and Holden nodded once. He was on edge... but not quite nervous enough to *not* watch Dana as she followed Jules around the side of the dilapidated building. She was wearing a fitted blue jacket, but it only came down just past her hips, and he could still admire the way her butt moved in her jeans.

As they disappeared around the corner he headed for the front door. It stood ajar, and looked as if it could never close all the way. The door didn't quite seem to fit the frame.

It scraped across grit on the floor as he forced it open. He saw curved scrape-scars in the timber floor boarding.

"Anyone here?" he asked. But the building's insides swallowed his voice, offering no echoes at all. He left the door open behind him to provide more light, and because he didn't want to hear that pained scraping again, ventured inside.

"Hello?" Curt called outside. There was no answer from anywhere, inside or out. And as Holden's eyes grew accustomed to the gloom, his sense of unease only increased.

"Holy shit," he muttered. It seemed as if he'd landed in redneck heaven.

He thought that perhaps it had once been a shop, but he couldn't imagine anyone wanting to buy anything from this place anymore. He couldn't imagine anyone wanting to *stand* in here, for more than a couple of minutes. The smell was rank, a spiced blend of fusty age and progressing rot, and flies buzzed here and there. *Why are the flies in here?* he wondered, and he had a sudden image of finding the proprietor dead and decaying on the floor somewhere, maggots crawling in his eye sockets and rats gnawing at—

"Hey!" he called, looking for movement, listening for acknowledgment. There was neither.

Wooden shelving and tables provided perimeter storage, and there were also two island units. Tinned goods were stacked here and there, the labels so faded by damp and age that he couldn't make out most of them. Tomatoes, perhaps? Corn? From metal poles braced across the ceiling hung several animal pelts, and one table seemed to be taken with various experiments in taxidermy. Several boxes and glass jars held what might also be a part of the experiment; in one glass jar something floated, its shape and origins vague in the opaque fluid.

There were meat mincers and slicers fixed to another tabletop, flies dipping in and out of both, dark speckles marking the hardened remains of old meat. One shelving unit in the corner was stocked with glass jars, some containing pickled vegetables of some kind, another holding what appeared to be boiled animal bones. It was as if the shopkeeper had suddenly tired of selling food and fuel and taken to stuffing animals in his spare time.

"Gruesome," Holden said to no one in particular. He walked to the rear, where a glass counter displayed a selection of hunting knives. He drew his finger across the counter, leaving a clear line of glass in its wake.

Well, this is nice, he thought. *All we need now is some old fuck warning us not to go any further.*

"Thar's danger in them thar hills," he growled, then he laughed, but the giggle he emitted was too high and nervous for comfort.

Fuck it. Time to go.

◇ ◇ ◇

"Why here?" Dana asked.

"Because I *hate* going in the Rambler!" Jules replied. "And besides, the keg's in there. I can't piddle next to what we're drinking. It's just... *euch*."

She shivered. This place was spooky and grim, but exciting too. There was something about it that had her blood flowing. It was almost... exotic.

"You think the toilet here's gonna be any better?" Dana asked.

"I don't like to pee when all my friends are two feet away from me," Jules persisted. They'd passed around the corner of the building now, and were threading their way through a scatter of old stuff lying all around. Leaning against the building's wall to their left was a large roll of barbed wire, with some dried husk tangled in it. She tried to persuade herself it was a mass of old plant, but the tiny splayed claws testified otherwise. To their right a camper van was all but buried in a large bank of bushes. Its color was no longer discernable, the tires were smothered beneath plant growth, and the rear window was obscured on the inside by drawn curtains. The thing that spooked Jules most about it was the open side door. If it had been shut she'd have thought no more about it, but open seemed to suggest that the thing was still in use. That there might be someone in there.

Hello? she tried to say, but no noise came from her mouth.

"So you're gonna pee in the Toilet From Out of Nowhere," Dana said, a quaver in her voice.

Jules reached for a side door in the building, assuming—hoping—that it was the bathroom. She *really* needed to pee.

"I'm quirky," she said, pulling on the handle. "At least this has gotta be—*hoah*!"

The smell hit her instantly, then the sight of the bathroom revealed behind the creaking door, and for a moment both robbed her of words. There was a toilet… and nothing else—no basin, not even a cistern. The walls were dark and coated with slime, the floor was wet with thick brown fluid... not *pure* shit, she thought, but an overflow of the stuff that filled the toilet. Thick, fluid, *shifting*, the sludge topped the toilet and dribbled slick down its surface, turning what might have once been white a uniform brown.

Behind her, Dana gagged.

Jules took a small step forward, fascinated, wondering just why the sludge in the pan was moving. And then she saw the scorpion, struggling in the fetid muck, slowly drowning. *And unless that thing's* full *of drowned critters, it's weird that we open the door just in time to see this*, she thought. It was almost as if…

She turned and looked around, past Dana, past the camper van buried in the undergrowth, along the lane that led away from this place up into the wooded hills, then back toward where she could just see the nose of the Rambler.

Dana watched her with raised eyebrows. Jules opened her mouth to speak, but before she could say anything they heard a muffled, "Fuck!" from somewhere around the front of the building.

"Seems we've found the attendant," Jules said softly. Walking close together, she and Dana retraced their steps. Suddenly, her need to pee had abated.

◊ ◊ ◊

I've got a bad feeling about this, Holden thought, and he uttered another nervous giggle. Heading back outside, he saw Marty and Curt through the doorway, trying to work one of the pumps. Marty was holding the nozzle in the mouth of the Rambler's fuel pipe, while Curt circled the pump, reaching out now and then to run his hands across the flaking painted surface. Looking for a switch or lever, Holden guessed, though he seemed to find neither.

"I don't think there's gonna be—" Holden began, voice raised to carry out as he approached the door.

Suddenly a shadowy figure filled the doorway,

blocking most of the light, and a voice said, "You come in here uninvited?"

"Fuck!" Holden gasped loudly. "Dude..."

"Sign says closed," the attendant said, because that must have been what this man was. Tall and broad, old and weathered until his skin looked like a leather jacket left out in the sun too long, his left eye terribly bloodshot and swollen. His lips and chin were stained and glistening with chewed tobacco and drool, and he scowled in anger and disgust.

He blocked the exit completely, and that was what worried Holden the most, more than his grotesque face and pissed attitude. *If I want to get out and he doesn't want me to...* He was just about to start looking around for an alternative escape—jump through a window, perhaps, or maybe he'd find a door hidden behind a pile of badly stuffed animals at the back of the shop—when the attendant grunted and turned around, walking out to face the others.

Holden let out a gasp of relief. That was when he realized he'd been holding his breath.

"We were looking to buy some gas?" Curt said, taking a few steps toward the old man. Marty hung back, still holding the nozzle in the Rambler's fuel pipe. "Does this pump work?"

"Works if you know how to work it," The attendant said. He glanced to his left and paused, and Holden took the opportunity to slip from the building. He circled around the old man until he was standing just a few feet to Curt's right, and past the guy he saw Dana and Jules appear cautiously around the side of the building. Both were wide-eyed and slightly panicked.

What have they seen? he wondered. Dana glanced at the attendant only briefly, then past him at Holden. They swapped nervous smiles.

The attendant didn't move to help Marty with the fuel. The moment felt frozen, and Holden wanted to move it along.

"We also wanted to get directions..." he said.

"Yeah, we're looking for..." Curt began, frowning, looking at Jules and asking, "What is it?"

"Tillerman Road," Jules said, taking a step closer to the attendant. Holden could see her nervousness, but he also knew that she wouldn't want to seem afraid. Her hands were fisted by her sides, holding on to control.

The attendant just peered at her, but something about him changed. He'd become still—jaw no longer chewing, body no longer swaying—as if the name had hit home. He looked Jules up and down, and Holden almost saw her skin flinching back from his gaze.

Then the attendant sighed and muttered, "What a waste." He walked toward the pump, moving with an exaggerated gait as if neither leg belonged to him. Curt stepped aside, and the old man plucked a ring of keys from his pocket—far too many for this shack, surely?—and unlocked a latch on the pump. Marty stayed where he was, regarding the man with hooded eyes.

Sometimes it's good to be stoned, Holden thought, and he smiled slightly, thinking how much Marty would appreciate the sentiment.

"Tillerman Road takes you up into the hills. Dead end at the old Buckner place."

"Is that the name of—?" Jules began.

"There wasn't a name," Curt said.

"Ready?" the attendant said to Marty, and when he nodded the old guy flicked a switch, then said, "Okay, pull the handle." Marty pulled, the pump *thunked* and shook for a couple of seconds, and then the pungent smell of fuel filled the air. Holden wondered how old this fuel was, and whether it had an expiration date, and wished he were back in the city where he didn't have to think about such things. The numbers behind the glass dome on top of the pump started turning. Holden thought he'd seen a pump like this in an old movie, once. Very old.

"My cousin bought a house up there," Curt said to the attendant's back. "You go through a mountain tunnel, there's a lake, would that be...?"

"Buckner place," the attendant confirmed, leaning on the pump and spitting a brown slick at his feet. "Always someone lookin' to sell that plot." He looked over his shoulder at Curt and smiled, exposing bad teeth stained brown, gaps here and there, and a thick gray tongue that looked to Holden like something trawled up from the bottom of the sea. "An' always some fool lookin' to buy."

"You knew the original owners?" Jules asked.

"Not the first," he replied, looking the girls up and down again. "But I've seen plenty come and go. Been here since the war."

"Which war?" she asked.

"You know damn well *which* war!" he shouted. He took two steps toward Marty and closed his hand over the nozzle, Marty just letting go and stepping back in time. He caught Holden's eye and shrugged, hands held out.

Holden tried to smile at him, but the atmosphere didn't feel light enough.

"Would that have been with the blue, and some in gray?" Marty asked. "Brother, perhaps fighting against brother in that war?"

"You sassin' me, boy?"

"You were rude to my friend," Marty said, his voice level, gentle as ever.

The attendant grew still again for a second, and Holden thought, *Cogs turning in there, stuff happening, he's processing what he didn't expect.* Then the old man looked at Jules again.

"That whore?"

Curt took a quick step forward but Holden was already moving, aware of what was about to happen. He splayed his left hand on Curt's chest and held it there until his friend looked at him. He was angry but, Holden was pleased to see, also a little freaked. That was good. That would prevent this weird shit from descending into something more.

"I think we've got enough gas," Holden said coolly.

"Enough to get you there," the attendant said, removing the nozzle. "Gettin' back's your own concern."

The girls came over behind the old guy and climbed back into the Rambler. Curt threw a twenty at the old man's feet, aiming for and hitting the slick of tobacco juice. He glanced at Holden, then nodded at the Rambler. Time to go.

Holden couldn't have agreed more.

Marty was the last one to climb back into the vehicle. The old man was still standing beside the fuel pump, apparently dismissing the money at his feet, still chewing, still staring at them with one good eye and one flushed with blood.

"Good luck with your business," Marty said, climbing the steps. "I know the railroad's comin' through here any day now, gonna be big. Streets paved with... actual street." And as he started swinging the door shut, Holden heard him mutter, "Fucker."

Curt was already firing the engine, and even in a vehicle so large he managed to leave a wheel-spin in their wake. *Now will come the joking*, Holden thought. *An unpleasant situation cast aside with bravado, mocking, and rude quips.*

But they drove away in silence, none of them catching another's eye, and it was only as they turned a bend and started the long climb into the hills that the tension started to filter away.

THREE

Marty lit up a spliff, offering his pre-rolled joints around to everyone else. No one took him up on it, though he thought for a second Holden was going to. They smiled awkwardly at each other.

Yeah, Marty thought, *he knows too. He knows that was super-weird and fucked up back there. Like, how the hell does that dude stay in business? And where the hell did he just pop up from? And why was he...?*

"Why was he looking at Jules like that?" Marty whispered. Across the small table from him, Dana and Holden heard the question but did not respond. Probably because they'd been thinking the same thing themselves, and there was no comfortable answer.

Bland rock played from the radio, Jules hummed in the front passenger seat, Curt cut in now and then with a few badly-sung lines from some song or another. Feigning normality.

"Don't give up the day job, dude," Marty said.

"At least I'll *have* a day job!" Curt said. "I won't spend my days stoned, wandering the woods, being at one with nature, and wondering how amazing it is that I'm actually alive."

There was silence for a few seconds, and then Marty responded, "I pity you, man." And everyone laughed.

That's better, Marty thought. *That's much better. Laughter's the second-best medicine*. He took another drag on his joint and held the smoke down, breathing out slowly. He was relaxed again now, leaning back in his chair with his head resting against the window. The sun caressed his scalp, and it was good. Holden had fetched them another beer each, and he felt a warm glow, starting at the center of him and reaching all the way to his fingertips and the ends of his toes.

Dana and Holden were sitting close, and though they affected indifference, Marty could see that each time the swaying Rambler nudged them into each other it sent a thrill through them.

Lucky guy, he thought. Dana was cute as hell and a lovely girl. A *beautiful* girl. They'd been friends for over a year, and to begin with he'd believed that she viewed him as some sort of a joke. Many people did, mostly the shallow types—the plastic people, he called them—who spent more time concerned with what the outsides of their heads looked like, rather than bothering to care for the insides. But he'd soon come to realize that, though gorgeous, Dana was not like that at all. An intelligent girl, both deep and somewhat mysterious, she kept a distance from him rather than regarding him as a joke.

Maybe her parents had had a thing about drugs of any kind, and it was a hangover from that, or perhaps... but no, he'd stopped thinking that long ago. Perhaps it was because she felt something for him and was afraid to grow too close? *Yeah, right*. Looking at Holden and Dana now, he could see how distant she kept from guys she liked.

But out of their awkward beginning had emerged a strange, close relationship. Marty was sure that Dana knew what he felt about her, and how intense was the first impression she'd made upon him. And Marty was getting to know her more and more every day. Of all the friendships he'd made at college, this one felt as if it would last longer than all the others.

Lucky guy, he thought again, and when Dana caught his eye he glanced away.

"Guys, take a look," Jules said.

Marty sat up and, with the others, leaned to look out the front windshield. To their right was a steep ravine, and ahead of them loomed the dark mouth of a tunnel set in the mountainside. It looked impossibly small. The ravine ended in a sheer, bare cliff face, above which rose a steeply wooded hillside, boulders, and rock spurs protruding between greenery like boils on a craggy face. And across the other side of the ravine, another tunnel mouth emerged onto a road ledge.

Must curve through the mountain, he thought, and he wondered who would have built such a tunnel instead of a simple bridge.

"Hey," Marty said, "do we really have to go—"

"Yep," Curt said. He slowed the Rambler as they approached, concentrating, and turned on the headlights. The darkness was pushed back as they entered the tunnel, and to Marty it felt as if they were being swallowed by the mountain. It seemed like an incredibly tight fit, but there was no scraping or crunching, and Curt steered confidently into the darkness.

Marty closed and opened his eyes again several times, enjoying the brash contrast between darkness and the artificial lights of the Rambler's dashboard. His friends were mere shadows in the barely lit cabin, and he knew that he'd look the same to them.

Halfway through the tunnel, when the faint glow of daylight started to show ahead of them, he suddenly sat up as the hairs on his forearms and neck stood on end. A shiver went though him, like a subtle electric shock, tingling his balls and tickling the insides of his nostrils. He immediately sniffed the joint, wondering if some alien substance had found its way in, and—

◇ ◇ ◇

Above the mountainside and ravine, a small bird's free will took it along the route of the rough mountain track. It swept above the wooded mountainside, unconsciously following the tunnel as it rode thermals. Singing as it flew, stomach full from a recent feed, it struck something in mid-air, something that flashed into view for a second like a vast blue, pulsing grid, and with a shower of fiery sparks the bird plummeted, dead. Its wings were scorched, its insides fried. Its brain had been carbonized, and any thoughts it once held were more remote and immaterial than shadows.

Nothing made the bird fly this way, nothing urged it north instead of east or south or west, but it died nonetheless. Free will was, perhaps, its undoing.

◇ ◇ ◇

"Oh... *oh*!" Marty heard someone say, and he thought it was Dana. No one else spoke, but he felt the brief, intense level of discomfort in the Rambler; people shifted in their seats, and the silence grew heavier.

Then they were out the other end and heading across the mountainside, the steep drop still to their right, and the glaring sun cleared away any dregs of darkness.

What was that? Marty wanted to say. *Weird magnetic field? Radiation from the rocks? Someone walking over my grave?* But when he looked around at the others he saw smiling faces, and a growing excitement that they were getting closer to their destination. Curt and Jules were singing badly again, Holden was drinking, and Dana stared dreamily from the window.

So Marty took another pull on his joint instead, and he didn't even look back.

They drove for another ten minutes. The ledge wove upward, turning back on itself and zig-zagging them up the mountainside. The view that was revealed alternately to their left and right was staggering, opening up across the ravine to expose miles of wooded countryside, hills peeking above the trees here and there, and dark green valleys hiding their secrets from view. After a short climb they reached a ridge, and then the track weaved them into a forest of towering trees.

Curt drove, Holden and Dana pretended not to notice where their skin touched, and Marty smoked. He was thinking about dynamite and digging machines, and men working with shovels and picks, and just how long it had taken to forge that tunnel around the end of the ravine, following the natural contours of the land except deeper inside. And the road that had twisted and turned its way up the mountainside; that wasn't an easy build, either. He thought about stuff like this a lot. And sometimes, such thoughts ended with a simple determination to smoke some more.

He lit another joint and leaned back in his seat, dozing.

Curt startled him awake with a shout.

"Behold! Our home for the weekend." Holden and Dana went first, squatting between Curt's and Jules's seats, and then Marty stood behind them, one hand on each of their shoulders to hold himself up. Dana gasped, Holden hummed in appreciation, and Marty had to admit to himself that, yes, this was quite a sight.

The lake lay to their left, surrounded by trees that cast stick-like shadows across the water from the southern bank. Elsewhere the sun glared off of the water, rippling here and there where fish or frogs jumped, shimmering with a million diamonds of light. There were a couple of small, bare islands sprouting low shrub growth, and on one a solitary tree cast its shadow over the water. A wooden jetty stood out into the water, a rough but sturdy-looking structure. There were no boats moored there, and taking a cursory look around the lake Marty could see several possible hiding places among the reeds at the lake's edge.

It wasn't huge, but the plant growth around its edges was lush. The stretch where the Rambler was now drawing to a halt must have been artificially cleared, and Marty found his attention drawn to the right to see why.

The cabin stood maybe a hundred feet from the lake, in a clearing that probed deep into the woods. For a few seconds Marty thought, *Right, that's like a timber store or something, and the real cabin's behind it in the trees, because if that's the place where we've got to sleep...* But then he looked closer and saw net curtains in the building's windows, and its allure slowly grew on him. They weren't coming out here for a hotel visit, after all. No room service or gourmet restaurants here.

It wasn't the most attractive building he'd ever seen, but it could easily be home. *For a couple of days, at least.* Single-story, with large eye-like windows on either side of the door. Several rickety steps led up to the wide decked porch area, where a small pile of firewood was stacked beneath the overhang to dry. Tall fir trees skirted the rear and both sides of the building, hiding it away from anywhere but where they were now parked.

Curt killed the engine and opened the door and, without speaking, they all climbed slowly from the Rambler.

Bird song, a gentle breeze through the trees, their crunching footsteps, something splashing out on the lake... there was no other noise. No traffic grumble or roaring of aircraft high in the sky.

Nothing.

It was, Marty thought then, idyllic.

"Oh my god, it's beautiful!" Jules said, leaning into Curt and adding quieter, "One spider and I'm sleeping in the Rambler. I mean it. *Uno spider-o*."

"This house is talking a blue streak," Marty whispered.

"So let's set up camp," Holden said. "And the most important feature: keg." He clapped Marty on the shoulder and grinned, and Curt accompanied them back into the Rambler to get the beer. They maneuvered it from the confined space and manhandled it from the vehicle, and by the time they'd deposited it on the cabin's porch, Dana already was there, turning the knob.

The door swung open with a deep, grinding creak. *You're velcome to stay zer night*, Marty thought, but as the others followed her inside he held back, appreciating the sky above him and the sense of space he still felt all around. In there they'd be... confined. He didn't shiver—not quite—but something felt askew. Had felt that way since meeting that weird old coot at the tumble-down gas stop, then coming up through the tunnel and winding track. Shit, maybe his batch of weed was contaminated with something. He'd heard about it happening before.

Once inside and settled, maybe he'd think about switching stashes.

The main room beyond the front door was living room and kitchen combined, and Dana was walking around slowly, touching nothing, as the others entered. To the right was a dining table and chairs, and a kitchen counter featuring poorly crafted wall and floor cupboards with a retro-fitted sink, the single tap dripping steadily. At the end of the counter stood an antique wood-burning stove, probably built before Marty's grandparents were even born. Its bulk and solidity seemed somehow out of place beside the rest of the kitchen, as if it was the only part that bled quality.

"Oh, this is awesome!" Curt said.

"It is kinda cool," Jules replied. "You gonna kill us a raccoon to eat?"

"I will use its skin to make a cap."

To the left in the huge room was the living area, with mismatched sofas and chairs arranged around the large stone fireplace. It looked comfortable, but strangely unloved, as if it were a place used for necessity rather than desire. Hanging back in the doorway, Marty spotted a wolf's head on the wall—courtesy of the old guy at the station, perhaps? It had been stuffed growling, and was just about one of the most vicious looking things he'd ever seen. That would get a shirt thrown over it before dusk, he was damn certain of that, by him if no one else. Its eyes seemed alive.

Directly opposite the front door a bare, wide hallway ran to the rear of the cabin, with two doorways leading off from either side. Between it and the kitchen there was a rectangle in the floor that appeared to be a way into the cellar. A few worn rugs littered the floor. The window at the hallway's end was obscured by nets and dust, and whatever lay beyond was dark, as if the woods back there cut out all sunlight.

Dana paused before the stuffed wolf's head, then moved on. Her footsteps were soft and gentle, hardly heard, and Marty wondered what lay beneath the timber-boarded floor.

Jules strode confidently along the hallway to check out the bedrooms. She grabbed a doorknob and twisted.

"Dibs on whichever room is—OW!" She jerked her hand back and stared at the bubble of blood welling on her fingertip.

I'm still not inside, Marty thought. *The others are and they're fine, they're at ease with the place, but I'm still not...*

"Curt, your cousin's house attacked me," Jules exclaimed with mock severity.

"I smell lawsuit," Curt said.

"When was your last tetanus shot?" Holden chuckled, and Marty noticed how close Dana had drawn to him. Not quite touching.

"Thanks, that's very comforting," Jules responded.

"Jules is pre-med," Curt said sadly, stroking his girlfriend's hair. "She knows there's no coming back from this. I'll miss you, baby. I'll miss your shiny new hair."

Dana glanced around then and looked at Marty, drawing him into their group again. He blinked, a little startled. He'd been off in his own world again.

"Marty? Are you planning on coming in?"

"Maybe," he said. "Maybe." But he waited until the four of them picked up their bags and headed down the hallway before he made his move.

Once across the threshold he sighed, looking around and listening to the others joking and chatting in their rooms.

He looked at the wolf and growled.

◇ ◇ ◇

Holden took the first room on the left, next to Dana's. He was excited. It had been a weird journey up from the city, the lowest point being that ignorant fuck at the gas stop. But now that they were here he could feel them all relaxing, and it wouldn't be long before they made this place their own.

Unpack, change, get the keg into the living room, sort out food for this evening, have a few more drinks... and maybe even one of Marty's joints... and then the weekend would really begin.

And there was Dana. He could feel the charge between them growing, and now he was certain that she felt it too. She was as keen to be close to him as he was to her. It felt a little awkward in the company of the others—he'd invaded their group, after all, and he couldn't shake the feeling that Curt had brought him along as a potential fix-up. But he couldn't deny the effect she was having over him.

He only hoped she'd brought a bikini.

He glanced at a picture on the wall—some old Victorian scene—then threw his bag on the bed and winced at how much it creaked. Sitting on the mattress and bouncing lightly up and down, he felt certain the resultant squeaking would attract bears from miles around. He hoped Curt's and Jules's bed wasn't this bad, otherwise none of them would be getting any sleep. If what Curt claimed was true, they went at it like rabbits.

The room was an echo of the rest of the cabin—wooden walls, wooden furniture, with a few touches here and there to make it look more homey. There was a rug on the floor, one corner almost threadbare, and a woven cushion on the bed covers. He turned back the covers and shook them, pleased to see no moths exiting or spiders scuttling away. He ran his hand between the sheets and felt no dampness. At least *that* part of it seemed to be comfortable enough.

Looking around again, he found his attention grabbed once more by the picture hanging on the wide wall. He'd assumed it was an old horse-and-dog print, a country scene from a long time ago, maybe even imported from Britain. But looking closer, the detail started to stand out... and it was horrible.

It was a hunting party, and most of the members were shown dismounted, their faces flushed red with rage or freshly blooded, arms raised, hands bearing curved machetes that reflected gray sunlight where they weren't also darkened with blood. At their feet were several big, vicious-looking dogs, reminding him more of the wolf's head in the living room than the family pets he was used to. And at the focus of their attention was a lamb. Scarlet clefts had been struck into its back and flanks, and one dog had its slavering jaws clamped about the poor animal's throat.

It was only a picture, but Holden found it repulsive.

"Yeah, I don't think so," he said, taking the painting down. He bent and leaned it against the wall, picture now facing inward, and when he stood again Dana was staring at him through a hole in the wall.

He jumped, letting out a nervous laugh.

She stared.

"Wow," he said meekly, "I've heard about the walls being thin, but—" And then he trailed off when Dana bared her teeth at him, leaning forward as if to take a bite from his face. Frozen by the strangeness of this more than afraid that she was going to bite him, he let his shoulders relax when he realized what was happening.

Dana was examining her teeth. She picked between the two front ones, turning slightly left and right to get the angle right to see toward the back of her mouth. Ran her tongue across her upper teeth, the lower. Stared again, at herself.

One-way mirror, Holden thought, and there was a creepy delight in the discovery.

He watched as she ruffled up her hair a little, pouted, and then she seemed to become distracted, staring beyond the mirror and through him as she dwelled on something for a long few seconds. A small smile tweaked her lips, then she shook herself from the reverie and returned to her bed.

She started unbuttoning her shirt.

"Oh shit, ah no, ahh..." Holden said, torn between this golden opportunity and his common human decency. If he waited here and watched her strip, he could never tell anyone about the mirror. But if he made her aware, he might kick himself later.

Three buttons, four, that smooth plane of skin flowing from her neck down to her chest…

He had to make up his mind quickly, in the next couple of seconds, otherwise—

Five buttons, and the shirt fell open to reveal her tan bra, and if he waited another few seconds...

Holden cursed silently and banged on the wall. Dana froze, head cocked to one side, and Holden took that second to just look at her before calling through the wall, "Hold up!"

"What? Holden?"

"Dana... I just saw... come into my room. Bring the others."

Dana closed her shirt and redid a couple of buttons, frowning as she left her room. Holden heard her calling their friends, and he backed away from the wall and turned to the door, preparing to greet them and feeling more ashamed than he should have. He'd told her, hadn't he? Some guys would have watched all the way, jerked off and re-hung the picture, keeping the whole thing their dirty little secret. And some guys would have done that, then gone across the hallway to tell Marty.

He wasn't some guys.

But I waited a few seconds longer than I had to…

Dana stuck her head around his door and smiled uncertainly. She entered, and Holden pointed at the window into her room just as Jules came in, Curt and Marty following her.

"Tan bra," he said softly.

Jules got it first. She coughed surprised laughter and said, "You have got to be kidding me!"

"That's just creepy," Dana said as she caught on.

"It was pioneer days," Marty said. "People had to make their *own* interrogation rooms. Out of cornmeal."

Holden shrugged and ran his hands around the rough one-way mirror frame. "This is from the... seventies, judging by the weathering. Who did your cousin buy this place from, Curt?"

"We should check the rest of the rooms," Curt said, ignoring the question. "Make sure this is the only one. You *know* Marty wants to watch me and Jules pounding away."

"I didn't even like *hearing* that," Marty said, wincing as he turned and left the room.

"Beer," Curt said, eyebrows rising, false realization dawning on his face. "Beer! Beer is the only answer!" He turned and dashed from the room, Jules rolling her eyes and following him.

"Don't be an ape, Curt."

The brief silence after the others left was a little

awkward, and it needed more than a smile to break it.

"How about we switch?" Holden asked Dana. "Not that I'd... I mean I'll put the picture back but you might feel better if we switched rooms."

"I really would," Dana said, leaving his room.

Holden cursed silently as he grabbed his bag, following her out into the hallway.

"Thanks for... being decent," she said over her shoulder.

"Least I could do, since Curt and Jules have sold you to me for marriage." Holden cringed a little; *said too much?* Dana cringed, too, but then her soft laughter made it all right.

"They're not subtle," she agreed ruefully.

"I'm just here to relax. And so can you."

"Yeah, I'm not looking for... But I'm still grateful that you're not a creep."

"Hey, let's not jump to any conclusions there," Holden said.

"Tan bra?" Dana said softly, and though he couldn't see her face he knew that she was smiling.

Don't want to play this too *cool*, he thought, and on the back of that, *So* am *I a creep after all?*

"I had kind of an internal debate about showing you the mirror," he said. "Shouting on both sides, blood was spilled..."

They entered Dana's room—his room now—and he dumped his stuff on the bed.

"So you're bleeding internally," she asked, mock-serious.

"Pretty bad."

"Well, Jules is the doctor-in-training. You should probably talk to her."

"Yeah." He smiled, Dana grabbed her bag, and as she turned and left he saw an expression on her face that he thought was similar to his own. *Cursing herself*, he thought. *She wishes this chat had gone one step further.*

Smiling as the door swung shut behind her, Holden thought that he and Dana would get on very well indeed.

◇ ◇ ◇

Shit shit shit that was lame, Dana thought. But she couldn't help smiling. Even with a closed door between them, she could sense Holden behind her. Unsubtle though Jules and Curt had been about her and Holden, it seemed as if they might yet finish this weekend pleased with their powers of matchmaking.

In her new room she closed the door and dropped her bag onto the bed, wincing at the creaking of springs. *Hope Curt's and Jules's bed isn't that bad*, she thought. Then she picked up the picture Holden had removed from the wall, turned it around... and it was unbelievably gross. She had no idea why someone would want that hanging above them in bed. Maybe there was more to it. The artist might have been a local celebrity, or something. But though she looked closely for a signature she could find none, and it had the sort of paint-by-numbers feel of a mass-produced image.

It was spooky, but she had to re-hang it.

Otherwise—

She saw Holden in the next room, her view darkened just a little by dust on the one-way mirror. He wore an enigmatic smile, and was slowly pacing back and forth at the foot of his bed. Distracted, he pulled his shirt over his head and then stood there again, apparently unmindful of the fact that he was now in the viewable room.

He was in pretty good shape, for sure. Dana was holding her breath. The moment seemed to stretch, and then Holden dropped his shirt on the bed and pulled his swimming shorts from his bag, and began unbuttoning his jeans.

"Uhhh... ah!" Dana muttered. "God!" She was where he had been and, though she could stay here for another ten seconds to see what he had, he had only watched for so long.

Long enough to see my bra, she thought, and as she caught sight of Holden's briefs she hung the picture, obscuring the window and making sure it banged against the wall. He'd hear it and know that she'd covered the one-way mirror again... but he'd also know that she'd paused just for those few seconds, watching him strip off his shirt.

"Fair's fair," she said softly, grinning.

She took one last look at the grim print, and on the wall it seemed even worse. But it was part of her room now.

"Yeah, I don't think so," she said, plucking a knitted

throw from the bed and hanging it over the picture.

That was better.

Now, time to strip in private and slip into that sexy red bikini.

◇ ◇ ◇

Their whole world in my hands, Sitterson thought. *Their every private moment under my scrutiny*. And he giggled to himself, because he was starting to sound like that crazy fuck Mordecai.

"What's so funny?" Hadley asked. He was working at his own control panel, sugar from a recent doughnut speckling the skin around his mouth.

"You," Sitterson said with as much seriousness as he could muster, "and the joke that is your life."

Hadley muttered something as he turned away smiling, and Sitterson pushed his chair back so that he could view every display at once.

On the bedroom monitors, the college kids were all changing into their swimming costumes. He'd seen this enough times before, but the voyeuristic delight had never quite left him, and neither would he wish it to. He regarded it as a perk of the job, and knew that Hadley did as well. They didn't make it obvious, but neither did they purposely look away from the screens.

There was no privacy here; that had been denied these kids the second they drove through the tunnel, and in some ways long before that. So while he checked readouts on his laptop and tweaked a few settings here and there, he also glanced frequently at the bank of monitors.

Just to... monitor.

The cute brunette—and *damn*, was she cute!—turned her back on the covered painting as she changed, which gave him a perfect view. Sweet, pert breasts, as yet defiant of gravity and not weighed down with the responsibility of childbirth. Strong limbs, long legs, a flat stomach rippled with the subtle evidence of running and other exercise. And she shaved. Most college kids her age did, he'd come to learn. That didn't do it for Sitterson, but he knew that Hadley was a fan of baldies.

Glancing across, he grinned to see his companion's gaze fixed on the screen.

"Cute," he said.

"Yeah," Hadley agreed, smiling softly. "But it doesn't matter."

Sitterson looked at the other screens that showed activity. The Fool was sitting on the end of his bed staring at the far wall, a joint hanging from the corner of his mouth. He hadn't bothered changing, and most likely wouldn't join his friends in the lake. Which was a shame, because it would necessitate a slight change from Story. But it was also allowed for.

The jock and his blonde girlfriend were fooling around naked, whipping at each other's butts with twisted towels, wrestling, but Sitterson knew that she was teasing, putting everything on view but not making anything available. Not yet, at least. The jock didn't seem aware of this, and when his interest started showing Sitterson turned away and checked some more readouts. Even though he had the audio turned most of the way down, he still heard the guy's complaining voice, and the girl's admonishment, full of control and manipulation.

Poor fuck. Didn't he know they were all insane?

Rolling his chair back again, he checked out the other feeds: cabin, dock, lake, the RV, several views of the kitchen and dining area, four for the living room, basement, bathroom... it all seemed well, and when the kids started leaving their rooms he tracked their progress from screen to screen.

"All right," Sitterson said, "places everyone. We are *live.*"

"Engineering," Hadley said, voice calm and almost bored. "We've got a room change. Polk is now in two, McCrea's in four. Story department—you copy? We'll need a scenario adjustment..."

Moments later a voice came over the control room's PA.

"Have it back to you in fifteen..."

"Oh, and the Fool's not swimming."

"Got that covered," the same voice confirmed.

It's all under control, Sitterson thought, and control was what pleased him. Outside this place he was a mess—his bachelor's home, his history of relationships, his life—but he more than made up for it with his work. He was, Hadley had told him more than once, a pain-in-the-ass perfectionist. *Who the fuck else would you want working here?* That was his stock reply. And Hadley had never argued.

Footsteps sounded on the metal staircase and Sitterson glanced up.

"Ms. Lin!"

She carried a clipboard under her arm, as ever. An affectation, he knew, because everything she needed for the weekend's activities was stored on the palm-top she carried in her lab coat pocket. He wasn't sure whether the clipboard made her look more sexy or more terrifying, and the fact that he found both alluring sometimes unsettled him.

"We've got blood work back on Louden," she said without any preamble. "Her levels are good, but we're recommending a fifty milligram increase of Rohyptase to boost libido."

"Sold," Sitterson said. He always favored a bit of hot sex action before things kicked off. Another perk of the job.

"Do we pipe it in or do you wanna do it orally?" Lin asked.

Sitterson held in his laughter, closed his eyes and sighed. "Ask me that again, only slower."

"You're a pig," she said. The tone of her voice didn't change at all, and sometimes he seriously considered Hadley's assertion that she was a robot. "Guess how we're slowing down her cognition."

Sitterson kept his eyes closed, knowing she'd tell him anyway.

"The hair dye." And was that a slight smugness to

her voice? He opened his eyes, impressed.

"The dumb blonde. That's artistic."

"Works into the blood through the scalp, very gradual." She looked past him at Hadley, her eternal doubter. "The Chem department keeps their end up."

"I'll see it when I believe it," he drawled without looking away from his control board.

Sitterson started shrugging, but halfway through the PA sounded again.

"Control?"

"Go ahead," Hadley said.

"I have the Harbinger on line two."

Hadley looked across, but Sitterson held up his hands, shaking his head.

"Christ," Hadley said. "Can you take a message?"

"Uh... I don't think so. He's really pushy. And... to be honest, he's kinda freaking me out."

Hadley gave a defeated sigh.

"Yeaaaahh. Okay, put him through." He hit a button on his panel and threw Sitterson one last, cutting glare: *You owe me.*

Sitterson finished his shrug and smiled.

"Mordecai!" Hadley said into his microphone, suddenly more upbeat and animated. "How's the weather up top?"

"The lambs have passed through the gate," a voice said, grizzled and grumbling—Sitterson always had been impressed by the guy's performance. He was a true method actor—the bloodshot eye never needed encouraging, and he really was a smelly bastard. Where the hell the Story guys had found him, he didn't know. He didn't *want* to know. "They are come to the killing floor," Mordecai's voice continued, echoing around the control room.

Hadley nodded, hand hovering above the disconnect button. But Sitterson had taken enough calls from Mordecai before to know that this was far from over.

"Yeah, you did great out there. By the numbers. Started us off right. We'll talk to you later, oka—"

"Their blind eyes see nothing of the horrors to come. Their ears are stopped; they are God's fools."

"Well, that's how it works." Hadley hung his head. His voice sounded with defeat. Sitterson chuckled.

"Cleanse them. Cleanse the world of their ignorance and sin. Bathe them in the crimson of—" He paused, then asked, "Am I on speaker phone?"

"No, no of course not!"

"Yes I am," Mordecai said. His voice raised, from subterranean grumble to eighteen-wheeler roar. "I can hear the echo. Take me off. Now."

Sitterson started laughing, clamping his hands over his mouth to try and hold in the mirth. Beside him Lin, ever the ice queen, was maintaining her cool. Mostly. But even her features were warmed by the subtlest precursor of a smile.

"Okay," Hadley said. "Sorry."

"I'm not kidding," Mordecai's voice grated through the speakers. "It's rude. I don't know who's in the room."

"*Fine.*" Hadley tapped the microphone. "There, you're off speaker phone."

"Thank you."

Sitterson was trying not to cry, but the more he held his laughter the greater the pressure built. *Hysteria is a sign of the loss of control*, Lin had told him once, and he'd roared with laughter as she'd left the control room. He hadn't disagreed; he'd merely laughed. He wished he knew how she stayed so calm. Perhaps she took some of her own chemical creations, though such indulgence was *strictly* forbidden.

"Don't take this lightly, boy," Mordecai continued from the gas station. "It wasn't all by your 'numbers'; the Fool nearly derailed the invocation with his insolence. Your futures are murky; you'd do well to heed my—" He paused again, then his voice lightened to a whisper; gravel on concrete. "I'm still on speaker phone, aren't I?"

That was it. Sitterson couldn't hold it anymore, the laughter bursting from him in an explosive cough of air. Even Lin was smiling, and from down the curved staircase Sitterson heard Truman, the stiff soldier, coughing as he tried to contain his own hilarity.

"No," Hadley said, "you're not. I promise."

"*Yes I am!* Who is that? Who's laughing?"

Sitterson felt tears running down his cheeks and he leaned forward in his chair, pounding his head on his console. *Hysteria is the sign of the loss of control.* As he glanced up at one monitor and saw two of the kids soundlessly running along the wooden dock toward the lake, he wondered how mirthful each tear really was.

◇ ◇ ◇

Holden was racing her. It was simple fun, but for Dana, there was still that competitive edge that was a hangover from all the athletics she did in her early teens. So she ran hard, feeling the boards flexing and creaking beneath her feet, and sensing Holden's shadow just behind to her left.

"No way you win," he gasped, and she cried out in delight as she put on a final burst of speed, launching herself from the end of the dock and feeling one of those moments of unadulterated, ecstatic glee that comes only rarely, and never for long. She pinwheeled her arms and legs, trying to crawl further through the air before the calm waters of the lake drew her down.

She tried to take a deep breath before she entered the water, but she was laughing too much. Beside her she sensed Holden flying with her, and then the water closed completely around her. And it was colder than she had ever felt before.

Surfacing, gasping, spitting water from her mouth, it took her several seconds to find her breath.

"OH! *Cold!* That's what cold feels like—"

"Fight through the pain," Holden gasped, treading water beside her. "It's worth it. I'm nearly convinced it's worth it."

Dana found her breath at last, the cold quickly numbing her senses. She turned in the water and looked back toward the cabin, where the others were approaching at a more leisurely pace along the dock.

Curt and Jules were wearing their bathing suits, while Marty was still in his tee-shirt and shorts. He had a towel slung casually around his neck, but he seemed to have no intention of joining them.

Right then, she could hardly blame him.

"Does it seem fresh?" Jules asked, voice etched with concern. "Lotta funky diseases sitting in stagnant lake water."

"What?" Dana asked, "*this* water?" And to emphasize her point she took a deep gulp of it, swilling it around her mouth before spitting it out in an arc. Cool and fresh, it was tinted with a tang of something wonderful. "This water's *delicious*."

"Oh my god, she's right!" Holden gasped. He took a mouthful too, spitting it in an arc toward Dana. She flinched back and it splashed her shoulder. "It tastes like... vitamins. And hope."

"C'mon Jules," Dana called. "Life is risk!"

"Yeah, I might just risk lying out in the sun for a while." She paused a few steps back from the edge, uncertain.

Curt stepped to the edge of the dock, face falling as he looked down.

"What is that?" he asked, almost to himself.

Dana, treading water, edged back from the dock and further into the lake. She could sense the depth increasing beneath her as she moved, and it was thrilling.

"What?" she asked, a hint of concern tickling the back of her neck.

"In the lake," Curt said. "I swear to god I..."

"Yeah, right," Dana said, not willing to admit that he had her spooked. He looked so damn serious, and— But then she glanced sidelong at Holden, saw his smile, and knew that it was a game.

"No, *seriously*!" Curt said dramatically. Jules edged forward and stood beside him, looking nervously down at the rippling surface. "Right there. Don't you see it? *There*. It looks just like—" He put his hands firmly on Jules's back, and as he pushed and she squealed in terror, he said, "My girlfriend!"

Jules flailed at the air as if trying to hold herself back to the dock, and she went in that way, arms and legs thrashing and mouth open to scream. She surfaced quickly, spluttering and turning so that she faced the dock.

"Oh! *Oh my god!* I'm gonna kill you!"

His expression not breaking for an instant, Curt pointed just between where Jules had landed and Dana was still treading water, trying not to laugh out loud at her splashing, angry friend. *She'll never be angry at him for long*, Dana thought, and realized how these two suited each other so well.

"Look—there's something *else* in the lake—" Curt said, launching himself straight at where he was pointing, and splashing Dana and Holden as he landed. He surfaced and raised his arms, treading water just with his strong legs. "It's a gorgeous man!" he shouted, and at the far side of the lake a small flock of birds took flight from the trees.

"You are *so* dead!" Jules said, still gasping against

the cold. She swam to him with three powerful strokes and tried dunking him.

"Don't kill the gorgeous man!" Curt cried. "They're endangered!"

Dana laughed, and looked up at Marty standing alone on the end of the dock. He eyed them all warily, holding the towel splayed around his neck.

"Marty, get in here!" she said.

"Nah, man. I'm cool. Just seeing the sights." He sat on the edge of the dock and dangled his feet, his bare toes just reaching the water. He leaned back with a joint smoking gently in the corner of his mouth, and Dana wondered how he managed to live on a permanent high. Some people chose that way, she guessed. But for her, *life* was a high.

Especially today.

She glanced at Holden, caught his eye and smiled, turning in the water and swimming out for the lake's center. And for a while before he followed she was all alone, and this beautiful place was her own.

FOUR

And now, it was time for the betting to begin.

Sitterson loved this part. The play had begun, and tens of thousands of man hours' preparation had led to a single moment. Everything had gone smooth as clockwork up to now, and it looked as if they were going to pull through well.

There were some who had doubted his own seemingly lax approach to the job; they questioned his flippant manner, and the way he seemed to make light of the darkest things. But those doubters were here now with everyone else. Ready to bet. Gambling on souls. It was, as he and Hadley had discussed during many evenings over many beers, their own particular version of gallows humor.

Take this too seriously and you became withdrawn and traumatized, and that could only lead to mistakes.

Sitterson *never* made mistakes, and his naysayers had seen that soon enough. He might joke and bet, laugh and use sarcasm or innuendo as a defense, but when it came to holding down his end of the project, there were none who could be trusted more. Hence his position in Control.

"Last chance to post!" he called, stepping up onto the console. All eyes were on him and the wads of cash he held, and this was about the only time he liked being the centre of so much attention. "C'mon people, dig deep. Betting windows are about to close!"

The control room was bustling. Truman had fussed to begin with, hassled at having so many people entering the room. But they'd all passed muster with his card reader, so there was really little he could say. He'd refused to place a bet, peering at Sitterson with veiled disgust and shock when he'd been asked. And now he stood and scanned the room with cold eyes.

Hadley remained in his wheeled chair, but there were several people clustered around him, as well, holding out betting slips and cash for him to pluck away and enter into his notebook.

"Who's still out?" Hadley called to Sitterson.

Sitterson looked at his clipboard.

"I got Engineering, I got R&D, I got Electrical—"

"Ha!" Hadley called. "Did you see who they picked? They're practically *giving* their money away."

"Yeah, you're one to talk, Aquaman."

A guy from the Chem department handed his form to Sitterson. He wore a lab coat that was stained a rainbow of colors across the stomach and up the sleeves, and Sitterson wondered what fumes the guy was leaving in his wake.

He looked at the form and frowned.

"I'm not even sure we *have* one of these."

"Zoology swears we do," the Chem guy said.

Sitterson shrugged and took his money.

"Well, they'd know." A few feet away he noticed a bit of a scene developing where a young man he didn't recognize—a guy with 'Ronald' stitched onto the breast of his lab coat, though that made Sitterson none the wiser—was protesting loudly to Hadley.

"No, no, I told you, they've already been picked," Hadley said, slowly and patiently.

"What?" Ronald asked angrily. "Who took 'em?"

"Maintenance."

"Maintenance! They pick the same thing every year."

Hadley sighed theatrically and stood from his chair.

"What do you want from me? If they were creative, they wouldn't be in Maintenance. If you win, you're gonna have to split it. You wanna switch?"

Ronald's anger brewed, peaked, and then seemed to filter away as he looked past Hadley at the giant viewing screens and the blurred action they displayed.

"Nah," he said. "Leave it. I got a feeling on this one."

Hadley raised an eyebrow at Sitterson, who laughed in reply and jumped down from the console. With all of the bets placed, he wandered over to where Lin stood talking with the still-glowering soldier, Truman.

"Not betting?" she asked Truman just as Sitterson approached.

"Not for me, thanks." It was obvious from his expression that he didn't approve of the idea. Strangely enough, she seemed to disagree.

"Seems a little harsh, doesn't it? It's just people letting off steam." She nodded at Sitterson, then past him at Hadley. "This job isn't easy, however those clowns may behave."

"You should listen to her," Sitterson said grave-faced. "She is wise."

"Does The Director... do they know about it downstairs?" Truman inquired.

Hadley joined them, expertly shuffling a wad of cash into a neat pile in his left hand while his right folded a slew of betting slips. "The Director isn't concerned with stuff like this," he said. "Long as everything goes smoothly *upstairs* and the kids do... what they're told..."

"But then it's *fixed*?" he asked. "How can you take wagers on this when you control the outcome?"

Sitterson and Hadley both glanced back at the screens, their work, their responsibilities and charges. Sitterson didn't feel an ounce of regret at taking bets on them, and he knew Hadley didn't either. Lin might be cool and prim, but she'd been right—they were blowing off steam. And there were worse ways.

Up on the screens, the five kids were in the cabin's living room now, having returned from the lake, showered, dried, and dressed again. The sound was muted for the moment, but there were still three people in the lower part of Control wearing headphones to monitor the conversation. They always had to be ready for any sudden changes.

"It's not like that *at all*," Hadley said. "We just get 'em to the cellar, Truman. They take it from there."

"They have to make the choice of their own free will," Sitterson added. "Otherwise, system doesn't work. Like the Harbinger: creepy old fuck practically wears a sign saying 'YOU WILL DIE.' Why would we put him there? The system. They have to *choose* to ignore him. They have to *choose* what happens in the cellar. Yeah, we rig the game as much as we have to, but in the end, if they don't transgress..."

He shrugged.

Hadley was counting the money, but he finished Sitterson's sentence as if this little speech was well rehearsed. And it was. They'd given it to new doubters at least three times before.

"...they can't be punished. Last chance, Truman. Window's closing."

"I'm fine," the soldier said, shaking his head.

Hadley and Sitterson exchanged amused glances, then Hadley turned back to the people milling around Control.

"All right!" he yelled. "That's it, gang. The board is *locked*." He handed the cash to Sitterson, who combined it with his own wad, tied an elastic band around it, and slipped it into a drawer in his console. It felt like a good amount this time, and he was pleased. Not only did that raise the excitement, it also meant everyone would be on the ball, focusing on their jobs.

None of them could afford to have anything go wrong.

Sitterson looked at the screens again and shouted, "Let's get this party started!"

◇ ◇ ◇

Music thumped. Curt worked the keg filling plastic cups for them all.

They'd lit the fire upon arrival, as well as some oil lamps, and the back boiler was already pumping out water hot enough to cook a cat. After running up from the lake, sun slowly setting behind them and goosebumps speckling their skin, they'd taken it in turns ducking into the shower for a warm-up before dressing again.

Curt and Jules had gone first, and that's when the music had been turned on—Marty, Dana and Holden had only been able to listen for so long to their groans and the banging on the wall. It had been uncomfortable, but funny as well, and the three of them had shared a smile and a few choice comments.

Holden had sat beside Dana on the sofa, towels wrapped around them as they waited for the shower, and their bare legs had touched without any awkwardness. They hadn't even kissed yet, and still they were beginning to feel like a couple.

Holden was sitting opposite her now, and his skin was still tingling from the contrast between the cold dip in the lake and the hot shower afterward. All of them were showered and dressed. Marty sat beside him on the sofa with a beer between his knees and the ever-present joint pinched between slightly-yellowed fingers, unlit at present. As Dana leaned forward and picked up her cup, her still-wet hair fell forward to frame her face, and she smiled at Holden over its rim.

"Let's get this party started!" Curt called, handing a beer to Jules. "Truth, dare, or lecture!" She danced across the room in time to the music that was pumping from the stereo.

"I've played truth or dare before," Holden said, "I just don't get the third part. What's 'lecture'?"

"Well, the lecture is our own addition," Dana said. Her smile was softer than ever now, and he could tell that the beer was going to her head.

"It's the X factor," Marty said.

"It redefines the whole concept!" Jules said, still jigging.

"Come on," Dana teased, leaning forward again and perhaps wishing that she and Holden were sitting together. But he was happy to forego proximity in exchange for eye contact. "You're the newbie, so you ask first. We'll show you how it's done."

"Okay, uh, Marty," he said, still a little hesitant. "Truth or dare or lecture?"

Marty sighed, as if even that took too much effort.

"I could go for a lecture about now."

Holden smiled, but inside he sighed.

"Lecture. How'd I guess." That was just the pressure he didn't want from a room full of people he hardly knew. Eyes were on him, though, and he maintained the smile as he thought about what he could possibly say.

"Wait, hang on," Marty added. He sat up slowly, plucked a lighter from his shirt pocket and lit the joint, taking a massive hit. For a moment he held his breath and seemed to stare at nothing. Then he nodded, waved the joint at Holden, and nodded again as if to say, *All right, bring it on.*

"You guys really know how to party," Holden said, chuckling as the others all raised a beer cup in toast. "Okay. Marty. I don't like to, you know, *lecture*, but we've been friends for so *many* minutes now that I feel I can be honest." He pointed at Marty. "You are not Marty. You are 'Pot Marty.' You are living in a womb of reefer and missing out on the real joys of life. I'll tell you, I've learned a lot out on the football field. I've learned about achievement, teamwork, homoerotic butt slapping and good clean fun. Curt here, he doesn't smoke weed. Because he knows it doesn't make you a winner, and because it interferes with his enormous daily dose of steroids."

"I eat them like candy," Curt confirmed seriously.

"Maybe, Marty, you should take a hit from the *life*-bong, and don't take your finger off the life-carb till the chamber's filled up with..." He waved at the air, losing track, searching for something, anything to help him through. "...with... with *opportunity*. For the love of God let me be done."

"Yes!" Dana squealed.

"Bravo!" Jules said, clapping where she stood and

spilling half of her beer. As the group's applause continued, Holden let out a sigh of relief, smiling, and locking eyes with Dana yet again. They both looked away almost awkwardly, as if each glance was becoming more and more loaded.

That's just the beer, he thought. *And Marty's pot fumes*. But he knew that wasn't *all* it was. He wondered if she'd been thinking the same as him as they'd sat listening to Jules and Curt going at it in the shower.

Marty exhaled a huge cloud of smoke.

"Thank you for opening my eyes to whatever it was you just said," he said earnestly. "Jules! Truth or dare or lecture?"

"Let's go dare!" she said. She and Curt were leaning on the back of the sofa now, arms around each other's waists, and Holden could almost see the glow of love between them. He took another long swig of beer.

"All right," Marty nodded, looking around the large room, thinking. "I dare you to make out with..."

"Please say Dana," Curt whispered, "*please* say Dana..."

"...that moose over there!" Marty said, pointing at the stuffed, snarling wolf's head they'd all noticed upon first arriving.

Er, Holden thought, glancing from Marty to the stuffed head and back again. *Maybe I shouldn't be the one to tell him*.

"Um, Marty," Dana said, "have you *seen* a moose before?"

"*Whatever* that mysterious beast is—"

"It's a wolf," Curt said.

"Yeah, it's a wolf," Holden confirmed, grinning.

"*I'm living in a womb of reefer*," Marty complained quietly. "Leave me alone. Okay, beastie, creature, whatever… Jules, I dare you to make out with *the wolf*."

Jules drained her beer cup in one huge glug, threw it over her shoulder and clapped her hands in an *I'll do it!* gesture.

"No problem," she said, and the group cheered.

As Jules walked away from the seating area around the fireplace and toward the stuffed animal head, she put on an exaggerated swagger, swinging her butt gently from side to side. She reached the wolf and walked on by, raising her head slightly in mock-aloofness.

Damn, she's good, Holden thought, and he could see why Curt coveted her so much. Hot, and fun, but… But Dana still shone brightest for him. He watched her watching Jules, and enjoyed that, too.

Jules paused and looked back over her shoulder at the wolf, pointing at her chest. "Who? Me?" She cocked her head as if listening, then continued, "I *am* new in town, how did you know?"

The friends laughed, cheering her on with *whoots* and whistles. But Jules kept her back turned now; she only had eyes for the wolf. She twirled her hair around one finger and stood with a hip thrust out.

"Oh my god, that is *so sweet* of you to say," she purred. "I just colored it, in fact..." That tilted head again, and she was such a good actress that her friends all went quiet, listening for the voice she pretended to hear.

"Yes, I'd love a drink, thank you," she said. She took a step toward the wolf then tripped, stumbling slightly. "Whoops! I seem to have dropped my birth control pills all over the ground..."

Holden clapped, the others hooted and hollered, egging her on and enjoying the great display. Dana glanced back at Holden to see his reaction, and her own eyes were alight. She turned back to Jules, and Holden checked out her back, butt, and legs where she was kneeling up on the sofa.

Jules caught his attention again, turning her back on the wolf and bending down as if picking something from the ground. She arched her back and swung her butt left and right, then stood again, backing up until the growling head was directly over her shoulder. She nuzzled the creature, cheek to cheek.

"Oh Mr. Wolf, you're so big. And *bad*." She nuzzled some more, then lowered her voice, so low that they all had to fall silent to hear what Holden was sure would be the climax of her little play. "No no no, there's no need to huff and puff..." She turned and took the wolf's head in her hands, thumbs stroking across the growling muzzle. "I'll let you come in."

And then Jules leaned in and gave the wolf a kiss so passionate that, for a moment, Holden swore they could have heard a pin drop to the floor.

Curt shouted, and the others followed, jumping to their feet and cheering, whooping and whistling. *I shouldn't have got turned on at that*, Holden thought. *I really shouldn't.*

Jules let go of the wolf's head and turned to the group, performing an extravagant bow before spitting out dust, fur and the taste of who-knew what.

Holden stood beside Dana, and she leaned into him and said, "Bet Curt's glad they got their moment in earlier in the shower."

"Yeah," Holden whispered back, "imagine competing with a wolf?"

Curt hurriedly poured Jules another beer and she took a swig, swilling it around her mouth before swallowing with a grimace.

"I didn't know it was possible," Holden proclaimed, "but I think you just officially won Truth or Dare."

"Or Lecture!" Dana added.

"The night is still young!" Jules said. "Now then... *Dana*—"

"Truth!" Curt called.

Holden noticed Dana's frown as she glanced at Curt, and immediately the atmosphere thickened a little.

"What's that supposed to mean?" she asked.

"I'm just skipping ahead," Curt said, suddenly realizing his misstep. "You're gonna say 'dare,' she's gonna dare you to do something you don't like and then you'll puss out and say you wanted 'truth' all along."

"Really." Dana studied Curt, and Holden shifted uncomfortably from foot to foot. *Not like him to be a dick*, he thought. Maybe his friend was drunker than he thought. Curt was the only person in the room he'd known before today, but suddenly he seemed like a stranger.

Curt nodded. "Or lecture."

"Oh, no, I wouldn't want one of *those*," she said tartly.

Holden looked around at the others. Jules had a somewhat bemused expression on her face, perhaps more to do with how things had moved on so quickly from her performance than at what was being said. And Marty was frowning, his usually relaxed expression troubled. He turned from Curt to Dana and back again, and seemed about to say something.

Curt, too, shifted and raised his head a little, mouth opening to speak, before Dana cut him off.

"Okay, Jules. Dare."

Good for you, Holden thought, and then he cried out as a huge *crash!* came from the corner by the kitchen. Jules screamed, Curt span around, Dana stepped back into Holden, his hands grasping her arms automatically and squeezing. She huddled back into him and that was their first embrace, her shaking, his heart pounding, and neither as a result of each other.

Even Marty jumped, though a second after the others. A cloud of ash flowed down from his joint, speckling the front of his shirt and jeans.

"What the hell was that?" Jules exclaimed.

"It's the cellar door," Dana said. In the kitchen and dining area, just to the left of the dining table and close to the hallway leading back to the bedrooms, a rectangle of darkness had appeared in the floor.

Holden blinked a few times, as if dust was obscuring his vision, because for a moment he thought it was simply an area of blackened boards. *There's nothing below us*, he thought, but then sight of the shadowy, upturned hatch drove that strange idea away.

Dust motes, agitated by the sudden opening, drifted in the air, dancing around the ceiling lights and the several lamps they'd lit and stood around the place. The amount of light in the room made it seem even darker down there.

Dana shifted out of his embrace, but only so she could reach down and squeeze his hand. He squeezed back, taking comfort from the contact as well.

Spooky… he thought, and Holden was not someone easily spooked. As one, they moved around the sofa and other easy chairs and edged toward the cellar door. Jules glanced back at Dana, wide-eyed. She didn't even acknowledge the fact that her friend was grasping Holden's hand.

"I thought... it was locked," Marty drawled.

"The wind must have blown it open," Curt said.

Jules laughed nervously. "What wind?"

They gathered close to the hole and looked down. There was a set of wooden stairs leading into the darkness, the first three or four steps visible, the rest hidden away. The wall to one side of the staircase seemed to be lined with sacking of some sort, gray and dusty. The smell that rose from the hole was age, and something else, something...

Alive, Holden thought. But that was stupid. He

was smelling rats and other critters, their shit and their dead, their lives hidden away beneath this dilapidated old place. That was all.

"What do you think's down there?" he asked.

"Why don't we find out?" Jules said, shrugging. She seemed to notice Dana and Holden's hands then, and smiled. "Dana?"

"What?"

"I dare you." Jules pointed at the hole in the floor.

Dana looked around at everyone. She was nervous, that was obvious, but she was trying to brave through it. Curt nodded, Marty continued frowning, and she looked to Holden last of all. He squeezed her hand tighter, trying to communicate.

This is stupid, you don't have to.

Then she let go of his hand and took a step toward the hole.

"Fine," she said.

The group, the cabin, and the darkness below held their collective breaths.

◇ ◇ ◇

This was the last thing she wanted to do, but there was no way she was going to lose. It wasn't bravado or even a desire to impress Holden; it was what Curt had said. He'd made her out to be a whining wimp, and she wasn't that at all. Not as wild as Jules, perhaps. Not as daring. But once dared, she had no alternative.

So she went down, but even as she did so, she

wondered in the back of her mind if she should have simply refused and nailed the hatch shut.

"Dana," Marty said as she stepped down onto the first tread. He plucked a small flashlight from above the kitchen sink and handed it to her. She switched it on and discovered that the light was weak and puny, so she wiped the front clear. That made no difference; the batteries must have been low, so she decided to turn it off until she really needed it.

"Yawn," Curt said, and Dana didn't even grace him with a look. *What the hell was wrong with that dick?* Too much beer, maybe. Or maybe back in the shower, Jules hadn't been quite so accommodating as they'd all assumed.

The second tread creaked loudly, and the third, the creaks providing background to her journey down. The smell closed around her, and the heavy, warm atmosphere—heated, perhaps, by pipes passing beneath the floorboards to the cabin's various rooms. She gasped, and the warm air she tasted reminded her of stale wet dog. She turned the torch on, but it was barely effective, the light serving more to deepen the darkness further around it than to illuminate close by.

"How long do I have to stay down here?" she called.

"Oh, you know, just 'til morning," Curt said, and she cursed him silently. *Prick*. Later, she decided, she'd ask Jules just what was wrong with him all of a sudden. She only hoped her friend knew.

Half a dozen more creaking stairs and then she was at the bottom, standing on a rough, packed soil floor that was covered in dust and grit. Shining the light around she caught vague glimpses of shapes in the darkness, inanimate shadows, each of which seemed to possess a hulking, waiting stance. Even squinting she could not make out much: an old shelving unit, vague objects bundled here and there; a bookshelf leaning with damp, its shelves stacked with books whose titles had long since worn away; the flared mouth of an old gramophone.

She could see nothing more, yet she had a feeling there was plenty down there. She sensed the size of the room, yet even her breathing was dampened by the contents piled within.

So she moved away from the staircase and into the darkness, the torch her only companion.

Away from the stairs, the complete darkness gave the flashlight more power. Its beam penetrated further, and soon Dana confirmed just how packed this basement was, and how random its contents seemed to be. The light glinted from metal tools stacked against the wall and hanging from hooks along its length. Most were rusted, bright metal showing only here and there, and some of them seemed to be broken. She made out the gramophone in more detail, an old wind-up device that would likely fetch a decent price at an antique market. Beside it was a landslide of old musical instrument cases, some closed, most open to reveal their barren insides. Scattered across the pile like snowdrifts on a hillside, heaps of sheet music lay in silence.

Moving to the left, Dana's heart leapt as the light fell across a humanoid shape standing behind a layer of thin, dusty net curtains. She held her breath and was about to flee when she saw that the shape had no head. She exhaled slowly and advanced, sweeping the hanging curtain aside. It was as light as a spider's web.

Beyond, the decapitated dressmaker's mannequin stood propped against a table, one of its feet broken off, as well. It wore a half-stitched dress, a lace affair that might once have been beautiful but which now was browned by damp and time. Dana wondered whom the dress had been intended for and how many times they had tried it on, standing motionless while a dressmaker pinned and folded, measured and cut. Whoever it had been, she guessed they were long dead now.

On the table beside the mannequin were several china dolls, their faces mostly broken and cracked. She found them more sad than troubling. Children had once played with these things and now, like the dress's vanished owner, they were gone, leaving only their broken toys behind.

"Dana? Hey Dana..."

She moved further around the room, ignoring the soft calls from Jules. The cabin above was a different world now, a long distance in time and space from this trove of old treasures. Though disturbed, Dana also found herself entranced by this collection of a life's leftovers. There was a toy chest with toys spilled around its base, including wooden animals, spinning tops, musical instruments, and gaily painted puppets. One corner seemed to be taken with a circus act's equipment, and Roberto: The Limbless Man stared out at her from a billboard and several posters. Circus games, their origins and uses lost to memory, stood either side of Roberto's posters, beautifully built, their garish colors fading down in the basement.

Bookshelves, furniture, hat boxes, mirrors, paintings, lamps, sculptured animals in wood and metal, a rack of movie reels—

And then the torch passed across a ghostly face staring right at her.

Dana screamed and dropped the torch, scrabbling to snatch it up again and backing against a wardrobe, its corner and joints soft and weakened by decay. Something fell inside the wardrobe—it sounded *wet*—and she slid away, torch and attention still fixed on the face.

Those eyes so probing so harsh so knowing*!*

"Dana?" Holden called from above. Footsteps rang on the stairs and timber creaked, and it sounded as if his voice and steps were coming in from a great distance, not just twenty feet away. Even as she realized that the glaring face was a portrait she was willing Holden to her, and hoping he would make the journey in safety.

Weird idea, she thought, and then Holden was by her side, holding her arm and looking at the portrait as well. It was actually a daguerreotype, she saw, of a young woman maybe fifteen years old. Her clothes were turn-of-the-century, and she stared with a grimness that typified portraiture of the time.

"You okay?" Holden asked. More clattering and creaking, and the others arrived behind him, even Curt looking concerned. *Changed* his *tune*, she thought.

"Yeah. Sorry. I just... scared myself. It was stupid."

"You called for help," Curt said. "Voids the dare. Take your top off."

Marty struck a match and lit an old oil lantern hanging on the wall, adjusting it so that the flame burned bright. It smoked for the first few seconds, burning off oil that had been coagulating for years, and then the orange light diffused through the room.

The others all gasped, and Dana caught her breath.

It's even more amazing than I thought.

"Oh my God," Holden muttered.

The basement occupied at least the floor area of the cabin above, perhaps more, and every dark corner seemed to be filled with creepy clutter.

"Look at all this," Jules said, and she was the first to slowly start examining the piles of stuff.

"Uh, guys," Marty said, "I'm not sure it's awesome to be down here." He stood at the bottom of the staircase, the oil lamp back on the hook beside him, and he looked as if he'd be darting back upstairs at the slightest provocation.

But the others weren't paying any attention. Jules and Curt were off on their own, each focusing on different parts of the basement, and Holden still stood beside Dana, peering around in wonder. He took a step and picked up an ornate music box from the pile of children's toys. Removing his glasses from his pocket and slipping them on, he turned the box this way and that before pausing, seemingly holding his breath.

"Dude, seriously, your cousin's into some weird shit."

Curt was across the basement holding a conch shell in his hands, turning it this way and that, and he brought it halfway to his ear—*You can hear the sea if you press an old shell to your ear*—before changing his mind and quickly putting it back down. He picked up a melon-sized wooden sphere that lay behind it. It was inlaid with dusty brass rings and lined with angular joints, and he turned it in his hands as if trying to find a way in.

"Pretty sure this ain't his," he said. "Maybe the people who put in that window..."

Dana couldn't take her eyes off the portrait of the girl. It was propped on a hardwood stand, and a black sheet hung over the portrait's frame as if it had once been concealed from view. On the small vanity table that stood before it was a variety of personal effects: an old hairbrush; a silver mirror; and a leather-bound book.

"Some of this stuff looks *really* old," she said.

"Look at this," Jules said. She had moved across to the dressmaker's mannequin, less spooky in the lamplight but still strange with the unfinished garment still tight upon it. She touched something hanging around its neck, an amulet, and as she held it in her hand she said, "It's beautiful."

"Maybe we should go back upstairs," Marty said. He was still standing at the bottom of the staircase, looking around nervously, hands clasped in front of him. *He's actually scared*, Dana thought, and the idea disturbed her. When no one answered him he said, "I dare you all to go upstairs?"

And then Marty froze, and a small smile crept through his fear.

"Oh wow, take a look at this," he said, and he walked a few steps to where a bunch of old film reels were stacked. Beneath them was a super-8 projector, and piled beside it several small suitcase-style containers that Dana thought might contain more reels. The plinth they stood on was circular and built up of regular stones, its tabletop a board of thick, roughly cut wood. It looked like an old capped well.

Dana frowned, wondering what a well was doing in the basement of a house; or rather, why a cabin would be built *around* a well.

Marty plucked a reel from its rack and started examining it.

"Porn?" Curt asked, but Marty didn't reply. He started unspooling it, holding the film up to the light and moving it slowly through his hand, mouth open in wonder.

"What is it, Marty?" Dana asked, but whatever story was playing before his eyes, it seemed to hold him entranced and distant from them.

So Dana turned and approached the portrait, staring into the girl's eyes and trying to blink back the certainty that they stared back. Perhaps it was something to do with the way the portrait had been formed, the material behind it, or the manner in which it had been slightly faded by the basement air, but the girl's eyes seemed so alive.

She picked up the book and brushed dust from its

cover, revealing the word "diary" in extravagant gold lettering. Opening the cover, she looked up, suddenly afraid of what she might read.

I should close this, she thought. *Put it back where it belongs, place it exactly in the rectangle of dust it left on the table.*

And we should all stop doing what we're doing...

She looked around at the others, all of them seemingly entranced by this place and consumed by the small part of it they were each examining. Holden was winding the small handle on a music box, and the haunting metallic music filled the air, pinging from note to note and somehow bringing tears to Dana's eyes. Curt was frowning as he worked sections of the wooden sphere, pulling rings, sliding wood against wood, clicking sections into place as he worked on transforming it into something else.

Jules had removed the golden amulet from around the dummy's neck and was holding it to her own neck, staring into a dusty mirror to see how it looked, and Dana thought that in the mirror her friend looked as old as everything else down here. Jules searched for the clasp as if to try it on for real.

Don't try it on, Dana thought, her own desperation surprising her. She tore her eyes away and saw Marty unwinding more and more film, leaving it to stream around his feet as he watched his own private moments against the lamplight, mouth and eyes wide, and she knew that even if she shouted right then it might not be enough.

The music box's music filled the basement, an incidental theme to Marty's movie, and Curt's puzzle box, and Jules's effort to undo the amulet's clasp—

Dana looked down at the diary and started reading, and from the very first word she imagined them being spoken by the girl in the portrait.

Then she wrenched herself free.

"*Guys!*" she called. The music box stopped, and the others all paused in what they were doing. When they looked at her, Dana saw some measure of relief in their eyes, as if they each had found their tasks challenging and draining and were glad to be distracted. "Guys, listen to this," she said. The others came and stood around her, and then it was just Dana and the book.

She had opened the diary at random, and the words sprang out at her and clasped hold, taking her away from her own time and back to when they were written. Above her the cabin was different, and if she hadn't had her friends around her she wasn't sure she could have held on.

She took a deep breath and started reading.

"'Today we felled the old birch tree out back. I was sorrowed to see it go, as Judah and I had sat up in its branches so many summers...'"

"What *is* that?" Jules asked.

Dana paged back to the inside front cover. She'd already read the inscription there, but she didn't want to get any of it wrong.

"It's the Diary of Anna Patience Buckner, 1903."

"Wow," Curt muttered.

"That's the original owners, right?" Jules asked. "That creepy old fuck called this the Buckner place." No one commented, no one questioned.

Dana continued reading from where she'd left off.

"'Father was cross with me and said I lacked the true faith. I wish I could prove my devotion, as Judah and Matthew proved on those travelers...'"

"Uh, that makes what kind of sense?" Marty asked.

"You know," Holden said, "it's uncommon that a girl out here was reading and writing in that era."

"'Mama screamed most of the night,'" Dana continued. "'I prayed that she might find faith, but she only stopped when papa cut her belly and stuffed the coals in.'" She stopped, breath held, and looked up at the others. No one said a word. The silence was heavy and loaded, and she wanted to read on. She looked back down. "'Judah told me in my dream that Matthew took him to the Black Room so I know he is killed. Matthew's faith is too great; even Father does not cross him or speak of Judah. I want to understand the glory of the pain like Matthew, but cutting the flesh makes him have a husband's bulge and I do not get like that.'"

"Jesus," Marty gasped, "can we not—"

"Go on," Curt said.

"Why?" Marty asked.

"Suck it up or bail, pothead! I wanna know."

Dana looked around—at Curt, her friend who still seemed to have become a dick, and the others—and finally at Holden. He gave her a small nod.

We should have closed the hatch and nailed it back

down, she thought, and then she flipped forward a few pages and continued reading.

"'I have found it. In the oldest books: the way of saving our family. I can hear Matthew in the Black Room, working upon father's jaw. My good arm is hacked up and et so I hope this will be readable, that a believer will come and speak this to our spirits. Then we will be restored and the Great Pain will return.'" She looked up, breathing a sigh of relief because she was almost at the end. "And then there's something in Latin," she said.

"Okay, " Marty said, "I am drawing a line in the fucking sand here—do *not* read the Latin." He frowned, looking around as if a bee had buzzed his ear. "The fuck…?" he said, waving one arm around his head. Marty started across the room toward Dana, face set, hand coming up to snatch the book from her hand.

Curt stepped forward, planted a hand on Marty's chest and shoved him back. He went sprawling, crashing into a bookshelf and covering his head as books fell on him in a shower of dust and dead, curled-up spiders.

"Fucking baby!" Curt shouted.

"Curt…" Jules said.

"It's a *diary*!" he shouted, louder. "Just a *diary*!"

"It doesn't even mean anything," Dana said, desperate to defuse the situation. Marty looked scared, and Curt looked... he looked mean. Tall, angry, and mean. "Look," she continued.

"Dana..." Marty said, voice tinged with hopelessness.

Dana shook her head and tried to laugh, but it

didn't work. So she simply read the inscription to show Marty—to show *all* of them—that they'd been creeped out for no reason. *Get this done and get the fuck out of this basement*, she thought. *Yeah, that's right. Get the fuck out and...*

"*Dolor supervivo caro. Dolor sublimes caro*," she intoned. The words read, she closed the book.

Nothing happened.

Someone sighed, then started quietly sobbing. And when Holden gently took her arm and guided her back up the staircase, she realized that it was her.

◇ ◇ ◇

Outside the cabin, in the forest where free will could not hold, there was movement.

The forest floor was soft with layers and layers of old leaves, those on the surface still almost recognizable as such from the previous fall, those deeper down little more than mulch. Deeper still, soil and mud, through which things crawled and ate and mated and died. There was no breeze and yet the surface leaves shifted, pushing upward in a small mound and then breaking apart as something forced through. Gray and gnarled, a hand, fisted around the haft of a rusted knife.

It rose further and bent at the elbow, lying flat across the ground as the body below heaved itself upward.

Elsewhere, rising from shallow graves, other bodies came. One, a boy, carried a scythe. Another, an obese woman, bore a broken, ragged saw. A man, followed by a huge form—a zombie, by any commonly recognized definition, dead people rising again under unnatural animation—which shrugged itself free of leaves and mud. The journey up from the ground had not been difficult. The graves were not deep, the leaves above them not so old.

A final shifting in the forest gave birth to a one-armed girl. In her one good hand, a hatchet. Anna Patience. Her eyes were far deader than those of her likeness.

They stood for a while like trees, and from a distance in the early evening darkness that was what they resembled. Dead trees, perhaps, broken off below the branching, just stumps, home to insects and spiders and slugs, waiting to rot and crumble and fall. But though *some* of that was true—they *were* home to small creatures, and all had gone some way toward eventual disintegration—the image of trees vanished quickly when they began to move.

Anna Patience was the first. A stumbling step, her one good arm swinging and slashing the air with the hatchet it bore.

Her teeth bared by the shriveling of her lips, she made for the light of the cabin.

FIVE

On screen, the zombie family had come together and were shambling their way toward the cabin. They didn't acknowledge each other, because perhaps they couldn't. But obviously there was an instinct at play here, and perhaps a need, because as they drew closer to the cabin they started to groan and grumble... almost as if in excitement.

Sitterson shivered, then smiled. And turning away from the large viewscreen he spoke loudly.

"We have a winner!"

The crowd cheered in anticipation. They surrounded him and Hadley. Pretty much everyone was there, as always, waiting to see how the bet would play out and who would win the wad of cash even now clasped in Hadley's hand. It was a pivotal part of each event, and once it was done they could move on.

"It's the Buckners, ladies and gentlemen! Buckners pull the 'W'!"

Most of the crowd groaned in disappointment. Betting slips were torn and thrown, and Sitterson glanced at Lin in amusement as she watched the littering with barely restrained disapproval. They milled and muttered, shrugging and offering one another sad smiles of loss.

But at the back of Control, close to the banks of computers, several men in work clothes and with tool belts clasped around their waists threw up their hands and cheered in triumph.

"Don't be sore losers now, folks," Sitterson said affably. "Looks like congratulations go to Maintenance!" The guys nodded to him and grinned, and he eased back his chair and scanned the betting board.

It was the same every time—disappointment and celebration. And it was always at this moment that he drew into himself a little, backing away from his surroundings and the people filling them to muse upon what all this really meant. The betting board seemed glib and amusing, a physical acknowledgment of what they were doing here.

The first column listed every department that had chosen to bet: Electrical, Engineering, Security, Zoology, and several more. At the bottom of the column were persons whose departments declined to take part, but who as individuals couldn't go a cycle without being a part of the big wager.

And listed in the next column, as if in a confession, were the eternal options: vampires, werewolves, floating witches, aliens, zombies, Kevin, clowns, wraiths, scarecrows, angry molesting trees, mutants...

Sitterson closed his eyes and breathed deeply.

What all this really means... he thought, and he opened his eyes again. No need to dwell on it. He had work to do. So he turned to the crowd again.

"And Maintenance split the pot with... Ronald the intern!" he continued. He handed a handful of cash to one of the cheering men from Maintenance, and Ronald the intern sauntered over from the back of the room, beaming with delight but looking shyly at his shoes, to collect the other wad.

The cheering died down, and people began filing from the room, some shaking their heads and others muttering under their breath. The excitement over, it was time to get back to work.

Sitterson and Hadley exchanged a smile. The pot had been good this year, and their ten percent commission would sit well in their pockets.

Then they turned back to their control panels. Sitterson tapped his keyboard and was just about to access a lakeside camera when he felt a tap on his shoulder.

He turned to face a short, pretty woman with brunette hair tied in a tight bun behind her head. She wore a lab coat, and a mask hung around her throat. Her striking blue eyes were wide, and the beginnings of a charming smile froze and died on his face as he sensed her simmering anger.

"That's not fair!" she said. "I had zombies too!"

Sitterson's smile rose again, because he knew he could deal with this. And off to the side he sensed Hadley's sudden interest. He stood and went to the betting board, even picking up a long thin pointer because he thought it would make him look more official. He heard a chuckle from his friend but chose to ignore it.

"Yes, you had 'zombies.' But this is 'Zombie Redneck Torture Family.'" He tapped the board to indicate what he meant. "Entirely separate thing. It's like the difference between an elephant and an elephant seal."

The woman opened her mouth to protest, scanning the felt-marked phrases he was pointing to. Then her shoulders slumped and she turned to go, and Sitterson felt a pang of regret that she hadn't argued more. She was cute. Maybe she'd have started to swear. He liked cute women who swore.

"There's always next year," he offered as she went. Still no cursing.

Truman stepped aside to let the woman through the door and closed it behind her, checking through the viewing port to make sure she really was walking away. *By the fucking book*, Sitterson thought. When Truman turned back and stared at the screen, he saw the soldier's fear beneath the cool slick surface, and the doubts that must be plaguing him were something known to Sitterson. He had struggled through the same fears and doubts his first time. And though he might silently mock the man, right then he empathized.

"They're like something from a nightmare," Truman said.

"No," Lin disagreed. She'd remained in Control after everyone else had left, observing the betting and the results, waiting for the high-jinks to be over so she could get on with her job. "They're something that nightmares are from. Everything in our stable is a remnant of the old world, courtesy of..." She pointed down. "You know who."

"Monsters, magic..." Truman said, his voice trailing off.

"You get used to it," Lin said, and she almost smiled.

"*Should* you?" Truman countered. Lin did not reply, Truman returned to watching the screen, and Sitterson turned his back on both of them.

He'll have plenty of sleepless nights after this during which to philosophize, he thought, recalling again his first time. *Plenty*.

He walked across to Hadley, who was staring up at the screens, despondent now. Sitterson knew exactly what was eating him.

"I'm sorry, man."

"He had the conch *in his hands*!"

"I know. Couple more minutes, who knows what would have happened."

Hadley sighed, frustrated.

"I'm *never* gonna get to see a merman."

"Dude, be thankful," Sitterson said. "Apparently those things are terrifying. And the clean-up on them's a nightmare."

Hadley nodded and shrugged, but Sitterson knew that he'd react like this every year until he had his way. Still…

"So, the Buckners, huh?" Hadley said, pointing at the monitor.

"I know," Sitterson muttered. "Well, they may be zombified pain-worshipping backwoods idiots, but..." And he smiled.

"They're *our* zombified pain-worshipping backwoods idiots," Hadley said, grinning again as they walked back to the control panel.

"Yeah! And they have a hundred percent clearance rate."

"True. We may as well tell Japan to take the rest of the weekend off."

"Yeah, right," Sitterson said, laughing. He glanced over at Lin. *Still not smiling! Maybe she really* is *a fucking robot. Has one of them escaped?* "They're *Japanese*. What are they gonna do, *relax*?"

"I don't know," Hadley said, sitting back down at his console. "Maybe they can do some group calisthenics or something."

"Ha!" Sitterson said. "So, let's see how they're doing then, eh?" He went to his desk and accessed his computer, and a moment later the big screen in the middle of the wall flickered from an image of the cabin's basement to a clinical, well-lit school room.

There was movement at the top—it looked like a black and white mass shifting and throbbing in the corner of the room—and then several Japanese school children broke from the mass, running terrified as a young girl floated through the air toward them. It looked as if she was hanging from an invisible noose, but Sitterson knew better.

Her bloated, pale face and black eyes spoke volumes, and her long black hair, sopping wet and dripping as though soaked by an invisible hose, dragged along the floor behind her, shimmering as if with a life of its own.

The school kids tried to open the classroom door but it was locked.

Behind the floating girl, in the far corner, several black and white shapes were also splashed with red.

"Hmmm," Sitterson said. "Looking good." But he couldn't help feeling a simmering jealousy.

He tapped a key and brought the image back to the cabin. The kids were back up from the basement. The blonde was slipping a CD into the stereo. The basement hatch was down, the dining table and chair dragged to sit on top of it.

As music blared, Sitterson spoke.

"And so the end begins."

◇ ◇ ◇

Marty took the armchair. He was alone, after all. He puffed determinedly on his joint, watching everyone else through a haze of smoke, and wondered what was going on. Closing his eyes, he tried to move back from where he was. Concentrate on things without the pot affecting his judgment. But still the music pounded through his senses, and the impact of dancing feet vibrated through the floor, and he opened his eyes again without arriving at any conclusions.

It was some blandly modern rock crap that Jules had slipped into the CD player. Marty didn't even know the band's name, though he'd heard the music enough times, blaring from the music systems of those who didn't know better. Its members were probably multi-millionaires who owned six houses and who finished each and every gig in the shower with a dozen girls each, all of them willing to do something different. A production line of sex. He chuckled silently to himself, but the idea seemed more disturbing than funny. Music without soul and balls was not music at all, it was noise.

Dana would think the same. He watched her on the couch, reading the book she'd found and leaning against Holden, but the frown on her face had nothing to do with the vacuousness of the thundering vibes. It was something altogether different, and Marty sat up straighter as he tried to translate her expression.

She knows there's something weird going on, too, he thought. He took another toke on the spliff, and for the first time in a long while wondered if he was smoking too much.

Jules was dancing around the large room. She sure could move, he'd say that for her. She had a gorgeous body—which he'd once had a brief opportunity to explore with his own two hands, though his memory of it, as with most of his memories, was somewhat hazed—and she was working it now, thrusting out her chest, shaking that long newly-blonde hair, wiggling her ass, stomping her feet, then using the MTV-friendly guitar solos to grind her hips and work her groin. There was a film of sweat on her face which only made her glow more, and she'd popped a couple of buttons on her shirt to expose more cleavage. Her bra was visible, and the mounds of her breasts moved heavily in time with her movements.

"Sweet," Marty muttered, his voice lost to the music. But maybe it was *too* sweet. Jules was cute and all, a little air-headed maybe, but generally decent and honest. He'd never thought of her as desperate.

Curt was dancing with her in that awkward, self-conscious way most guys had. He wasn't a natural mover, but he was doing his best, following behind Jules and cupping her butt when she wasn't writhing and twisting too much, squeezing, and running his hands up and down her stomach and chest from behind when she gave him the opportunity. She was the seductress and he was the poor, led fool. It would have been pitiful if Marty didn't know Curt well enough. Last thing *he* was, for a fact, was desperate. He was going along with it because he wanted to go along with it, and that was that.

Jules moved into the seating area, knocking the table slightly with her legs and spilling a slick of beer, arms raised and hands entwining each other like dancing snakes, hips twisting. She moved in front of Holden and performed a quick, suggestive lap-dance for him, bending over to wave her ass in his face, then turning and stretching one foot up onto the couch's back right next to his head. She flexed to and fro, running both hands along her leg to her foot and back again.

Dude, you look so awkward, Marty thought as he watched Holden. The guy was looking anywhere but at Jules—though Marty thought he did see his eyes flicker just briefly to her cleavage a couple of times, and once to her crotch, denim shorts stretched tight by her movement. He looked sidelong at Dana, who was still involved in the diary but obviously not too thrilled at the display.

"Go baby, oh yeah!" Curt called. "That's the goods right there, fuck yeah!"

"This is so *classy*," Marty said.

"Like you wouldn't want a piece of that," Curt scoffed.

"Can we not talk about people in *pieces* anymore tonight?" Marty held up his joint, raised his eyebrows as if to make a point, then took another puff.

Jules slipped away from Holden, and his relief was obvious. She turned on Marty this time, moving luxuriously, running her fingertips up her stomach and over her chest. Her nipples were obvious against the strained shirt.

"Oh, are you feeling lonely, Marty?" she asked. She plucked the joint from his fingers and sucked hard. "Marty and I were sweeties in our freshman hall," she said over her shoulder.

"We made out once," Marty said. "I never did buy that ring."

Jules pouted.

"But we're still... close." She blew smoke in his face, lips close to his, and then handed him back the joint. She'd smoked a third of it in one hard puff, and he wondered how the hell she wasn't coughing her guts up on the floor. She danced away, back to the open area between sofa and dining table, where Curt awaited her with his questing hands.

"You know, I have a theory about all this," Marty said.

"That's our cue to bail!" Curt cried out, throwing up his hands and showing the sweat patches on his tee-shirt. "Tommy Chong has a *theory*. You can tell it to Egghead Holden here, if he's not too busy devirginizing Dana."

Dana pressed her lips together, stood, and dropped the book on the couch. She paused for a second, looking into the fireplace at the fire that was burning down because no one had thought to add any more logs.

We can't look after ourselves, Marty thought. Dana shot a quick glance in his direction, then turned to her roommate and spoke up.

"Jules, do you want to lie down?"

"That's exactly the *point*!" Curt said, shoving Jules toward the door. "Mush! Mush!"

"Don't push me around," Jules protested, but she wasn't upset, and she even made her objection sound suggestive.

"Not around, baby," Curt said. "Straight line. Right

there. Out there. Pretty stars!" He reached around her and tugged the door open, and the breath of air made the dying fire glow brighter for a few seconds. The two of them left the cabin and it suddenly became motionless, music still blasting, a knot in the fire popping.

Then Dana sighed and crossed to the kitchen to pour another beer.

Marty hauled himself up from the chair. Holden was still on the couch, avoiding his eyes, tapping his fingers on his knee.

"Hey..." Marty began, but Holden picked up the leather-bound diary and started flicking through it, pausing here and there as if he'd found something interesting. "Dude, it's cool," Marty said, but walking across to Dana he felt the lie in that.

Reaching the place where she stood, he handed her his own beer cup and she started filling it. She didn't look at him or speak.

"Do you seriously believe that nothing weird is going on?" he asked, surprising himself with the bluntness of the question.

"A conspiracy?" she asked wryly. She smiled, but it was without humor. He saw the strain in her beautiful face.

"The way everybody's acting!" he said.

"I'm sorry about downstairs," she sighed, waving at Holden and the diary.

"It's cool, it's not..." Marty shrugged. "I mean, when did Curt start with this alpha male bullshit? He's a sociology major; he's on a full academic scholarship!

Now he's calling his friend an "egghead," whose head in no way resembles an egg..." He looked over at Holden. "Except... ahhh. Okay, kinda, from this angle, it's..." He smiled and held his own head in an effort to keep it from becoming egg-shaped.

"Curt's just drunk," Dana said.

"I've seen Curt drunk," Marty said, serious again. And serious hurt his head. "Jules, too. And this ain't them."

"Then maybe it's something else," she said, pointing at his joint with one hand and taking a sup of beer with the other. She had a line of foam settled across her top lip, and Marty found it unbearably cute.

"My secret secret stash is a gateway to enlightenment," he said. "It's not a devolvafier." He glanced at the stuffed wolf's head, still unreasonably disturbed by the terrifying growl it had found for eternity. "Moose, back me up on this. Dana, you're not seeing what you don't wanna see—the puppeteers."

"Puppeteers?" That caused him to toss her a puzzled look.

"Pop-tarts?" he asked, frowning, putting one hand to his head and wondering what he was on about. *Backtrack a little here*, he thought. "Er... did you say that you have pop-tarts?"

Dana laughed.

"Marty, I love you, but you're really high."

"*We are not who we are*," Marty said, deadly serious. He closed his eyes and tried to find where that had come from, but there was a part of him removed now, conducting this conversation and tweaking his emotions while the real Marty sat back in the armchair, chilled and smoking and without a care... "I'm gonna read a book with pictures." He ambled down the corridor to his room, feeling Dana watching him go.

What does she think, the gorgeous Dana who can never be mine? He wasn't sure. Wasn't even sure what *he* thought. A lie down, that's what he needed. A rest. Rest those eyes, that mind...

Rest.

◇ ◇ ◇

Dana watched him go. Marty. He was sweet, and a great friend. She'd never wanted to spoil their friendship with anything more, and she never really thought of him that way. But usually when he was high he didn't freak her out so much. The few times she'd tried pot she'd gone pale and sweaty, her heart-rate had increased, and she'd ended up puking or lying on her bed for the next three hours while it left her system. Marty was a pot veteran; she'd never seen or heard of anyone smoking as much as him, without it seeming to impede his judgment or consciousness. Not *too* much, at least.

Alone in the room with Holden, it felt peaceful at last. She turned down the music and glanced over to see if he had noticed, but he seemed involved with the diary. So she took over two beers and sat beside him again, holding one out for him. He took it and nodded his thanks, but still didn't take his eyes from the book.

When he did speak, it wasn't anything Dana was expecting to hear.

"'The pain outlives the flesh. The flesh returns... or re... has a meeting place... towards the pain's ascension.'" He was obviously reading from the diary, brow furrowed, one finger following the words.

"What's that?" she asked.

"The Latin. That you—"

"You speak Latin?" she asked, surprised.

"Not well, and not since tenth grade. Weird how it comes back." He sipped his beer, frowning at the book a little longer before closing it and tossing it to one side. It landed on the sofa and flopped open again, to the exact page he'd been reading. Dana noticed, but Holden didn't seem to.

Finally, he only had eyes for her.

"Well, it's been a weird time. I'm so sorry about... tonight." She shrugged. "You know. Everybody."

"Do I lose points if I tell you I'm having a pretty nice time?" he asked.

"No, you can tell me that. No points lost." She sipped her own beer, and watched Holden get up and stoke the fire. He threw on more logs and used the poker, rooting around and blowing gently on the glowing embers until the crackle of flames rose again. They were small to begin with, but they would spread. Warmth bled outward from the fire again, and Dana relaxed deeper into the sofa.

Holden sat back down beside her, closer than e

and placed his arm across the back of the sofa behind her. It wasn't a secretive move, and his hand rested easily on her shoulder. Dana leaned sideways until her head touched his shoulder and thought, *Maybe it'll be an okay evening after all. Maybe Curt just needs to get laid, and Jules is drunk on first-night excitement, and Marty... Marty's just high.*

But then as the flames sparked higher she thought of Holden's translation of the Latin she'd read out: *The pain outlives the flesh*. And even through the fresh heat she felt goosebumps prickling her arms.

◇ ◇ ◇

Jules ran. Perspiration was cooling all over her, chilling her, making her muscles seem frozen and her skin prickle with a million points of ice.

Footsteps pounded behind her, closing, closing, and she put on an extra spurt of speed. The darkness did not slow her, and neither did the feel of spider webs breaking across her face and neck as she ducked between trees. Maybe she was more drunk than she thought, or perhaps it was just the thrill of the chase. The chase, she'd always known, was better than the catch, and maybe that was why she'd always had guys in the palm of her hand.

There were her looks, sure; she knew she was a scorcher. But she also knew what guys wanted, and *when*, perhaps better than they. There was a difference between leading them on toward nothing, and racing them toward something.

So she ran, giggling, breathing hard, skirting the lake to her right and curving around into a part of the woods they hadn't seen before. And just when she judged the moment was right she slowed a little, feeling Curt's arm close around her waist as he skidded to a stop and swept her from her feet. Her legs kicked up and he turned, bringing her around to stand again before him.

In his other hand he was still carrying his beer cup, most of it spilled now, but some still glinting in the bottom. He was grinning. Breathing hard. She wasn't sure she'd ever seen him quite like this, but then she also felt...

Different, she thought. *And horny as all hell.* The afternoon's shower escapades had, it seemed, been just a prelude.

"Come here!" he said, pulling her close, the remaining beer slopping from the cup.

"Ah! Don't spill on me!"

"Thought you liked it when I spilled on you."

"Your beer, pig." But Jules giggled, writhing in his grasp.

"Did I get a little beer on your shirt?" He kissed her deep and hard. "I guess it'll have to come off." He threw the beer cup away and started plucking at her buttons. She pulled back playfully, shirt stretching.

"Not here," she teased.

"Oh, come on..." He paused and looked around, grinning. "We're all alone." He pulled her shirt open but she caught the edge and held it together again, stepping back, enjoying the chase just a little more. She was aching for him, but the ache would be more satisfyingly tended the longer this preamble continued. Curt knew that too, but his eyes were almost animal with lust now.

"I'm chilly," she said, pouting as Curt advanced on her. *Like a big bear*, she thought. *Here comes* my *big bear.*

◇ ◇ ◇

A groan passed through the crowd of assembled onlookers. The girl backed away again, shirt tight across her chest, even though they could all see the sweat beaded on her face.

It was going well. It was going to plan. But Sitterson was keen to speed things along. Time might be running out, and he wanted to see—

"Okay, that's enough," Hadley said, standing from his desk. "Everybody out. You've all got jobs to do." He waved them toward the exit, and nodded to Truman to hold the door open for all of them.

Just like Hadley, Sitterson thought, smiling. *He's never liked watching the fucking with too many people around him.*

After the other workers had been herded out his friend sat again, then wheeled his chair expertly across. Sitterson knew immediately what Hadley was going to ask.

"We got temperature control in that sector?"

"On it," Sitterson said, smiling. He'd already been notching the temperature up, subtly but noticeably. He opened a window on his computer and nudged the touch-screen thermometer up a little more. "It'll be tropical in there within minutes," he said.

"Nice," Hadley replied. He was back at his own station now, tapping away on his own computer. "Okay, engaging the pheromone mists."

Chem guys are doing well this time, Sitterson thought. *I'll have Tom compliment the Ice Queen on that. But here's the next big test for them.* The mists were notoriously glitchy. A breath of a breeze from somewhere—their control of the environment was extensive, but not complete—and the effect could be lost entirely. But this time...

This time he was feeling good about things.

It was all going according to plan.

He smiled. He'd long ago shed the guilt he ought to feel over what would happen next.

◇ ◇ ◇

Damn, it's warm, she thought. The air around them was hazed with a subtle mist, and maybe that had raised the temperature a little, a damp heat that seemed to have spread all across and through her body. *Oh, fuck it, this has gone on long enough*. She breathed in through her nose, still holding the edges of her blous closed, but feeling the heat growing in her stomach a groin. Her legs were weak, her fingertips tingling.

She opened her eyes and looked at Curt, her lust reflected there.

He came close for another kiss and she let go of her shirt, wrapping her arms around him, sliding them up beneath his shirt to feel his muscled body slicked with a sheen of sweat. Their mouths met and passions merged. Jules kissed with her eyes open, relishing the sight of him and eager to be a part of their surroundings. It was so warm... so comfortable... so conducive to love.

She tugged hard at his shirt and felt buttons pop, and his low laughter gave her license to pull harder.

"It's so dark," she muttered, for some reason feeling the need for one last, weak protest. "I'm gonna get twig-butt. Take me inside." When all the time she was thinking, *Have me now, fuck me* now!

"Baby, this is why we came here," Curt breathed into her mouth. "It's romantic." He turned her, one hand on her tight stomach, the other gently pulling her open shirt down so that he could nibble on her. He knew how wild that drove her, and he ran his teeth down her neck and along to the nub of her shoulder, biting softly and holding her up when her knees weakened.

Her breath came fast and—

◇ ◇ ◇

—Sitterson coughed, trying to cover his embarrassment. He was supposed to be a professional, but *damn*, this was hot. The jock was a jerk, but the girl was gorgeous.

He thought perhaps the Chem guys had allowed a bit too much aphrodisiac, but that was one mistake he didn't mind.

"Music, and moonlight, and love and ro...mance." he sang softly to himself, tapping some computer keys and tweaking a small level on his control panel.

On the large viewing screen, behind the writhing, still-standing couple an area of moss and soft green ferns seemed to glow from within, only slightly but enough to draw their attention. Neither of them even looked as they edged that way, and he sat back and cracked the knuckles on both hands.

He looked across at Hadley.

"Eh?" he asked, nodding at the screen. "Eh?"

Hadley nodded.

Damn, I'm good, Sitterson thought. *And now—*

◇ ◇ ◇

Jules felt dizzy with lust. Curt eased her down onto the ground, and the moss and ferns seemed softer than the mattress back in the cabin, warmer, there were no creaks, and the gentle scent of nature drifted around her as they explored each other's bodies.

She heaved herself up and they rolled, Curt beneath her now. She propped herself on one elbow for a moment, her hand traveling down across his washboard stomach and delving beneath his belt. He held his breath, she held back for just a moment, the she closed her hand around him and he groaned.

Damn, he's as horny as me, she thought. As his hands ventured inside her shirt she started to work him and—

◇ ◇ ◇

—Sitterson turned a dial less than a degree, increasing the humidity infinitesimally, and it was an adjustment he knew many other people would have never found cause to make. But that was why he and Hadley were the best. They were more than just technicians, they were craftsmen, as concerned with the journey as the outcome itself.

He knew very well that the chase was better than the catch.

Sitterson hummed to himself, then whistled a little, glancing across at his partner and swapping a contented nod. They were such a great team. If he had his concerns, Hadley would pick up on them right away, and the converse was true.

"Okay," Hadley said softly, "boobies, boobies."

"Show us the goods," Sitterson muttered.

From behind him came Truman's uncomfortable cough. Sitterson had known this moment would come; he'd sensed the confusions in the kid, and more than that, the doubt. There'd been others like him before, and mostly they were given other tasks in the facility, taken away from Control where they could see everything that was going on and given menial tasks that held no obvious outcome. But there had also been two others who'd come this far and then refused to go any further.

They'd been taken care of. Sitterson had succeeded in forgetting even their names. But he'd also vowed to coach any new guys past such dangerous concerns.

"Does it really matter if we see—?" Truman began, and Hadley cut in quickly.

"We're not the only ones watching, kid."

"Got to keep the customer satisfied," Sitterson added, glancing over his shoulder at the soldier. "You understand what's at stake here?"

"Sorry," Truman said, nodding.

Sitterson turned back to his screen, considered asking for some coffee, but decided that—

◇ ◇ ◇

—Her lust was all-consuming, her breath fast, and she yearned for him, lifting her butt to allow him to pull off her jeans. He bent forward and ran his tongue up her right leg, her thigh, passing her panties and gripping the elasticated waist instead. He pulled it up and growled, letting it snap back across her stomach, and Jules laughed.

Then the growl faded away as he dipped his face down between her thighs, and Jules's head fell back as she felt the first touch of his tongue.

◇ ◇ ◇

"Oh," Truman said, but Sitterson ignored him. That was another thing with these newbies—the first few times were porn. *He pretends he knows what's at stake*, he thought. *But the sight of a hot chick getting eaten out drives all that from his mind.*

Sitterson adjusted a dial, tapped some buttons on his computer, checked some readouts. All seemed good.

"Oh!" Truman said again.

Hadley upped the volume on the speakers, Control was filled with groaning, and Sitterson grinned. Bastard was just winding the kid up. And... well, Hadley got a lot out of this, too. Sitterson guessed all the married guys did, because it was allowable. It was part of the job.

For just a moment he imagined Lin lying there on the moss with his face pressed between...

But that was too much of a distraction, at least for now.

"Looking good," he said, checking more readouts. He glanced up at the screen again, humming softly.

"Looking good."

◇ ◇ ◇

Jules sat up and pushed Curt aside, sitting astride him and undoing the final couple of buttons on her shirt. She teased... touching her stomach... fingers stroking the edges of the fabric while Curt panted beneath her. And then she pulled at both edges and let it drop from her shoulders, quickly slipping down her strapless bra and exposing what she knew were just about the best breasts in the Northern hemisphere.

And Curt was a guy. Though he'd seen them a thousand times before, he still caught his breath and looked up at her in silent, worshipful wonder.

"You look so—"

◇ ◇ ◇

"—good," Hadley said. "Wow."

"Yeah," Sitterson said, "great tits." But it was the voice of a man admiring a particular work of art. The girl leaned forward, the guy wrapped his arms around her.

"Score," Hadley muttered.

"Eat that, Stockholm," Sitterson said.

Beside him, Hadley sighed. Sitterson checked more dials and readouts, then he glanced to the left where he'd seen movement on one of the other monitors. Hadley had seen it as well.

"Oh," Truman said again. "She's...wow."

Any moment now, Sitterson thought. And just for a moment he looked away from the screens, allowing himself a moment to close his eyes and compose himself, readying himself for what was to come. He almost told Truman to do the same.

But like he'd had to do, the kid would need to learn the hard way.

◇ ◇ ◇

Curt rolled her over and slid his hand into her panties, his fingers expert at touching her where and how she most desired. She groaned out load and looked up at the tree canopy, her left hand freeing him from his jeans as he worked at her, her right hand splaying out on the ground and clasping a handful of the scented, warm moss.

I wonder where the stars have gone? she wondered.

Something slammed into her hand and she could no longer move it. It felt warm, then suddenly cold again.

Curt's fingers were inside her, but she no longer felt them. She grew cold again. The ground pricked against her bare skin.

And then the pain bit in and she screamed, looking at her hand and seeing the thick rusty blade that had passed through her palm and pinned her to the ground.

"Curt!" she screamed, bucking him off, because nothing else she saw around her made any sense. "*Curt!*"

SIX

For the first few seconds Curt could not move, or speak, nor could he feel his heart beating. Like him, it was frozen in shock.

When it did kick back in he almost collapsed from the impact, coughing as it pummeled his ribs, trying to rise from his knees, and painfully aware that the love of his life was about to die in front of him.

They were being attacked, but not by people. These things might once have been people but now they were…

Dead, Curt thought. *They must be, because they've got things crawling out of their mouths and holes in their skin, their faces, their heads, and—*

And Jules was screaming for him again, almost naked and sitting up, trying to pull away from where a skinny, small boy had impaled her against the ground with a *fucking knife*! The boy—

—*Zombie!* Curt thought, *That's all they can be, what they must be—*

—wore old-fashioned clothing, had long hair caked in mud, and when he glanced back at Curt his eyes were milky white and terrifying.

He held Jules's wrist and tugged his rusty blade from her hand, eliciting a scream that chilled Curt to the core.

Behind her, a lumbering, fat woman reached around and pressed the rusted teeth of a saw against her throat.

Staring at his lover's terrified, screaming face Curt could not avoid seeing what happened just behind her, as the zombie woman's stomach seemed to flap open and spill three burning coals from a cauterized interior. They tumbled onto Jules's head and fell down her back, and the pleasant country air was suddenly alive with the stench of burning hair and scorched skin and flesh.

The woman pressed herself against the back of Jules's head and pulled the saw across her neck. The teeth snagged on skin and parted it with a terrible ripping sound, like wet cotton being torn.

And Curt shoved aside his shock and leapt forward.

He dove past Jules and knocked the zombie woman aside, seeing as he did so that there was a huge third shape lumbering toward them from the shadows.

"*Fuck away from her!*" he screamed. The mother-zombie fell aside, saw *twanging!* at the air. Jules's scream had died out and she was leaning forward, but as he turned to help her the kid-zombie's arm swung and the knife's rusted blade buried itself in Curt's arm.

He roared in fury, shock keeping the pain at bay for the precious few seconds it took him to try and pull it out. He couldn't, so he grabbed the kid-zombie's arm instead and tugged hard. The thing came close, no expression at all on its face—and that was the worst thing right then, worse than the shock and Jules's crying and the idea *What the fuck is going on here?*—the complete lack of expression on the faces.

No signs of life, Curt thought, and he grimaced as he punched the kid-zombie in the face with his left hand.

He felt the nose give way and parts of it crumbled off. It didn't seem to faze the kid-zombie at all, but it did shove him back so that he let go of the blade.

Curt stepped in front of Jules and tugged the blade free of his arm, screaming as he did so, bending to see how bad the damage was, mind working at twice its normal speed as he tried to figure out just what the fuck he was going to do next. *Carry her no can't carry her too slow fight them all maybe but that punch didn't*—

He heard a chain rattle, looked up, and saw that big-zombie had arrived. He was maybe six and a half feet tall, almost that around, and unlike the others he did exhibit some basic human emotion.

He grinned.

Something dropped from his hand and hit the ground at his feet, connected to his hand by the chain Curt had heard rattling. It was heavy, and metallic, and though the trees filtered the moonlight Curt could still see the ugly teeth of an old-fashioned bear trap, broken, just one jaw left. As he wondered what had happened to the other jaw, big-zombie swung the makeshift mace and chain with terrifying speed.

Curt fell forward and tried to protect Jules, but the heavy metal whacked the side of his head. He fell, grunting, seeing the shadow of the weapon pass by above him as it ricocheted from his skull. *Flat side not teeth side*, he thought with vague relief, trying to rise to protect himself from another blow. But dizziness hit him and he stumbled, blinking blood from his eye and mumbling, "Ju... Jules..."

"Curt!" she shouted, and her throat sounded raw.

In front of him, Curt saw Jules trying to stand, reaching for him with one hand while the other clasped the bloodied mess of her throat. Her nudity made her pathetic now, and their loving seemed a million years away as he watched the bear trap swing around again and bury its teeth in her back.

She screamed and arched forward, reaching back to try and pry the thing loose, blood spewing from her ripped throat and down across her chest and stomach. And when she fell forward Curt thought it was because she was trying to walk toward him, but her legs would not obey.

He shook his head and cleared his vision, dashing forward to grasp her hand but only just missing as big-zombie started to haul her backward.

Her fingers dug into the earth and rucked up furrows of rotting leaves and damp soil.

Curt lunged forward again... and then felt the cool sharpness around his throat. He snapped his head back from the blade, connecting with something dry and soft that crunched as it broke, and then the blade was pulled tight against his throat, something hard pressed against his back, and he was pivoted from his feet. He struggled and thrashed, thinking of Jules's gashed neck and trying to protect his own, but there was nothing he could do.

Not even scream.

He could only watch as big-zombie stomped on Jules's back and pried the bear trap from her flesh, blood gouting into the night air. She was pleading and whimpering now, bubbles forming at her throat as she did so, and as the kid-zombie grabbed her hair and pulled back her head, she was looking directly into Curt's eyes.

It's holding me so I can see this, and then it'll kill me.

Mother-zombie held the broken saw blade against Jules's throat again, and Curt thought, *This is when it ends, the joke, the trick, some freakish new TV show maybe, and the guys will come out from the cabin laughing at how easily we were taken in by a bunch of fucking zombies coming out of the woods and—*

Mother-zombie began sawing at Jules's throat. She struggled, her eyes rolling back and mouth working but saying nothing, but she was held fast. The saw hacked through skin and flesh, and Curt heard the flow of blood as her carotid artery was severed. Then he heard the first hard scrape of rusted metal teeth against bone.

"Oh God," Curt whimpered, unable to close his eyes however much he tried, "oh God, oh God, oh—"

◇ ◇ ◇

"—God," Truman said, "oh God, shit, shit, shit..."

The sounds coming through the speaker were turned up, because it had to be that way. Wet, tearing sounds. The bubbly hiss of the girl's last breath. The saw tearing into bone, catching, jarring.

From Hadley and Sitterson, only the uncomfortable shuffling of men who had seen this before, but who could never quite get used to it. Sitterson was looking down at his hands, which were hovering above the keyboard in case any last-second tweaks needed performing, though he knew from all he had seen and heard that all was going well.

The girl had stopped making those noises because her throat and windpipe had been cut through, and now came only the terrible scraping sound.

"This we offer in humility and fear," Sitterson intoned, "for the blessed peace of your eternal slumber. As it ever was."

"As it ever was," Hadley echoed softly.

Sitterson pulled at the thin leather thong around his neck, lifting the pendant from beneath his shirt. It was made from white gold, cast into the shape of a five-pointed symbol. Not a pentagram, but something more arcane, something older. He glanced at it briefly, concentrating on one small arm of the deformed star, and then kissed it before dropping it against his chest once more.

From the corner of his eye he could see Truman

watching, but he did not turn to face the young man. Why should he? There was nothing on offer there.

Behind him, Hadley had crossed to the mahogany panels at the far end of the room, built into the plain concrete wall and the ancient rock of the ground behind them. Sitterson turned slightly and watched his friend open the first panel, sliding it back on smooth runners, to expose the ornate brass apparatus. Without hesitation Hadley grasped the lever and eased it downward, pushing against pressure, and kept his hand on it until it clicked into place against the lower pin.

And deeper down in a place that could never be seen Sitterson knew what was happening: in the mechanism older than Man, a small metal hammer struck a glass vial, cracking it from top to bottom and releasing the blood retained inside. The blood ran into a brass funnel that extended into a long, long pipe, running even deeper through rock and dark spaces, emerging eventually into a place deeper still.

Here, the blood poured onto a slab of marble leaning against the wall, and in the total blackness it began to fill the intricate image carved onto the marble slab's surface.

Sitterson opened his eyes, not aware that he'd been daydreaming. His heart was thumping.

I mustn't go down there, he thought, *not even in my dreams!*

"The boy," Hadley said, and Sitterson nodded, sniffed, wiped his hands across his face. He had to get himself together.

This had only just begun.

◇ ◇ ◇

Calm, Curt thought, looking down at the blood-spattered leaves at his feet, and realizing with detached shock that his dick was still hanging out of his trousers. That seemed somehow sad. *Stay calm, stay still, let them think I've given in, that's my only chance...*

The kid-zombie and mother-zombie were ambling toward him, kid holding the rusty blade, mother holding the saw that glimmered with Jules's blood. Beyond them he could see her body, the ruin of her head and throat hidden by the big zombie. He was moving strangely, but Curt couldn't see what he was doing. He was glad. But not seeing didn't mean that he could not imagine, and every zombie movie he'd ever seen gave him hints.

The small zombie and the woman zombie hissed as they drew closer, giving their faces inhuman expressions for the very first time, and then they raised their blades.

Curt—the sportsman, the football star, the fit guy who all the girls loved to love—grabbed the father-zombie's arms and heaved himself up, planting a foot on each of the approaching monsters' chests and kicking hard. They sprawled to the ground, and Curt fell back onto the zombie holding the scythe at his throat. He used the momentum to roll backward, head slipping out from beneath the blade and his feet landing on the ground just past the zombie's head.

Jumping upright, amazed at his own escape, he stared at Jules for a couple of seconds, aware that big-zombie was turning to look at the commotion. On his face, blood.

Curt turned and ran. And just as he thought his legs had helped him escape and that he might actually make it—back to the cabin, back to friends, where they could pull together and defend themselves against these bastard things—the scythe sliced into the leg of his jeans, opened the skin across his ankle and tripped him.

Curt cried out as he hit the harsh, spiky ground. He wondered what saw teeth would feel like when it was tugged murderously across his throat.

◇ ◇ ◇

Little Nemo in Slumberland was hardly the height of literary endeavor, but Marty liked the little dude. There was lots about Marty that the others didn't understand, and lots they probably couldn't, even if they bothered putting their minds to it. But he was a guy who, with the aid of mind-enhancing drugs, understood himself completely. And there weren't may people who could say that.

Like Curt, for example, with his close-cropped hair and square jaw, defined muscles and eyes that said, *Love me, please*. Or Jules, sweet Jules with her pert little titties, ever-changing hair and an awareness of herself that stretched only so far as others saw her.

Friends, but distant from him.

Dana, maybe. Dana had come closer than anyone, their friendship a complex thing but one which he relished, and treasured.

"Nemo, man," he said, "you gotta wake up. Your shit is topsy-turvy." He sighed and dropped the book to his chest. "Ah, I feel ya, Neems. Gotta ride that bed." He stretched, and through the roaring of blood in his ears as he yawned—

"*I'm gonna go for a walk.*"

The voice wasn't his.

Marty sat up, eyes wide. He looked around his room. Bed, chair, cupboard, weird picture on the wall, that was it.

"Okay, I swear to fucking *God* somebody is talking." He ran his hands over his eyes, weary. Yawned again. *Just that*, he thought. *Just me yawning*.

But there'd been that time earlier, when the others were arguing and he thought he'd heard a whisper on the air...

"Or I'm pretty sure someone is... ah..." Marty shook his head.

"*I'm gonna go for a walk.*"

Marty stood and looked around the room, arms waving about his head as if to flick away an annoying fly.

"Enough! What are you saying? What do you want? You think I'm a *puppet*, gonna do a *puppet* dance—fuck all y'all! I'm the boss of my brain, so give it up!" He waited for something else, but there were no more voices, no presence in his room. He snorted. "I'm gonna go for a walk."

He slammed his door behind him and stalked along the corridor. The large room beyond was subtly lit with candles and the newly-stocked fire, and for a second Marty stood at the end of the hallway and watched Holden and Dana. They were kissing, and it was the sweetest thing he'd ever seen, soft and passionate. It didn't seem to fit their surroundings.

There's something old and hard here, Marty thought.

"I don't wanna..." Dana muttered. "I mean I've never... I don't mean *never*, but not on the first..."

"Hey," Holden said, "nothing you don't want." He leaned in to kiss again and Marty had to turn away, walking across the room and heading for the outside door. To his left the hatch into the basement remained firmly closed, but he couldn't help thinking that something had come out of there with them.

To his right, the lovers on the sofa glanced up at him with coy surprise.

"He's got a husband bulge," Marty said, frowning, not quite sure where that had come from. *Jealous much, dude?* Then he pulled open the door and stepped outside, gasping momentarily as he met the cool air. The door closed behind him and the cabin's interior was instantly far away, a memory of someone else walking across that room and saying that strange thing. *Who the fuck calls a boner a husband bulge?* he thought, and though the memory of where he'd heard that phrase was fresh, he did his best to avoid it.

He walked on and left the cabin behind, pausing at the first stand of trees. It was quiet, and he looked up between the trunks.

"I thought there'd be stars." He sighed, smiled. "We are abandoned." He unzipped and started pissing, watching the swirls and whorls of steam as it drifted off between the trees, lit by weak light from the cabin.

Behind him, a breaking twig.

Marty stopped in mid-stream and looked around. Just trees. He glanced left and right, remembering something about peripheral vision being better at night. Nothing moved, and there were no more sounds.

He sighed again, looking forward to getting back inside and rolling a new joint, and as he finished pissing and zipped up Curt barreled into him.

"Run! Fucking run!" He was clasping Marty's arms too tightly, hurting, bunching up his shirt and tugging hard as they danced on the spot and Curt tried hauling him toward the cabin,

"What's—?"

"Go!" Curt yelled again. He looked a mess—blood on his arm, head cut and bleeding somewhere, leaves, dirt, and he looked fucking *terrified*. As Marty was sizing him up Curt changed tactic, letting go and pushing Marty toward the cabin instead.

His panic caught, and Marty ran.

From the shadows to their right, a figure darted at them. It was... a girl, but there was something wrong. One arm was missing. And in her other arm, she carried a hatchet. Her hair was long and lank, clotted with leaves and mud, and her face was *all wrong*. Marty skidded to a halt, staring, trying to make sense of what he was seeing, but Curt put on a burst of speed and swung his arm across the girl's throat. She flipped backward and sprawled, never letting out a sound.

"Dead bitch!" Curt shouted. He span around, grabbed Marty's arm, and pulled him up onto the porch.

"Curt, your dick's—"

"Inside." Curt flipped the catch and booted the door open.

◇ ◇ ◇

He's got a husband's bulge, Marty had said, echoing the weird language in the diary from downstairs. At the time Dana had thought it strange, but as soon as Marty had closed the door Holden had held her again, pulling her close and cupping the back of her head as he kissed her sweet and deep.

And now here she was, hand resting gently against his husband's bulge and the night ahead of them alight with possibilities.

The door smashed open. Dana and Holden knocked teeth as they sat up, and she was about to shout at whoever was fucking around when she saw Curt. He was on his hands and knees inside the door, and she had never seen him like this before. Never seen him looking so *scared*.

"Curt!" she gasped. She and Holden went to him, and the blood and wounds registered instantly. Blood streaming down his arm, a gash in his head. And his hands... it looked like he'd been digging.

"Jesus, what happened?" Holden asked.

Curt's eyes rolled in his head, and he seemed unable to focus on either of them.

"Door!" Marty screamed, skidding through the door as he attempted to slow and slam it behind him. He spilled to the floor, but Curt had already turned and kicked the door closed.

What the hell is this? Dana thought. For a moment she wondered if it was a joke, and that they'd all start cracking up soon, pointing at her and Holden and rolling around on the floor. But she didn't think that for long. Not with the way blood was pulsing from the slash in Curt's scalp. And not from the terror in Marty's eyes.

"Anna Patience," he muttered. "Her. Her!"

Dana darted to Curt's side.

"Where are you hurt? Is all this blood yours? Where's Jules?"

Curt pushed her hands away, shaking his head. He stood slowly, shaking, glancing around as if any shadow could hold danger. He zipped his fly, and firelight reflected in his eyes, dancing shapes. Dana thought he was crying, but she wasn't sure.

"It's okay, Curt. You're okay..." Holden tried to calm him, holding his upper arms and catching his eye.

"No," Marty said, gasping for air. "We're not okay.

What's the opposite of okay?"

"What are you talking about?" Dana said, because they were scaring the shit out of her now. "Curt, *where's Jules*?"

Curt shook his head. Blood spattered his shoulder and the floorboards, but he didn't notice. His eyes still seemed to be looking elsewhere.

"She's gone," he said, remembering something terrible. "We gotta get out of here!" He started toward the corridor leading to the back of the cabin. "There's a window back here, we go through there, into the woods, run like fuck and—"

"No!" Dana said. "Wait!" This was madness. She knew she should listen to Curt and Marty, but she... wanted to open...

I need to see for myself.

She reached for the front door, turned the handle and started to pull it open.

"Dana, don't open that!" Marty shouted. She had never heard Marty shout before, and in a way that scared her more than anything. Marty losing control was just not right.

"I'm not leaving here without Jules," she said. And it was that simple. She swung the door open.

Standing on the porch, framed by the doorway, was the biggest, deadest man she had ever seen.

"Big-zombie," Curt whispered, saying it like one word, as if he'd already had cause to name this thing.

The huge man—big-zombie—stared for a few seconds, and no one reacted.

His eyes are rotten things, Dana thought, and then she noticed that he was holding something in his right hand. It didn't register for a moment what it was, but perhaps that was only because of the blood. Then he threw it at Dana, she caught it, felt the wetness, the tangle of blood- and gore-knotted hair, *blonde* hair... and she looked down into Jules's battered face.

Jules, her face, her head, it's heavy, her eyes, she's damaged... she's bruised her eye, it's sore, and her lovely lovely hair, very fabulous, no? No longer fabulous because of the blood and leaves and...

She screamed and dropped the head. It seemed to fall in slow motion, and if seemed as if her own scream was issuing from the grotesquely open mouth, turning as it fell so that Jules's accusing eyes focused on the shape blocking the doorway. The head bounced from her foot and rolled back toward the door, and then big-zombie kicked it back into the room as he took a lumbering step forward.

He's going to get in and—Dana thought, but Holden's fear galvanized him. He dove forward, balance unsettled but using his momentum to shoulder into the door, his right foot tangling in Jules's hair and swinging her head across the floor in a blood-smearing arc. He slammed the door shut again, falling against it just as the thing smashed into it, rattling the frame, splintering wood.

Holden slipped the bolts and fell back, kicking his foot frantically to dislodge it from the head's hair.

Big-zombie slammed into the door again. Timber

splintered and fell away from the frame, and Dana actually heard the creak of bending metal as the bolt warped under the immense pressure.

A few more like that... she thought, and then Marty was at the door with Holden, helping him throw the top and bottom bolts as well. They wouldn't hold for long, but perhaps they'd give them some time to—

She saw her friend's head from the corner of her eye. Jules was staring at her. Dana sucked in a few deep breaths to try and calm herself, but all they did was feed the scream building in her lungs once again. Holden and Marty leaned against the door, grimacing with each impact. The air in the room seemed to vibrate every time big-zombie struck.

Dust was in the air, and most dust is human skin, and the scream was coming.

She opened her mouth—

"Dana! C'mon!" She turned away from Jules, and Curt had heaved the couch over onto its back. He was trying to shove it across the timber floor to pile it behind the door, and in his grimace of effort she saw the first glimmer of madness. His eyes kept flickering to Jules's head, and the blood still glistening around his right eye emphasized its size and deepness.

He's losing it, Dana thought, and she swallowed her scream.

They pushed together, neither commenting when the couch knocked the head aside. Marty and Holden pulled back at the last moment, and Dana and Curt shoved the couch until it was wedged just beneath the doorknob. Flush with the wall and door, it would provide some small measure of barrier.

But not for long.

Wham! Big-zombie struck again, and the whole cabin seemed to shake and creak. More dust drifted down from the ceiling, hazing the air and dancing in candlelight. *Five minutes ago this light was so romantic*, Dana thought. She glanced at Holden, he threw her an uncertain smile, and she realized how shocked they all were.

Fisting her hands, she felt the tackiness of Jules's blood between her fingers and on her palms.

"What *is* that thing?" she cried.

"I don't know," Curt said. "But there's more of them."

"More of them?" she asked, glancing at Marty.

He nodded.

"I saw a young girl. All... zombied up. Like him." He nodded at the door, seemingly unembarrassed by his choice of words, and no one mocked him. "And she was all 'Little House on the Prairie,' too, but she's missing an arm..." He trailed off, frowning. Even another impact from big-zombie couldn't upset that brief, loaded moment of silence among the four of them.

It can't be, Dana thought, but at the same moment she knew it was.

"Oh God," she said. "Patience. That diary we found..."

"'The pain outlives the flesh,'" Holden quoted. "She must have... bound a mystical incantation into the text so someone would come along, read the diary aloud and—"

"And I did it," Dana said quietly. She glanced at Marty. "You told me not to, but I did it." Marty only shook his head, his expression sad, not accusing. But she didn't need someone else blaming her in order to feel the sudden flush of guilt.

"Look, brainiac," Curt snapped at Holden, aggression hiding his terror. "I don't give a limp dick *why* those things are here. We gotta lock this place down!"

"He's right," Marty said, nodding. Shivering. Dana could see them *all* shivering now, and she felt it in herself. For now it was adrenalin coursing through them, and they had to take advantage of that. Once the shivering became due to fear and pain, their bodies would grow cooler, their muscles would weaken, and whatever chances they had at survival would grow much less.

Wham! Another impact against the door. The frame shook, wood cracked, but the sofa was wedged tight beneath the handle.

"We'll go room by room," Curt said. "Barricade every window and door." He headed toward the back of the cabin, alone, then turned and waved them to him. "Come on! We gotta play it safe. No matter what, *we have to stay together*!"

Damn right! Dana thought. The thing outside impacted the cabin again, and again, and she couldn't imagine being alone.

Crash... crash... crash...!

Dana turned her back on her friend's dead stare.

SEVEN

Sitterson knew that Hadley would be panicking right now. That was just his style. Once the real game began, he became edgy and nervous, seeing the few obscure ways things could go wrong, instead of the many ways they were going right. It was Hadley's way of working, that was all. How he kept focused, maintained his composure.

But that still didn't prevent it from pissing off Sitterson.

Least they could do was enjoy themselves a little.

Hadley slumped down in his chair, one hand to his forehead.

"Calm down, I got it," Sitterson said as he tapped some keys. "Watch the master work." He brought up three new windows on his computer, then tapped a switch on his control panel array.

"There." He sat back in his chair, hands laced behind his head, and glanced across at Hadley.

"What?" Hadley asked.

Sitterson sighed and nodded at the large displays.

"Eyes on the screen," he said. "The camera never lies."

◇ ◇ ◇

This is so fucked up, Marty thought. Things had gone from laughter to panic in a matter of minutes, and now there was running and shouting and screaming and dying, and he wasn't sure just when things had changed. Seeing Curt outside, of course... bleeding, panicked raving... that had been when reality had become more terrifying for him. But he had a feeling that everything had begun to change much earlier than that.

Curt's behavior with Jules had been so unlike him, and even earlier, down in the basement when they'd been looking through all that weird old stuff, something had seemed not quite right. The stuff down there was stacked and piled and stored so haphazardly that Marty couldn't help but see some order in it all, as if it had been placed that way. Maybe he was the only one who *could* see that, and it was his laid-back approach to life that encouraged him to find order in chaos, but he thought not. Not completely, at least. There had been something more.

Something like design.

Now Curt was leading them to the back of the cabin to make sure all the doors and windows were secure and blocked up. And though Curt was the jock everyone looked up to and respected because he was cool, good-looking, and generally a great guy... even that felt wrong.

Holden and Dana moved close together, not holding hands but touching fingers as they walked. Marty coveted their security.

Thump! The thing hit the cabin again, and Curt came to a halt just at the beginning of the corridor, looking around as if suddenly lost.

"What's the matter?" Dana asked, her voice terrified.

Curt seemed confused. He shook his head, frowning, running one hand through his hair and spattering a dozen tiny blood droplets onto the cabin floor.

"This isn't right..." he muttered. Then he looked at the others almost as if he no longer trusted them, face hard but eyes afraid. He settled on Marty. "This isn't right. We should *split up.* We can cover more ground that way."

Hold on now... Marty thought.

Holden and Dana swapped a glance, and Marty saw something change in their stances. The fear was still there, the tension, but for a few seconds... it looked as if they were listening to something else. Some inner voice that whispered things they did not understand.

Are they hearing voices too? Marty thought, but even thinking it made him feel slightly ridiculous. He was the dope-head, as Curt was always so keen to tell him. He was the one who heard the fucking voices.

"Yeah..." Holden said, and Dana nodded at him. "Yeah, split up. Good idea."

"Really?" Marty asked. And behind them, the living room window exploded inward. He ducked and span around in time to see glass slivers jingling to the floor and timber frame shards spiking inward. And through the ruin of the window protruded big-zombie's arm. His fist was clenched around a handful of glass and wood, but there was no blood.

Beyond, his shadow pressed close.

"I got it!" Curt shouted, running at the window. "You guys *get in your rooms*!" He shouldered into a bookcase and it started sliding toward the window, screaming across the floor, books tumbling, while the zombie's arm thrashed to clear more broken glass and framing.

"Wait..." Marty said, but his voice was lost amid the chaos.

Dana and Holden shared a glance, a nod, and then Dana said, "Let's go!" They headed for their separate rooms on the left, parting without even a hug, and for a moment Marty couldn't move.

This isn't right, he thought. He looked back at Curt, who was now shoving against the bookcase while big-zombie leaned in the window and pushed back, seeking entrance even while Curt strove to prevent it.

"Go!" Curt screamed at Marty, angry at his indecisiveness. So Marty went, because there was little else he could do. Maybe Curt was right. Maybe they should all check their windows and doors individually, then go back and help him fight that big fucker.

But even as he entered his room and dashed to the

window, it was almost as if he could foresee what would happen next. *We'll be locked in*, he thought. And he turned back to his door.

◇ ◇ ◇

"Told you," Sitterson said, perhaps a little too smug.

"Yeah, okay," Hadley said. On the big monitors they saw the three kids dashing into their rooms as the fourth tried to hold back Matthew. Sitterson, humming, tapped a couple of keys and the views changed without a flicker, shifting to inside each room.

Dana entered her own room and dashed to the window, Holden stood in the center of his and took a few deep breaths, and Marty was the last, frowning, head shaking.

Curt was still battling Matthew the zombie.

Well, let him. Sitterson wasn't concerned. His placing right now didn't matter too much, and if things went too far at that end of the cabin, he could still be lured across to the other.

"Peas in separate pods," Sitterson said, raising his hands in triumph.

"Lock 'em in," Hadley said, and he was smiling as well. For now. He'd find something else to stress about soon.

Sitterson tapped a key and—

◇ ◇ ◇

—Marty's door slammed shut behind him. After the slam came the slide and *thunk!* of locks ramming home—not just in his door but in the others, as well.

He gasped and held his breath, listening for more. Weak light from the single light reflected from one half of the window, making the darkness outside even more complete. The other half stood wide open. He'd unlatched and opened it earlier when he was laid back on his bed smoking pot, having some vague idea that the fumes could spread through the air outside and chill the forest. It had been a little too *looming* for his liking, a little too *forceful*. Trees should be just trees, and shouldn't wear the shadows of guardians.

Locked in, he thought. *We're all suddenly locked in.* And glancing down at his door handle he couldn't even see a keyhole. There was a handle, that was all. So the locks must be…

"On the outside," he muttered. But that felt wrong, too. He tried to recall what the doors looked like from out there, and he was pretty sure they were the same—just a handle, nothing else.

No keyhole.

No lock.

In which case…

The cabin shook again with another terrible impact. Curt cried out from somewhere and more glass broke, and Marty's window suddenly seemed larger than ever. He moved then, slowly to begin with, two small, quiet steps, and then in his mind's eye he saw zombie-girl's face intruding through the window. He leapt the last few steps, grabbed the handle and pulled it close, flicking the latch to secure it shut. Something shattered behind him and he shouted, turning around and hardly prepared for what he might see.

He must have knocked the table with his leg as he rushed by, and the lamp on top had wobbled and smashed after he'd turned the latch.

Not that glass and thin wood will do much good against—

He looked down.

What the fuck is that?

It was a moment that punched him in the gut. Amongst all the chaos, thumping, shouting from outside, and his own terrified panting, it was the sight of the smallest thing that finally succeeded in knocking Marty's breath out of him.

The remains of the china lamp were splayed across the floor, and from its plastic heart a white cable led to the plug socket in the wall. The bulb had survived—shielded from impact by the bent-out-of-shape shade—and in its glare he saw a *second* wire.

It was thin and black, and there was something about it that seemed all wrong.

The wire snaked through the remains of the broken lamp, its end pointing directly at him. *An* end? *Shouldn't it be plugged in somewhere? Shouldn't there be a fixture?* But Marty's bullshit detector was on full, and he knew this was something that shouldn't be there.

He bent and picked up the wire, squinting at its end, and thought, *fiber optic*. The sense of being watched was suddenly very real. His place in things shrank to an almost infinitesimally small point. And he stood and looked around the room, thinking of the one-way mirror.

Curt's weird behavior.

Jules's brutal death.

"Oh, man," he muttered.

◇ ◇ ◇

"That's deep," Hadley said. "'Oh, man.'"

"He's not there for his philosophical insightfulness." The guy's face filled the screen now as he stared into the hi-tech camera, distorted by the closeness to the domed end of the cable, and for the first time ever Sitterson experienced a glimmer of fear.

It's almost like he's *watching* us.

He shoved it quickly down. He wasn't here to empathize.

But he couldn't ignore the obvious.

"Uh-oh," he said, "that's not good."

Hadley flipped down the microphone on his headphones and flicked a switch. "Chem, I need five hundred cc's of Thorazine pumped into room three, *now*—"

"No no no," Sitterson said, because he'd seen movement elsewhere. *Oh we're just too fucking good*, he thought, pointing at the large screen to the left. "Hang on." And yes, the movement was manifesting into a shambling, pale thing in the darkness, passing between the silent statues of trees and seeming to emerge from the very darkness itself as it approached the cabin.

Sitterson checked a few settings and smiled.

"Judah Buckner to the rescue," he said. And the brief pity he'd had for the kid was eaten away by the sight of Buckner's zombified face.

◇ ◇ ◇

He could have mouthed obscenities or flipped them the finger, but that wouldn't do anything to help him right now.

Now, he needed answers, and perhaps some clue as to how the hell they could *get the fuck* out of Dodge. But...

As he pulled the wire taut and started following it around the room—across the floor, along the skirting to the corner, then up to where a small hole was drilled in the ceiling's corner—the realization dawned that he'd been made to look like a complete dick.

He stared up at the ceiling and smiled.

Of course things had been out of kilter. The cabin was fake, maybe even the woods all around them were unreal, and everything they did and said was being monitored.

"Oh my God, I'm on a reality TV show." Every breath they took, the booze they'd drunk, the almost biblical amount of pot he'd already smoked, the kissing couple on the sofa, everything was for public consumption. The stuff in the cellar really *was* a set-up, planted there by scene designers who must've had multiple orgasms when they saw what was required of them in the shooting script.

Those things outside, the zombies, Jules's death and her head rolling about on the floor like that... all of that was thrown in just to scare the shit out of them. *And it worked*, he thought, but then he chuckled, too. Jules's and Curt's noisy fucking in the shower was probably the most-viewed clip on YouTube right now.

"My parents are gonna think I'm such a burnout."

And then he realized that he'd be the one they'd be focusing on right now, and if they didn't want him to ruin everything for the others, they'd have to—

The window behind him smashed, and Marty aimed a knowing smile at the fiber optic cable still in his hand.

They'll have to come and get me.

He turned to the window, ready to see the cameras and the presenter, so sun-baked that he or she had passed tanned and entered somewhere into the orange spectrum. Microphones thrust at him, producers with fingers at their lips silently pleading for him to *Keep the secret a little while longer*, and there would be transport to somewhere from where he could view the remainder of his friends' ordeal…

And though he felt cruel and immature even thinking about it, he couldn't wait to see what a job they'd made on the fake Marty-Slashed-Up-And-Dead mannequin.

The zombie wasn't quite as tall as the big one they'd seen outside, but his face was about ten times as horrific. *Good job, guys*, Marty thought admiringly, and then the zombie's arm extended and his hand closed around Marty's throat.

The fingers squeezed hard and Marty felt things *grinding* in there.

Not so tight! he thought, but he was already realizing his naivety.

What a dick.

The breath was shut off from his lungs, giving way to pain. The thing pulled him to the broken window, spun him around, closed an arm around his throat and tugged him backward.

As Marty folded at the waist and felt the jagged spikes of broken glass scoring and slitting his thighs and back, he was still cursing himself and his foolish thinking. There was *no way* this could have been reality TV. There hadn't been nearly enough sex.

How could he have been so stupid?

Marty screamed, and it felt as if he was shouting only for himself. The arm across his throat squeezed tighter as the thing tried to drag him backward through the window, and *no one* could make up that smell, *no one* could manufacture the fucking breath on that thing.

He struggled more fiercely, pulling himself back in a little even though the pain of the cuts on his back and legs was just starting to catch fire. The thing pulled even harder and Marty clung onto the window frame, refusing to let go or ease up his own pressure for even an instant.

These arms will not move however hard that thing pulls.

Judah! Marty thought. *That's the father zombie out there, the father of Patience, whose image started all this down in the basement with Dana.* It seemed to make sense, ridiculous though it was. And it seemed suddenly more real than any reality TV could be.

But the zombie pulled harder, tugging him so that his back creaked as he bent in half, hauled through the window, and as he lost his grip he reached around with his right hand for anything he could use as a weapon. He knocked clothes and a pouch of tobacco from the dresser surface, then his fingers closed around his thermos-shaped bong.

The cool night air suddenly kissed his bloodied skin as he exited the cabin. It seemed so much colder, and when he thumped to the ground and saw the thing standing over him, the idea that he'd ever thought it false was just so ridiculous.

Judah swung his hand down. Marty rolled, heard the harsh whisper of metal sticking into soil, looked at the zombie's hand and saw the blade being tugged from the earth.

A second later and that would have been right through my head. He half stood, but Judah's other hand knocked him across the shoulders, spilling him to the ground again. Marty didn't have time to turn his head and watch the blade swinging down for another try, so he rolled to the right and saw Judah stagger as he stabbed the ground again.

Marty kicked out at the hand holding the knife and heard something crumple and snap. But it seemed to make no difference. The zombie pulled the knife up again and turned slightly, and Marty knew that if he didn't find his feet he'd eventually be pinned to the ground with that cruel blade. And then...

"And then" he didn't want to think about.

He kicked out at Judah's legs, and when the zombie took a staggering step backward Marty found his feet, swaying slightly as if the ground was dipping and lifting. Judah fell toward him, one clawed hand reaching for his throat, the other raising the knife to strike again.

Marty shook the thermos shape in his hand, and felt and heard the familiar *click-clack* as it telescoped out into the giant bong. He'd sure had some fun with this, and it seemed a shame to smash it. But choice had been taken from him. Maybe it had been stolen long ago. Or perhaps he'd never had any choice at all.

He swung the bong into the side of Judah's head with all his might. The sound Judah made when he hit the ground was like a bale of hay dropped from several feet up; a crunch, and a few snaps. His hand still gripped the blade's rotten handle, and he writhed briefly before starting to struggle to his feet again.

Fuck this, Marty thought, and he turned and ran for the forest. He could lose this thing out there, outrun it—hadn't Romero said that zombie's ankles would break if they ran? He was the expert, right?—and then double back to the cabin, get inside, and plan with the others just what the fuck they were going to do now.

The things were strong but mindless, just living-dead freaks that needed a good shovel swung at their necks or a fire set in their—

Something punched him between the shoulder blades. He gasped and staggered forward, losing his footing and wondering what the hell the zombie could have thrown to have unbalanced him so much. And then he sprawled in the mud and leaves as the cool kiss of pain drifted in, and he knew.

Knife…

The knowledge invited the agony to settle upon him and he gasped, never understanding that such pain could exist. He felt entered and violated, the foreign object probing his innards, heavy and hot in his insides. He reached around with one hand, the movement shifting the rusted metal blade in his flesh. Crying out at last, his fingertips brushed cool metal. But he couldn't gain purchase.

He brought that hand beneath him and reached with the other, but was no more successful.

Get up and run! he thought. *Don't fuck around here, get up and run, if you can get… up… then do it and…* run!

Marty heaved himself up on both hands, screaming as his wounded flesh flexed around the piercing blade, and then he felt hands closing around his ankles. They pulled, he hit the ground face first, and then Judah started dragging him into the forest. Leaves crumpled beneath him, sticks and rocks scraped his groin and stomach and chest, filth getting into his open wounds, and he could barely find the energy to hold up his head.

"Help!" he screamed at last. But his voice was pitiful,

and he tasted blood in his mouth. "No! *Noooo!*"

Judah dragged him, not rushing, keeping a steady pace whatever obstacles he had to overcome. A fallen branch snagged on Marty's clothing and the zombie pulled on, eliciting a scream from Marty as a sharp stick pierced his stomach and snapped off. He gasped, crying out again, and tried to reach a hand down to explore the new wound. But though he managed to reach a hand beneath him, the dragging prevented him from feeling how serious the puncture was.

Warmth was all he felt, and wetness. More blood leaking from him to soak into this unnatural forest's floor.

Are they watching me even now? he wondered. *The death and pain's for real, but there was still that camera, so are they watching me now? Those controllers? Those bastards?*

"Help me!" he shouted. "Please!"

They passed over a small rise topped with heavily thorned plants. First he heard them snagging in Jonah's clothing and dried skin, and then they gouged and pricked at his own—thighs, scrotum, stomach, chest, and then his face, because he was feeling weaker with each second that passed by, and couldn't hold it up. His back was wet and hot around the knife wound, cooler elsewhere as the night air whispered across the blood. He could smell it, and see it beneath him as he left a bloody trail across the forest floor.

Marty coughed and spat a dark mass. Tears burned his eyes. The darkness grew darker.

"No... *help me*!"

And then the darkness grew deeper still as Judah went down. At first Marty didn't understand, but as things started to feel and sound different—the ground was damper, his cries and the dragging noises muffled by something surrounding them—he realized what was happening. Judah had risen from a hole in the forest floor, and now he was taking Marty back down into it.

He started struggling with all the energy and determination he had left, digging his fingers into the soil, clawing, trying to gain purchase as the zombie continued to pull. Trees and sky were being drawn away and total darkness hauled him down, and he'd never wanted to be out in that weird forest as much as he did then.

"*Help me!*" he screamed again, voice swallowed by the ground around him. He could see each extreme of the hole now as it framed the outside, and the inside smelled musty and of old decay long given over to time. His strength was leaving him. The knife drained his life and poured it into the ground around him. He smelled wet earth and blood.

One final scream and the outside was cut off from view, and Marty could do nothing but be dragged, and dragged, and dragged toward his doom.

◇ ◇ ◇

The screen grew still as the screaming boy was taken underground. They had cameras and sensors down there too, but there was no need to check on what was happening. Old Jonah Buckner was good at his craft, and if he couldn't extract the knife from the kid's back to finish the job, he had plenty more. Down there. In the darkness.

Sitterson swiveled his chair away from the control panel and started whistling, glancing around Control as he did so. Truman stood beside the door just down the curved metal staircase, as he had since the beginning. His eyes were wider than usual, and Sitterson thought he saw a trace of sweat on the soldier's top lip. But they'd have never been sent a raw recruit. Without even asking, he knew that Truman had seen action and had at least three years of combat postings behind him. He'd likely seen friends killed, and might have killed people himself. From a distance maybe, their deaths little more than clouds of dust and a quick dance. Or maybe he'd killed close-in, so he could look into the victim's eyes as he or she died.

But none of the action he'd seen would have been like this. Sitterson was only glad the soldier hadn't yet asked what lots of new ones tended to: *But why, when they're so defenseless?* Mainly because the answer was so glib. *They have to be.*

Still whistling, Sitterson watched Hadley go to the second mahogany panel at the back of the room, slide it open and pull the lever inside. He closed his eyes and kissed the pendant around his neck, knowing that a process was being repeated around and beneath him, blood flowing, grooves and carvings and etchings being filled, all in darkness as ever it was.

Sometimes in nightmares he dreamed of that shape slowly being traced in blood, the primitive human figure holding a goblet and dancing, carved into a chunk of stone as old as the world itself, and on waking he'd feel a deep dread more basic than anything he'd ever felt before, fearing that *he* was the Fool. Much of the dread came from the knowledge of what he had almost touched, because even dreams were no way to draw close.

And some of the dread came from the mystery of how he knew about the blood, and the carving, and the shapes they picked out.

He had learned to simply accept. Much easier that way. So he whistled, and Hadley returned to his desk, and Truman looked at his feet for a few seconds because he knew it had only just begun.

A rumble passed through Control, and two of the three large screens flickered for less than a second. The sensation passed as quickly as it had begun.

"They're getting excited downstairs," Hadley said as he lowered himself gently into his chair.

Sitterson nodded and looked around at Truman, who was standing almost to attention again now, though his eyes flickered left and right as if searching for something.

"Greatest Show on Earth..." Sitterson said. Then he returned to his controls, tapped a few keys and brought up the next screen.

Another rumble filled the room as the last girl did her best to survive.

◇ ◇ ◇

Somehow she was still functioning. Through all this the fear had clasped her cold around the chest, but she was still moving, still able to stand, still able to think. She had no idea how.

She looked at her hands pressed against the side of the tall dresser as she tried to push it in front of the window, and Jules's blood was already crisp between her fingers and tacky across the back. Perhaps that was where her strength came from: she knew that Jules would never want her to just give in.

So she shoved, and the wooden base of the dresser squealed across the timber floor.

Patience's mother was thumping against the window from outside. Two panes of glass had cracked, but the zombie seemed stupid, not realizing that she could shove her way through the glass. She pounded against the wooden frame and around the opening, mouth pressed against the glass, rotten tongue tracing grotesque patterns in the dust. If Dana could just get the dresser across the window…

She'd heard the screams and chaos from Marty's room. Then the silence. She tried not to think about what that meant, but how could she not? How could she ignore the idea that Marty might have—

Jules's dead eyes urged her to fight on, and the dresser slipped that much closer to the window.

"Keep bashing, bitch," Dana muttered, and then the sound of Mother's pounding changed. The whole room began to shake, dust drifted down from the ceiling, dark spidery shapes scurried to safety in shadows, and then the cabin swayed as a great grumbling sound filled the air. Dana looked around in disbelief.

Earthquake? You gotta be fucking kidding!

"What?" she gasped. "No! No, come *on*!"

The air seemed to vibrate and her vision blurred. She bit her lip—afraid for a second that she was fainting—but then the rumbling started to subside and the floor leveled beneath her. For a moment all was still and even the bashing from the window had ceased. *Let the ground have opened up and swallowed her whole*, Dana thought, but she was already shoving hard against the dresser when the pounding began again.

With one last effort she heaved the tall item of furniture before the window, standing in front of it and pushing so that it was flush against the wall on either side. As if that was a signal, Mother turned her attention to the glass and soon smashed it out, and Dana felt the dresser starting to rock. She leaned against it for a moment, absorbing the impacts, but they were turning harder and harder as the zombie became more determined to gain entry.

Timing the blows, Dana darted to the bed and dragged it up against the dresser, trying to wedge its feet against differing levels in the floorboards in the vain hope that it would jam the dresser in place.

But it was like putting sticking plaster over a compound fracture. It was only a matter of time until the bitch found her way in, and Dana already knew that the room offered nothing that she could use as a weapon.

At least I'm *still working*, she thought with unnatural calm. She was amazed that her heart hadn't exploded with the terror and her limbs hadn't simply ceased to function.

The dresser rocked and the bed's legs screeched as they were driven against the floor. Dana went to the door and tried it again. She'd heard the heavy bolts thumping in as soon as the door had slammed behind her, but before she'd been able to investigate the ghostly shape of Mother appeared at the window and started hammering. *So who the hell locked me in?* she wondered, working at the handle. It turned, but the door was stuck fast in its frame, with not even an inch of give. Solid, like a wall.

Now Dana started kicking at the door's wooden panels, aiming the heels of her trainers at the corners. The feel and sound of each kick was all wrong, as if the wood was simply a veneer, and beneath lay something solid, like metal. She felt panic starting to well up—

Keep calm, calm, I've come this far—

—and then the dresser tilted against the bed, scraping it across the floor with its leaning weight, and around the side of the dresser she saw Mother's gray weathered hand clasping at the room's air.

Dana had to make a quick choice: stay and fight with the door, hoping she could get out before Mother got in; or try to kill the zombie before it killed her.

How the fuck do you kill a zombie? she wondered,

and a hundred images from a hundred horror movies flashed across her mind. Destroy their heads, destroy their brains, burn them, decapitate them, take off their arms and legs and they'll still come at you, jawing themselves along the ground in their search for your flesh, your heart, your *braaaainnnns*.

She plucked up a bedside lamp and, as Mother peered from behind the leaning dresser, smashed it across her face. The zombie barely seemed to notice. She looked at Dana and continued working her way from behind the tilted furniture, two hands free now, torso, and one leg lifted clear and planted against the bed, ready to kick up and launch herself through the air.

Dana backed against the wall, because she was out of options. She closed her eyes briefly and thought of Jules, and wondered how much it would hurt.

Something thumped with a loud impact, and a shower of glass scraped across her shoulder and past her face. She gasped and jumped, looked down, and saw the bizarre hunting picture, face up on the floor. Then she heard Holden's gasps and grunts.

She pulled back a little and he knocked out the rest of the glass from the one-way mirror, using a lamp base as an impromptu club. He didn't smile when he saw her, only looked past her at Mother. From his room Dana could hear thumping, as well, but there were no zombies in there.

Not yet.

She let out an explosive sob and Holden looked at her at last, offering a brief smile.

"My door's stuck," he said.

"Mine too!"

"Come on." He held out his hand and Dana took it, and as she climbed through into his room she expected to feel Mother's hand clasping her ankle at any moment, the skin cold and rough, the strength impossible. But she fell through onto Holden's floor, wincing as errant glass shards sliced her scalp and scratched across the bridge of her nose. Holden slipped on something and went down with her, and for a moment they were close and she could taste the panic on his breath.

She checked out his room and saw the pile of furniture stacked against his own window.

"That didn't do much good for—" she began, and his wardrobe tilted inward and crashed to the floor. It threw up clouds of dust and shook the floorboards, and as she and Holden helped each other up she saw big-zombie standing in the shattered window frame.

"That'll be Matthew," she said, and giving the thing a name seemed almost stupid enough to laugh. Almost.

"Well he's big enough to—"

"The bed!" Dana said. And as Holden tipped it on its end and she helped him shove it against the window, she knew that it was futile. Matthew thumped at the mattress as they pushed it close, and she thought he was perhaps being playful, like a cat knocking a mouse around with only a shred of its full strength before killing it.

They leaned against the upended bed, looking at each other, and the sense of hopelessness was shattering. *I haven't even had a chance to take a breath*, she thought, and for a moment she almost kissed him. But that, too, would have felt so stupid, and so final.

So instead she looked around for something else they could use—as a weapon, or to help secure the bed against the wall—and that was when she saw the trapdoor.

"Er... Holden," she said, nodding to the side. It had been hidden beneath the bed up to now, and already she was thinking of all the stuff down there in the basement that they could use as weapons. Those tools, the chains, maybe even something from Roberto the Limbless Man's circus. And all the other stuff, the weird stuff.

That picture of Patience staring with dead eyes...

Mother appeared at the shattered mirror. She stood there for a moment, hands clasping at the jagged glass still stuck in the frame's sill, staring in at them. *Don't let her smile*, Dana thought. *I don't think I could handle a smile.*

But Mother did not smile. She started to climb instead, clumsily trying to shove one leg and her head through the small gap at the same time. It wouldn't take her long to figure it out.

"Go," Holden whispered, and Dana went to the trapdoor. She grabbed the small rusted handle set in one edge and pulled, fearing it would be jammed tight, and falling back in surprise as it swung up and open without even a squeak from the hinges.

Oiled recently, she thought. There was nothing but blackness below, and the smell of age.

She looked up at Holden.

"Better or worse, you think?" she asked.

"Lamp," he said, nodding at the small table beside where his bed used to be. It was still plugged in, so Dana leaned out and grabbed its shade, glancing back over her shoulder as she did so. Mother now had both legs over the mirror's sill and was trying to press her head through, as well, straggly hair caught on glass shards above. She was growling and keening.

Dana lowered the lamp, holding the cord and letting it dangle when it reached its extreme. She leaned down and looked into the basement. It was empty, just a dirt-floored space below the room. Maybe it connected to the main area they'd been in, somehow, or maybe not, but right then it seemed not to matter. She didn't think they had any choice.

"It's empty," she announced.

Holden shoved the bed into place one last time, glanced across at Mother still struggling at the smashed hole in the wall, then moved to his door.

"Curt!" he shouted. "Curt!"

Moments later the door knob twisted left and right, the door not moving at all. "Unlock your door!" Curt called, and Dana never thought she'd be so glad to hear his voice.

"I can't, it's locked!" Holden shouted. "Got Dana in with me. Get down to the basement, we've got a way down from here!"

"Okay!" Curt called, and Dana saw the doorknob fall still as he let go.

Holden took a quick look down into the barely-lit blackness, sat on the edge and tipped forward, holding the floor and flipping himself over to land on his feet. For a moment Dana was left alone in his room, Mother halfway through the jagged mirror and forcing herself past the remaining spears of glass, and Matthew shoving at the bed, its metal frame scoring the timber floor as it shifted with each impact.

Then Holden called to her and she sat at the trapdoor's edge, easing herself down into his arms.

It was suddenly quiet in that dark part of the basement, as if the noise from above was meant only for the bedroom. She heard Holden's breathing and felt his thumping heart next to her own, and he was holding her tight even though her feet were on the floor. She was glad. And then she looked around and saw *why* he was holding her, and knew they had made a terrible mistake.

The only light was from the lamp still dangling to their left, and it was barely bright enough to illuminate the whole room. But it showed them enough.

It was a torture chamber. A chair stood against one wall, fixed with rough metal clamps to the wall and floor. Thick leather straps protruded stiffly from the arms and legs. Chains and shackles hung from metal rings in the floor joists that made up the low ceiling. Several chains ended in cruel hooks, and others bore manacles, some of them set swinging by the sudden invasion of this place. The chair's seat seemed stained dark, though that might have been the light.

Against one wall stood a table, and on the table was a vast array of terrible, brutal tools and implements of pain. Saws, hammers, hooks, knives, chains, wooden stakes, pliers, branding irons, axes, cleavers, nails, bolts... A fine film of dust lay over everything, blunting the knives and dulling the intended use of some instruments, yet the small underground room seemed to echo with the horrors it had seen.

"This is the Black Room," Dana whispered.

"What?" Holden asked.

"From the diary. Remember? This is where he killed them." She was shaking now, not cold but terrified, because everything was coming together. Guilt made her feel sick, and the fear of what was to come strove to empty her of hope. "This is where he kills *us*."

"What are you talking about?" Holden asked. "This is just some sicko's—"

"I brought us here," she whispered, and the weight of responsibility was crushing. She could hardly breathe, thinking of Jules's head in her hands. Her vision swam as she replayed Marty's screams. "I found the diary, read from it, conjured them, and... you're all gonna die because of me."

Holden grabbed her upper arms and shook slightly until she looked at him. So strong, so solid, so there, even behind his fear she saw determination and strength. For a second she almost let it make her feel better.

"Nobody did this," he said. "Okay, it's bad luck. Horrible fucking luck. But I'm not gonna die and neither are you. We just gotta find the door."

"There isn't one," she whispered, and even though she hadn't looked she knew she was right. This wasn't part of the basement. It was a different place, and the distance between here and Holden's bedroom above seemed endless.

He glanced around, and Dana watched him searching for the door. *Bet he wishes he'd never tagged along now*, she thought, but she couldn't even smile. He turned back to her and nodded.

"Yeah. Nothing obvious. But there must be something in the wall. Just look."

His optimism shook her a little, and she closed her eyes and took a deep breath.

Maybe he's right, she thought. *Maybe we can't just give in*. And she moved to the table. She didn't want to spend too long looking at the tools and dwelling on their uses, so she picked up something that looked like a small crowbar and started running it along the walls, tapping. She listed to the sounds it made to see if they changed—anything that might indicate an alternative material in the construction could mean something different beyond.

She tapped and tapped, but found nothing.

"Curt?" she shouted. If he'd made it down into the basement by now, perhaps he was on the other side of one of these walls. She concentrated, trying to position herself in relation to the outside wall of the cabin, but the geography of the room above them had become confused.

One or both of them will be down here soon, she

thought, and the seconds seemed to tick away like memories of her life.

"Anything?" Holden asked.

Dana shook her head.

"No."

He crossed the room toward her. He'd been tapping, too, and she saw a shadow fall over his face even though he tried to fight away his own desperation. *He's doing it for me*, she realized. *He'll never say it's hopeless.*

"Hidden rooms were a staple of post-civil war architecture," Holden said. "There's gotta be a—" And when he was directly below the trapdoor a shadow swung in, a spiked metal smile on the end of a long chain, catching him beneath the left arm and across the back of his shoulder.

Holden's eyes went wide and he screamed.

Dana reached for him as the slack chain tightened and he was lifted from the floor. He swung a little as his feet left the dirt and knocked her back, and she clasped his hands and pulled. Above and behind him she saw up through the trapdoor where Matthew's huge shadow loomed, shoulders flexing and arms working as he pulled. The rusted teeth of the bear trap were embedded, it was only going to take a couple of seconds to haul Holden from the basement room, and then…

And then there'll just be me, Dana thought. She did not want to die alone.

She tugged at Holden's hands, knowing that each movement would be jarring those cruel metal teeth gripped within his flesh. But if she let the zombie drag him up and out he was finished, and Holden knew this as well.

Teeth gritted and bared he jerked his shoulders, stretching forward to help Dana each time she tugged. On their third try the shadow above them slipped and fell forward, and Holden dropped to the floor.

Matthew's girth lodged him in the trapdoor, his upper body hanging in the basement, hands still reaching for Holden where he'd fallen. The lamp swung wildly beside him, and the shifting light danced shadows across his face, almost as if he had expression. But there was no expression there. He moaned slightly, but that was the only sign of effort as he twisted and turned, futilely reaching for his prey.

Holden had managed to tug the broken bear trap away from his back, dropping it to the floor and slumping over weakly, when one of Matthew's questing hands snagged a fold of his ripped pullover. Holden's eyes went wide as he was snatched backward, and Matthew hissed in triumph.

"You like pain?" Dana asked. She stepped around Holden and stabbed hard with the crowbar. It punctured Matthew's face amidst the remains of his nose, driving him against the wall and pinning him there. Dana screamed into his face, "How's that work for ya?"

Holden fell free.

Matthew's hands grasped at the bar and started pulling, and Dana heard the sound of metal scraping against bone.

He's not dead, she thought, *bar through his head*

and he's not dead, not yet, not dead, not yet—

She plucked a long carving knife from the torture table and stabbed at Matthew's chest, neck, throat, face, head, hacking at him a dozen times, shaking with rage. She went for his heart, not knowing for sure that it beat; his brain, uncertain of whether he even thought in the normal sense. His hands finally swung down and he hung limp, but she kept stabbing anyway. She was furious at his lack of blood. If he'd bled, perhaps she would have felt... happier?

She wasn't sure; didn't think she could ever be happy again. She buried the knife deep in his left eye and hung on, exhausted.

"Remind me... never to piss you off," Holden said. And through everything, Dana finally managed a smile.

EIGHT

Hadley was standing behind Sitterson, watching the action on the giant screens that rose before them. He'd been pacing nervously for the last couple of minutes, and Sitterson had to resist the urge to swivel in his chair and tell him to sit the hell down. Things were going to be okay. The kids were doing pretty well in comparison to other occasions, true. But they'd gone from outside to inside, and inside to down, just as was intended.

And now that they'd got the better of the huge zombie Matthew, their defenses would be lowered for a while. They'd feel a flush of success, celebrate their resilience, rejoice in their humanity. Who knew, they might even fuck. It had happened before.

"Oh yeah," Hadley said. "Nothing to worry about. He *looks* dead..."

Sitterson smiled, worked at his keyboard, and turned a dial a quarter-clockwise. A graduated display on the small screen beside the dial showed a steady increase in power.

"And what do we do when the dead guy stops moving?" Sitterson asked. He was aware of Truman standing off to their left, more enrapt than terrified now by proceedings.

That's good, Sitterson thought. *He's learning fast*.

He pushed the button beside the dial. The charge peaked, then purged and dropped to zero. And on the screen—

◇ ◇ ◇

—Dana jerked her hand back from the knife, staring at her fingers and palm. Holden could hardly blame her. The damage she'd done to that thing, that *zombie*, was sickening. Whatever it was now, it had once been human.

She turned to him with a frown, hand still held out, and she was about to say something when he took her in his arms and held tight. He felt tears burning but swallowed them back. She relaxed into his embrace, her face slick with sweat and a sheen of blood down her left cheek, and he took as much comfort from the contact as she. Even the pain where her hand pressed against his injuries was refreshing, because it made him so alive.

"You smell good," he said, remembering their tender kisses and tentative caresses.

"I stink of blood and sweat," she mumbled against his neck.

"Yeah. Blood. Sweat. Mmm."

She *felt* good, as well, but he didn't need to tell her that. Her hands pressed against his back, never quite still, and she was feeling the solidity of him just as he was with her.

"Holden..." she said, her voice quivering, and she started to shake.

He should have comforted her. The words came to his lips but when he tried to speak they emerged as a sob, and in this silent pause when violence was no longer upon them, he felt his barriers beginning to tumble.

"Come on," she said, edging him toward the back of the room. "Come on."

The hanging shape of the slashed-up zombie was starkly illuminated by the dangling lamp, casting a horrific shadow against the far wall. His big hands almost touched the torture room's dirt floor. The chain wrapped around his wrist bit in deep, and the half-moon curve of the broken bear trap glistened and glimmered with fresh blood.

Holden frowned, because he wasn't aware he'd been injured that badly. There was *so much* blood on there.

"Come on," Dana said again, "we've got to try and—"

A rumble came from the wall, and for a moment Holden through it was another of those troubling earth tremors. But then he felt the vibration through his feet and heard the sound coming from a very definite direction.

Then a section of the wall started to fold away.

"Back!" he shouted, hauling Dana behind him in some deep-set belief that he should be protecting her. She's *the one who killed the zombie*, he thought, and he barked a brief, mad laugh as Dana dashed to the table and brought up a heavy, curved hatchet.

"You feint left, and I'll get it when it goes for you," she whispered. Holden nodded, tensed, and when the wall was fully open and the flashlight blinded him he darted to the left... straight into the thing's arms.

"Hey!" Curt said, squeezing his shoulders. "Hey, it's me."

"Curt," Dana gasped.

"Let's move let's move!" he said without even pausing to check out the room. Behind him, the chaotic mess of the main cellar was lit by two hanging bulbs, both swinging and dancing as Curt ducked beneath the joists for the floor above and brushed the wire with his head.

Dana followed, with Holden bringing up the rear.

Should've closed the door, he thought, even though he'd seen Dana doing a blade-job on the bastard thing. *If it gets out—*

"We're getting the fuck out of here," Curt said. He moved quickly across the cellar, knocking a bookcase with his thigh and spilling a slew of moldy books across the floor. Dana walked into a chandelier of fine chains hanging from an old wagon wheel, waving her hands around her head as if to shove aside spider webs. Holden went to help but she was through them, one hand fingering through her hair and bringing the dirty, bloody knots to his attention.

She's bleeding more than I thought. He wanted to embrace her again, and he promised himself that he would. Soon. They would hug soon, somewhere safe where terror couldn't tear them apart again, and where warmth and safety replaced the stink of age and the coldness of death.

Curt stopped below the storm doors that led to the outside, looking around, kicking a heavy shelf from the wall and hefting it as a weapon. A dozen ornaments spilled from the shelf and shattered on the floor, and as he went for the three stairs leading up to the doors he crunched them into the ground.

He turned around and glanced from Dana to Holden, sizing them up.

"Hurt?"

Dana shook her head, denying the blood. Curt pointed at her nose, her scalp. "Not bad," she said.

"I'm cut," Holden said. He hadn't yet explored his wounds from the bear trap, but he could still feel them leaking afresh. Once when he was a kid he'd fallen and scraped his knee, and keeled over in a faint when he looked down to see the slight dribble of blood. Since then he'd been terrified of blood— especially his own— and the last thing he needed now was to pass out.

He turned his left side to Curt, who looked him up and down without his expression giving anything away.

"Think you can you run?" he asked.

Holden nodded.

"Good. I open these doors and we go for the Rambler, okay?"

Dana and Holden agreed with a nod, Curt turned to the doors and shoved them open, and darkness flooded in.

No time to talk and plan, Holden thought. *This is controlled panic. None of us really knows what's happening here.*

Curt went first, the heavy shelf held across his chest ready to swing. He climbed the stairs, stood in the open beside the cabin, and looked around.

"Okay," he said, and Dana followed him up. Holden came last, ready to stand and look cautiously into the darkness between trees, but the other two were already sprinting for the Rambler.

And this is when control gets flushed down the toilet, he thought, remembering every horror movie he'd ever seen. *The creeping and peering around corners is over. Now we're just running.*

Holden's side and back hurt more when he ran, and the cool night air was chill across his flowing blood. But he concentrated on Dana, even smiling slightly as he realized that despite all this he was still checking out her butt, and they reached the vehicle without being attacked by any of the walking dead.

"What about Marty?" Dana gasped as they skidded to a stop.

"They got him," Curt said.

Marty? Holden thought, feeling a deep loss for someone he hardly knew. *Marty's—?*

Curt pointed at the door handle and touched his finger to his lips.

Holden looked and saw what had made him so cautious. Dirt on the handle, a wet slick with half a dead leaf trapped in it like a fly in amber.

Marty, Holden mouthed, but Curt shook his head. Whatever he had seen, it must have been enough to mean Marty couldn't possibly have recovered.

Curt hefted the plank over his shoulder and stepped back, looking from Holden to the door and back again, and Holden nodded in acknowledgment. *After three*, he thought, crouching beside the door and reaching for the handle. He mouthed one... two... three... then flipped the catch and moved aside.

The door swung open. Curt tensed, shuffling a half step forward. Shook his head.

"Okay," Dana said. "Okay. Now can we please get the fuck out of here?"

"Seconded," Holden said.

"Yeah," Curt nodded.

They climbed inside, slammed the door behind them, and Curt took the driver's seat. He whispered a prayer and the Rambler started first time. Its headlamps pushed darkness back between the trees. As he steered them out of the clearing, the lights splashed across the front of the cabin. The door was cracked and broken, but still solid in its frame. A lamp still burned in the large main room. There was little to show what had happened there.

Good fucking riddance, Holden thought as Curt swung the vehicle around and headed back along the road they had traveled so recently, and a lifetime ago.

◇ ◇ ◇

Oh fuck, Sitterson thought, *they've gone and screwed it up*. And much as he always enjoyed the tense competition between themselves and the Japanese, and the friendly rivalry to see who could produce the most perfect, most imaginative, most effective scenarios, he also liked to win. And what he saw on the screen meant that they weren't out of the woods yet.

And that brought immense pressure to bear.

Hadley had wheeled his chair over to sit beside his friend, an unconscious desire for closeness as they watched the Japanese effort fall apart on their central big screen.

The hideously screaming face of the drowned Japanese girl filled the screen, long black hair floating and waving about her head like a million individual snakes ready to inject their own unique venoms. Yet horrible and terrifying though the floating drowned girl was, both Sitterson and Hadley knew what was about to happen.

To this story, there would be no shock ending.

The screaming face started to relax. She looked bewildered, as if remembering that she had once been a little girl, not this screeching banshee-thing with hair that cast lethal shadows. A warm glow grew around her, driving away the monochrome of dark tendrils and white pasty skin, and imbuing her visage with a semblance of life.

Sitterson sighed as the view pulled back to take in

the entirety of the Japanese classroom. Several children knelt at its centre, carefully placing lotus flowers into a large bowl of water above which the floating drowned girl hovered. She seemed smaller now, her hair more lank than wild, her eyes sad instead of filled with vengeful rage.

The kids sang a song whose lyrics Sitterson did not understand, but his skin prickled with the happiness of the tune, the love it conveyed, and any other time he might even had felt a lump at his throat.

But not now.

"This is just too fucking fucked up," he said.

The floating drowned girl began to glow. For a moment her face dropped in fear, but then she smiled brightly as light enveloped her, spewing from her eyes and mouth where previously there had been only darkness. She waved her hands in the air as if swimming, and her hair drew back and hung across her shoulders, no longer obscuring her eyes.

The light grew brighter still, and then it faded away to a background glow that seemed to fill the whole classroom with sunlight. The girl faded away, as well.

A frog leapt from the bowl of water and flowers, sitting amongst the other girls and looking around.

They chanted something, and at the bottom of the screen a line of subtitles appeared. Sitterson wondered who in control was translating. He didn't really care. He knew the gist of what it would say.

"Now Kiko's spirit will live in the happy frog!"

The girls laughed and hugged. The picture flickered,

went to static and then cut to black. Sitterson hoped that somewhere in Japan, heads would roll.

"*Fuuhhhcck yooouuu!*" Sitterson shouted.

"Not good," Hadley said, shaking his head. "Not good." Sitterson turned to his friend and colleague, a useless anger brewing, and then something buzzed and something else flashed and he had an incoming communication.

"That'll be Lin," Hadley said, wheeling himself back to his control panel as Sitterson composed himself a little. He flicked a switch and a monitor on his desk lit up. Lin stared from it. It looked to Sitterson as if she'd had her hair pulled back even tighter since he'd seen her last. Maybe she had a machine that did it.

"You seeing this?" he asked.

"Perfect record, huh?" Lin said without expression.

"Naruto-watching, geisha-fucking, weird gameshow-having *dicks*! They fucked us!"

"Few injuries, but zero fatality," Lin said. "Total wash. Any word from downstairs?"

"Downstairs doesn't care about Japan," Sitterson said, sighing. *Move on*, he thought. *Accept it, stop stewing, stop blaming everyone else when everything is down to you and everyone else here and...* Move on!

"The Director trusts us," he said softly.

"You guys better be on your game," Lin said, voice even more impersonal than ever over the electronic link.

Before Sitterson could spit out something offensive Hadley cut in. *He knows me so well*, Sitterson thought as his friend spoke.

"You just sweat the chem, Lin," he said. "While these morons are singing 'What a Friend We Have in Shinto', we're bringing the *pain*."

"Fuck was up with that fool's *pot*, anyway?" Sitterson asked. "He shoulda been drooling, and instead he nearly made us."

"We treated the shit out of it!" Lin said, and her defensiveness was the first real expression he'd seen on her face. He shouldn't have enjoyed that—they all worked together, after all—but he did.

"Got 'em in the Rambler, headed for the tunnel," he said to Hadley, spotting the vehicle's movement on a big screen. He turned the central monitor back to focus on their own concerns, now that the Japanese were out of the picture. They never messed up, and deep inside he found that cause for concern.

But it also presented a challenge.

And what *a challenge*, he thought. But he couldn't go that way, couldn't let the implications get on top of him. Right now he needed to focus like he never had before.

"The Fool is toast anyway," Lin said from the monitor, as if that could excuse the mistake. "You better not fuck us on the report."

"Shit!" Hadley said.

"What?" Lin asked. "Shit why?"

Yeah, shit why? Sitterson thought, looking across at his colleague. Hadley glanced up and flicked his fingers across his throat.

"Work to do," Hadley said, and Sitterson could

hear the urgency there. "Gotta go."

"You guys are humanity's last hope, don't tell me—"

Sitterson cut her off.

Don't tell us what we are, bitch, we already fucking know.

"So?" he asked.

"There's no cave-in," Hadley said.

"What!?" *We can't fail we can't fuck up we can't let anything go wrong—*

Hadley worked his keyboard and pointed at the main screen. It was a view through the tunnel, a staggering transfer through the fifteen cameras along its length. It went from moonlight at one end, to moonlight at the other, with no obvious blockage in between.

"The fucking tunnel is *open*!"

Sitterson breathed deeply for a second, composing himself. Then he hit a switch and spoke into his microphone.

"This is Control to Demolition." He waited for a response but heard only static. "Shit, they're not even picking up!"

"What?" Hadley asked. The panic was brewing in him, the constant nervousness expanding. He looked gray.

"Don't worry," Sitterson said, though he was *more* than worried. He hit another button and spoke again. "Broadcast, can you patch me in to Demolition?"

"We're dark on their whole sector," an anonymous voice replied. "Might have been a surge in the—"

Sitterson cut them off. Sat there breathing for a

while. Looked up at the screen, tracking the progress of the Rambler as it careened around the forest track too quickly, wheels spitting grit and mud and the Jock driving it expertly.

He stood quickly, sending his wheeled chair rolling across the floor to strike the wall below the mahogany panels. Two open, three still closed. He blinked at them, then turned to Hadley, who was busy tapping away on his keyboard.

"See if you can bypass—"

"Fuck you *think* I'm doing?" Hadley snapped. Sitterson started to reply but decided better of it. Instead he turned and walked toward Truman.

"Get the door."

The soldier shifted uncomfortably from one foot to the other.

"Mister Sitterson, you're not supposed to leave the—"

"Open the goddamn door!" Sitterson snapped. He was standing in front of Truman now, the soldier's uncertainly evident, but his professionalism was also clear. He glanced down at the boy's pistol, then snorted. *What the fuck are you thinking?*

"You got family, Truman?" Hadley asked without looking up from his screen. He was sweating, leaning closer to the computer than ever, eyes alight with text and numbers and whatever else he was absorbing.

"Yeah..." the soldier said.

"Kids get through that tunnel alive, you won't anymore." Hadley didn't even glance up.

Sitterson nodded at the screen—the Rambler sliding around a curve, headlamps lighting the trees, wheels spinning—and decided to give Truman three seconds.

At the count of one he'd stepped aside and hit the panel to open the door.

"Good choice," Sitterson said, and he started to run.

Demolition was one level down, and the staircase was at the end of this corridor, past the dog-leg and past Chem. He reckoned thirty seconds. He wasn't as young or as fit as he used to be, but he ran faster than he had in years, ignoring the pains in his toes and shins, the burning of his lungs, the thumping of his heart.

Maybe three minutes 'til they reach the tunnel, he thought, running through their route in his mind. *That's if they don't blow a tire or hit a tree or skid into a ditch*. And with what was at stake, there was no way he could rely on anything so remote as luck.

"Make a hole!" he shouted at a couple of guards milling outside Chem. "Fucking *move*!" They pressed back against the wall and he ran by, wondering whether at that moment Lin might have glanced up at the door and seen his panicked shape rush by. Maybe she had. And if he didn't run *faster*, maybe she'd never have the chance to ask him what it had all been about.

In his earpiece Hadley's voice was shrill.

"I can't override! It's asking me to run a systems diagnostic!"

"By the time that's finished, *we'll* be finished!" Sitterson panted.

"Good luck, Buddy."

Sitterson smiled and ran faster, skidding around the dog-leg, pushing between two strolling workers and barreling through the swing-doors leading into the stairwell. He slid down the handrails, quick but cautious—a broken ankle now would mean the end of everything—and then back out into the corridor below. First door to the right was Sustenance, and when he drew level with the door to Demolition he kicked it open and ran inside.

There was a guard standing to the left, hand on the butt of his gun. Sitterson glared at him and rushed by. *Just you fucking dare*, he thought.

A second to scan the Demolition control room and he knew where the problem was. One large control panel was dark—power off—and from beneath came sparks and flashes. A man and a woman were working the panel, the man flicking a switch back and forth as if persistence could lure electricity back to him, the woman running diagnostic on a wired-up laptop.

Jesus Christ, where do we find these people?

"It's not the breakers!" the man said, glancing up as he saw Sitterson approach.

"Fuck is going on in here?"

"We don't know!" the guy whined. "Electrical said there was a glitch up top, one of the creatures?"

"The tunnel should have been blown hours ago!" Sitterson said.

The woman glanced up at him—pretty, terrified—and said, "We never got the order!"

"You need me to tell you to wipe your ass?" He

shoved the man aside, glanced down at the laptop screen. She was stuck on the fucking *password*. "How do we get past this?"

"We're fried inside," she said, a quaver to her voice. "We need a clean connection to the detonator—"

Sitterson snorted, dropped to the floor and crawled beneath the unit. If they needed a clean connection then why were they fucking around with switches and trying to run a fucking diagnostic! She was stuck on the password, for fuck's sake! He closed his eyes and breathed deeply, trying to chill, shedding the fearful anger and shifting focus to what needed doing and what *had to* be done.

After two seconds he opened his eyes again and pulled half a dozen quick-release bolts. Plastic covering fell away and a mass of wires and circuits was revealed.

"Okay, I need you to tell me exactly what went down first and how long after the other systems followed. And hand me a voltmeter."

"Systems Tech is trying a reboot on the—" the guy started, but Sitterson cut in.

"We don't have time. Talk me through."

As the guy talked, Sitterson started checking boards until he found the one that had fried. He noted the number and shouted up for a replacement. It took thirty seconds for the woman to drop one in his hand, and another thirty before he'd replaced it with wire clips. *Should be soldered*, he thought, closing his eyes as he connected the last wire.

Something hummed, and he saw some of the

surface indicators lighting up through the guts of the panel above him.

"We good?" he asked.

"No, that's just local," the woman said. "It's not linked.

"Shit!"

"Lin's here," Hadley said through his earpiece.

"Oh, great, she's just who we need right now. Tell her to go poison someone."

"The Rambler's a mile away from the tunnel," his friend said softly.

"Okay. Okay." Sitterson scanned the mass of boards and chips, wires and fuses, circuit connectors and relays. A flush of utter hopelessness hit him, but he shoved it aside with an angry growl. He applied the voltmeter here and there, noting where power had failed but also knowing that in each of these places, it shouldn't really matter. It was the relay to the detonator that mattered, and he'd just replaced...

"Is the detonator button still lit?"

"Yes," the woman said, "but I told you, it's just—"

"Local," Sitterson said. He shuffled further beneath the unit and probed with his penlight, sniffing, smelling burnt plastic.

There!

He held the penlight in his teeth.

"Gary, we don't have long," Hadley said in his ear.

"Uh-huh." He pulled the melted mass of wires apart.

"I mean it."

"Uh-huh." In the artificial light, orange and red

were too close, indistinguishable, so he stripped all four wires with his thumbnail.

"They're approaching the last bend. *Damn*, that kid can drive."

"Shud the huck up!" Sitterson growled, and he touched wires. Sparks flew, he flinched, and then from above he heard a brief, victorious yelp.

"We're up!" the man said.

Sitterson spat the torch aside and held the wires together.

"Blow it!" he shouted.

The woman smacked the big demolition button and Sitterson winced as he was shocked. *Been sweating, wet, this might kill me.* But the pain was brief, and when it passed he called out.

"So?"

"We're good," the man said.

"We're good," the woman echoed.

Sitterson twisted the wires and snaked his way out from beneath the unit. The guy and woman were staring at him, faces slack with almost unbearable relief. The man actually held out his hand to help him up. Sitterson stood on his own, wiping imaginary dust from his sweat-soaked shirt. He examined the burns on his thumb and forefinger, pus-blisters already forming there. That was going to hurt, but all was still.

Downstairs, all was still.

"Wipe your ass," he said and, leaving them to their shame, he smiled and left the room.

NINE

"Back up back up back up!" Holden shouted, and Curt slammed the Rambler into reverse, stomping on the accelerator and not even bothering to look in the mirror because he wouldn't be able to see anything anyway.

Holden and Dana crouched close behind Curt's driver's seat. *We should get in back and hide*, Holden thought, but that would have been unfair to Curt. Something kept them together. United by their near-escape, perhaps now they would all die together. At least being crushed by falling rocks was better than—

This is beyond the zombies, and we all know that now.

Ahead of them the tunnel was in chaos—ceiling falling, slabs of rock pounding down, walls blasting out, dust and grit billowing and scraping against the Rambler's chassis and windscreen. Visibility was quickly reduced to zero, and their only hope of survival would be if Curt steered them back out into the open air.

A big rock scraped down the front of the vehicle, fracturing the windshield and tearing metal. Nevertheless, Curt held the wheel straight, foot pressed all the way down on the gas. The engine screeched in protest. They shook from side to side, and at the rear of the Rambler one of the sunroofs shattered and let in a shower of stinging debris.

Holden twisted to look and winced as his wounds distorted, and fresh blood flowed.

Through the back of the Rambler he saw a flash of trees.

"Almost there!" he shouted.

The roof was being battered now, dented and ripped where rocks struck. *If the whole mountain comes down into the tunnel we'll be squashed without even knowing what happened*, he thought. He held Dana and kissed her, one hand around the back of her neck, another cupping her breast, and he felt her own desperate realization of their predicament.

If there was any way he'd wish to go...

And then they were out, and it was as if the weight of the world had been lifted from around them. There were no more impacts, and Curt looked back past them as he steered the vehicle far from the collapsing tunnel and up against the wall of the roadside cliff. He left the engine running and pulled on the parking break.

Their gasps mingled, and Holden did not let go of Dana's neck. Given a choice, he never would again.

"Well..." Curt said. He got up from his seat and

kicked the door open. Bent metal shrieked in protest. Dana followed, and she reached back for Holden's hand as they all exited to stand beside the battered Rambler.

Rumbles still issued from the tunnel's mouth, and a pile of debris had spilled out across the road. Dust rose in billowing clouds. Grit rained down around them like hard rain.

"They might be following," Dana said, glancing around nervously. Holden looked as well. The road was bathed in moonlight, but beneath the trees lurked the gloom that might hide anything.

"We drove really fast," he said. "Even if they can run they'll be a mile or two back, easy."

"Yeah," she said uncertainly, squeezing his hand.

"No!" Curt shouted. "No fucking way! This isn't happening! It's *right there*! He gestured across the ravine at the ground beyond, and freedom. They could even see the road curving out from the tunnel, and a ponderous cloud of dust was making the onward journey that now eluded them.

Holden scanned the cliff face opposite, then walked to the edge on their side. The bottom of the ravine was hidden in darkness. There could be anything down there, but then... there was anything up here, too. There were fucking *zombies* up here.

"You got any climbing gear?" he asked Curt. "Ropes?"

"Yeah, in my fucking dorm room."

"We can't climb this. This is limestone, it's slippery and it'll crumble under pressure."

"We can't go back," Dana said, standing beside them at the cliff's edge. "There's no way across?"

"What are we gonna do, jump?" Holden said, closing his eyes, shaking his head. "Sorry."

"It's okay," Dana said. "Not in the mood for a jump anyway."

"No? Zombies don't do it for you?"

"Dude," Curt said quietly.

"What?"

Curt nodded back at the Rambler.

"The dirt bike on the back," he said. "I'm good."

For a few seconds Holden didn't really comprehend what he meant. So he was good on a dirt bike, how did that help them if...?

"You're serious," Dana said, and then Holden got it. He looked from Curt to the other side of the ravine, then back again.

"You really think you can…?"

Curt shrugged, frowned then nodded. Nodded again, harder. "Yeah," he said. "Yeah I can. Now help me get the thing ready, will you?"

The three of them lifted the bike from the rack, and Curt checked it over to make sure it hadn't been damaged in the rockfall. *All we need now's a puncture*, Holden thought, but the bike had survived in good shape, protected by the bulk of the larger vehicle. Curt sat astride, fired it up and did a couple of gentle circuits around the Rambler, making himself comfortable and spinning the rear wheel a few times.

"Holden, we should stop him," Dana said.

"You think he'll listen to us?"

"No, but we should try."

Holden knew she was right. But at the same time he was looking at the jump and trying to judge the distance, the arc the bike would take, and the chances of Curt making it across. And the more he looked, the more he thought it looked good. There was a decent rise on this side just before the drop-off, and the other side was clear of trees and boulders. A good place to land, so long as he stopped before the cliff face over there. And then if the bike made it in one piece he could go for help, be back here within a couple of hours with cops and the army and—

But what if Curt didn't make it in one piece? What if he made it across but spilled, broke both legs? Would they really have to watch each other die?

"I dunno..." Dana said, shaking her head. And Holden knew that she was thinking the same thing. She hated Curt risking this, but she also knew it might be their only chance at escape. Even now back there in the forest, *things* would be coming for them.

"Okay," Curt said, skidding to a stop beside them and eyeing the ravine.

"Curt, are you sure about this?" Dana asked.

"I've done bigger jumps than this."

"You've got a smooth run," Holden said. "A slight rise here, and maybe a five foot differential on the other side, which is good. But you gotta give it everything."

"You know it."

"Curt..." Dana said.

He came down off his adrenaline kick for a moment and looked at her. *He's already lost so much*, Holden thought, and he wondered how a guy like Curt could still function having seen his girlfriend's head kicked around by a zombie. But it was precisely a guy like Curt who *would* continue to function after such a terror. Functioning—doing something—helped him forget, at least for a time.

Sitting by, doing nothing... that would eat him up.

"When I'm across and gone, you guys stay in the Rambler," he said. "If they come, just keep driving away from 'em. I'll get help. If I wipe out I'll fuckin' *limp* for help, but I'm coming back with cops and choppers and large fucking guns and those *things* are gonna pay." He glanced aside. "For Jules."

Dana leaned across and kissed him on the cheek.

Curt gunned the bike.

"Don't hold back," Holden said.

"Never do." Curt grinned at them and ran the bike back along the road a little, standing in the saddle and leaning to curve around to the right. He didn't wait and rev up, but let go instantly, knowing that even that small bit of momentum could give him the added speed he needed when he hit the drop-off.

Go on, Holden thought, *go on, you're the jock, the good-looking guy every girl wants to go out with and every guy wants to be. It's only right that you'll be the one to save us*. And as Curt powered past them on the dirt-bike Holden knew definitely, absolutely, that he would succeed.

He hit the slightly raised lip of the drop-off with the front wheel high, speed good, and Holden punched the air and yelled, "Yeah!" because the jump could not have been performed any better, it was perfect, when they got back to the world Curt would be able to make a profession as a stunt—

The bike struck something and exploded in mid-air.

"Noooo!" Dana screamed.

The fire and burning fragments spread far and wide as if he'd struck something solid, and beyond the extremes of the flames, sparking blue lines flicked into and out of existence. Straight lines, perfectly vertical and horizontal like a grid.

What the fuck what the fuck what the fuck—?

Curt didn't make a sound, and Holden hoped that he was already dead as he fell. Because he was on fire. His clothing was splashed with fuel, his hair singed away, his face aflame, and he twisted slowly as he plummeted into the ravine like a living flare, lighting the cliff walls all the way down. And all the way, those severe blue lines flickered in and faded out all around him.

"Oh God, oh God..." Dana chanted, and when Holden grabbed her arm her muscles were hard as steel, fists clenches so tight that he felt a dribble of blood issue from beneath her fingers.

"He hit something!" Holden gasped. "There's nothing! What'd he *hit*!"

The flames had fallen away now, going down with the remnants of the bike and his dead, still-burning friend. But between them and the other side of the ravine, something stood guard. *Curt*, he thought, and his face crumpled as he thought of his friend's ready smile and friendly manner. He took a couple of steps and saw a faint glow somewhere far below. But then he stopped, because he didn't want to see what gave that glow.

"Puppeteers..." Dana said softly. He'd never heard her sounding like this before. Tender, yes, and shy, and scared and terrified. But her voice now was tinged with defeat.

"Did you see it?" Holden asked. "What'd he hit?"

But she was looking at something far more distant than either of them could see.

"Marty was right. God."

"Get in the van!" Holden said urgently. There was just the two of them now, and if those zombies could *run*—

"Marty was right..."

"Dana, get in the fucking Rambler! We can talk about this later, but right now we have to get away from here. They'll be attracted by the..." *Explosion*, he thought. *Our shouting. The impossible explosion, and our useless shouting, because whichever way they turned*—

But he would not be defeated. Curt would have snorted even at the *thought* of defeat. He had died trying to save them all, and Holden would run and fight and do every single thing he could to honor his friend's sacrifice.

He grabbed Dana's hand and pulled her toward the van. She was slow—he was almost dragging her—and he wanted to shout and rage at her to not give up, *never* give up. But when they reached the Rambler she let go and opened the door, holding it open for him to jump in first. And though distracted, he could also see something new appearing in her eyes: anger.

Holden jumped into the driver's seat and Dana sat beside him. She was deliberate, almost calm. All the fear had dropped from her face. And she'd been talking about... puppeteers?

He gunned the engine and swung the Rambler around, away from the tunnel and back the way they'd come. Perhaps he'd pick out one of those fucking zombies in the headlamps and be able to run the thing over. Then reverse. Then run it over again.

"You're going back," she said.

"I'm going through," he said. "We'll just drive. There's gotta be another road, another way out of here."

"It won't work," she said. "Something will happen. A bridge will collapse, a road will wash away. We'll fall into a sinkhole."

"Then we'll leave the roads altogether!" he said, unreasonably angry at her sudden sense of defeat. "Dana, we'll drive as far as we can into the forest, go on foot from there—"

Dana shook her head.

"You're missing the point."

"I am?" He hated her fatalism; he was trying to help them here. And he had never seen that in her before. *I thought I was getting to know her*, he thought, glancing at her sidelong. "Hey," he said. "*Look* at me."

She looked. She even smiled a little, but it was one of the saddest smiles he'd ever seen.

"This isn't your fault," he said.

She laughed softly but it did nothing to lift the sadness.

"I know. It's the puppeteers."

"Please don't go nuts on me, Dana," Holden said. *Puppeteers? What the…?* "You're all I got."

She continued staring at him. He glanced at the road, back at her, and her relaxed, sad expression did not change. *She looks as far from mad as I've seen her since this began.*

"I'm okay," she said.

"Good. 'Cause I need you calm." He took a tight bend, fighting with the wheel, unused to the big vehicle and almost letting the rear end swing out from behind them. He'd have to go slow—if he wrecked or rolled the van that'd be it for them. The thought of being trapped inside while those zombie bastards bashed and hacked their way in... "No matter *what* happens, we gotta stay calm."

A rush of optimism hit him. He didn't know where it came from but he grabbed on, relishing the way it brightened his view a little, and made Dana feel just that little bit closer. They drove on, sweeping around bends and making their way back toward the cabin. And still flushed by optimism he smiled and opened his mouth to say, "Everything's—"

Something pressed against his throat. His voice ended. And the newly enlightened world grew suddenly dark.

Dark red.

◇ ◇ ◇

She'd sensed a changed in Holden, but she knew it was nothing like the sense of doom that had settled over her. They could drive, they could run, they could hide, but the Puppeteers would find them. They'd find them because they were controlling this, and perhaps even now they were being watched by someone or something she couldn't understand. In a way she hoped it was some*thing*, because if some*one* was responsible for all this... how sick must they be? How twisted?

She glanced at the road ahead of them, then looked back at Holden in time to see the shadow moving behind him. He was smiling as the scythe curved around his throat and flicked, opening his skin, tearing the meat of him, spraying the windscreen with a splash of blood, and she screamed, falling from her seat and pressing back against the side door as she saw who was there.

Father Buckner. The family killer, the murderer, the zombie, pressing his knee to the back of the driver's seat as he tried to tug the scythe free.

Holden's hands were still on the wheel, his eyes wide, body pulled back tight against the seat by the rusted blade buried deep in his throat. Blood bubbled there as he tried to scream.

Dana screamed for him, high and clear. Buckner did not even look her way. He tugged and shook and growled, throwing Holden's body around in the seat like a—

—like a puppet—

—and then the scythe came free with a wet sucking sound, and arterial blood geysered from the wound as Holden's terrified heart thumped and pummeled, splashing the windscreen and spattering across Dana's face and throat. She held up her hands and felt its warm impact, soft as a wet kiss across her wrist, and she screamed again because she knew what was to come.

Holden's hands lifted from the steering wheel as he tried to hold in his blood. They pressed to his ruined throat, finding meat and bone and gristle instead of skin, and the big wheel jerked and spun unchecked.

We'll hit a tree, Dana thought, *and Father will go through the windscreen and I'll pull Holden aside and—*

But the Puppeteers would never allow that to happen.

As she wiped thick arterial blood from her eyes a shadow whipped through the air and she heard *thwack!* as Buckner buried the scythe's point into the side of Holden's head.

Dana gasped at what had been done to the man she had kissed and caressed just hours before. His throat was open and spewing, one eye had erupted from its socket, and his face was distorted by the metal buried deep behind it.

At least he's free now, she thought as he slumped forward over the steering wheel, leaning to the right and turning the van to the left.

And then Dana tried to scrabble up to see over the

dashboard and out the windscreen, because she had to know where they were going. For a second she thought, *There's nothing out there at all... no forest, no sky, no stars... it's all make-believe...* And then she saw that they were going for the lake, its calm expanse speckled only with the memories of long-dead stars.

She braced against the dashboard moments before the van hit the water.

If they hadn't been moving so fast maybe they would have splashed down and floated for a while. But they hit hard and fast, and the already-fractured windscreen exploded inward. Lake water powered in, shockingly cold as it flowed down and lifted her up against her seat, pinning her there as the Rambler's momentum drove it onward and increased the weight of the water pouring in. She kept her mouth squeezed tightly shut. *Don't scream don't scream hold your breath and when we stop moving it'll be time to swim—*

Holden was thrashing in the seat beside her, and it was more than the water waving his limbs and battering his body. He was *still alive*! The zombie Buckner had gripped the scythe's handle and was now struggling to free it from Holden's skull.

How can he still be alive? Please let him be dead... I don't want him to be alive if he's like that, broken beyond mending.

The scythe came free with a terrible grinding sound, audible even above the thunderous water. Buckner swung it again, but without Holden's body as an anchor the water blasted him back into the Rambler, rolling and shoving him toward the rear as the vehicle quickly began to fill. Doors broke from hinges, chairs tumbled, and the whole van shook as it came to a standstill.

Lake water still poured in and they were sinking quickly. Beside her, Holden had turned her way, hands clasped to his throat and his ruined face turned toward her. *Fight through the pain*, he'd said when they first jumped in and felt such coldness. *It's worth it. I'm nearly convinced it's worth it.* There was no way he could fight through this pain, because on the other side was death.

For him, blessed death.

Please die please die, she thought, and she pushed from her seat as the water filled the cab. She scrabbled at the ceiling and took in a deep breath, and when she ducked back down the thunderous sound was muted, and the still-lit headlamps cast a ghostly glow through the cloudy water.

Holden had slipped from his seat and was pressed against the rear of the front cabin, close to the toilet door where they'd kept the keg on their journey up and where Buckner must have been hiding. And as she let go of the seat and the water pushed her that way, she saw him die. His mouth opened and bloody bubbles rose in a final breath. The water around him was clouded with blood, and it was quickly obscuring the already-poor visibility.

I've only got seconds, she thought, but she held her breath. She'd always been a good, strong swimmer, but that was no comfort here. If she died in this sinking van, it would not be from drowning.

Maybe it should, she thought. *Maybe I should just let go. I'm the last one, and there's no escape, and who- or whatever has been controlling all this—the puppeteers—surely can't see me now. So I'll cheat them their final sick victory. Grab onto Holden—he'll still be warm—and open my mouth to tell him about all the times we might have lived through together.*

But Dana had never been one to give in. And she could imagine her friends' reactions if she did.

So she kicked past Holden's corpse, but she had no real control. The van was shifting as it sank—

—*how deep is this fucking lake?*—

—and the water inside swilled and shoved her this way and that, forcing her up eventually against the ceiling, tumbling her toward the back, toward where she'd seen Buckner swept just moments before.

She grasped onto the rim of one of the ceiling vents, thrusting her face up into a small air bubble there, thankful that it hadn't been smashed when the tunnel caved in. She inhaled—it was stale and acrid, and she thought about stuff like battery acid, toxic fumes, and other horrible ways to die—and then she ducked back down.

Still holding on tight she looked to the rear of the Rambler. The water was almost impossible to see through, and the headlamps' light barely reflected back this far. She knew that he was back there somewhere, though, and she wondered whether zombies needed to breathe.

Of course not. If they did, the puppeteers would have never crashed them into the lake.

Anger replaced her fear with a burning, raging intensity. If she saw Buckner then she'd have gone for him, trying to rip him apart with her bare hands instead of doing her best to escape. It would be a poor revenge, destroying something already dead and sacrificing herself in the process. But she had no idea how much free will she still had. Perhaps she'd *never* had any.

But if the murdering bastard was back there, maybe the water's flow was still pressing him against the rear window. So she grabbed the handle that lifted the roof vent and started turning, trying not to gasp out precious air as she found sprains in her arm she didn't know she had.

It took seconds but it felt like hours, and as she pulled herself up to punch out the propped plastic cover, she thought she saw shadowy movement below her.

Don't think about it, get out, swim. She pushed her arms through the small opening and propped her elbows either side of the hatch, then pulled. Above her, the surface of the lake glittered with stars and the promise of air. As her hips squeezed through and the feel of open water welcomed her, the Rambler shifted violently beneath her, dragging her sideways and shocking a gasp of precious bubbles from her mouth. She thrashed in the hole, trying to swim herself out, and a hand closed around her ankle.

Somehow she held in the rest of her air.

Dana thrashed, kicked, using her hands to move her

body from side to side, shoving down with the heel of her free foot, and she knew that if he grabbed that one too, then he would only have to hold her for a few more seconds until she drowned. Then he'd pull her back into the sunken van and carve her up.

Kicking, her anger raw and red in her eyes, the pressure building in her lungs and her head thumping, she felt her heel connect with something more solid than water, but softer than something alive.

The hand released and she pulled through the hatch, swimming for the surface. When she broke through the cold air in her lungs was soothing, the starlight on her skin welcoming her back to the land of the living.

She trod water for only a few seconds before spying the wooden dock twenty feet to her left. And then she swam for her life.

◇ ◇ ◇

Ahhh, Sitterson thought, *time for beer*.

Sometimes at this juncture he'd feel an overwhelming sense of anti-climax, as if something momentous should happen, but never did. And even though he knew that this was all about making certain something momentous *didn't* happen, he'd feel an element of being let down. Cheated. All that effort with no visible result.

But not today. Today it had been closer than ever before. If he really let himself think about how close it had been, he'd probably collapse on the floor in a gibbering wreck and not be able to speak coherently for weeks. That time would come, he knew. Nights when he slept alone and the darkness closed in around him like a huge, crushing hand…

So, beer. Celebratory, and also to numb the possibilities that had been avoided. He flipped the lid from the cooler beneath his console, pulled a bottle and lobbed it to Hadley. Then he took out two more, one for himself and one for Lin.

Lin. Joining them to celebrate. He grinned. She'd obviously seen how damn close they'd come, too.

At the rear of the control room, two more mahogany panels had been opened, two more levers pulled, and deep, deep down the blood would have flowed, and the etchings would be filled. Old carvings given new life with someone's death.

Only one left. And that one…

Well, that one was optional.

"God *damn* that was close," Hadley said.

"Photo fuckin' finish," Sitterson agreed. "But we are the champions... of the *world*." He glanced at Truman and held up a beer. "Tru?"

Truman shook his head.

"I don't understand. We're celebrating?"

"*They're* celebrating," Lin said. "I'm *drinking*." Sitterson raised his bottle and took a swig, and as he did so he glanced at Lin. Damned if she wasn't almost smiling. He'd always wondered if she might not be the cold fish he once thought—she *couldn't* be as cold as she projected, or she'd be as dead as the Buckners—

and perhaps it had taken something like this to warm her up a little. He wondered just how much she'd been warmed up. Whether after festivities had truly taken off, she'd be up for a walk somewhere, a shared bottle of bubbly, a liaison in one of the small admin offices down the corridor.

He chuckled and drank more beer.

"I still don't understand," Truman said quietly.

Sitterson pointed at the large monitor, on which a bloodied, exhausted Dana could be seen swimming toward the wooden dock.

"Yeah, but she's still alive," Truman said. "How can the ritual be complete?"

"The Virgin's death is optional," Hadley said. "As long as it's *last*." He watched the screen for a moment, nursing his beer in his lap. "All that really matters is that she suffers."

Sitterson stood and leaned on the back of Hadley's chair.

"And that, she did," he said with genuine respect. Truman might never understand. The drink was a celebration, and an expression of relief. But it was also a toast to the swimming girl and her four dead friends.

"I'm actually rooting for her, believe it or not," Hadley said. "The kid's got spunk, which is more than—"

"This where the party's at?" someone said. The door was wide open now, and several people were peering inside with huge grins on their faces.

"Hey, thank god," Hadley called. "Tequila! Get

in here!" The people entered—lab smocks, suits, uniforms—one of them carrying a huge bottle of tequila. The new arrivals milled and shook hands, laughed and clapped each other on the back, and even Truman smiled when a cute lab tech started chatting with him, handing him a plastic cup half-filled with booze.

Sitterson watched them all and acknowledged the congratulations that came his way, smiling when a woman flirted mildly with him, laughing when someone from Story said he should go work for them. And all the time his eyes kept flashing back to the big viewing screens that continued to show what was happening down by the cabin in the woods.

I'm actually rooting for her, Hadley had said. Sitterson was too. But he knew that her death would be slow, painful... and soon.

◇ ◇ ◇

Somehow she found the energy needed to swim. In high school she swam for her school in the state championships, helping them streak to a win in the four-by-one-hundred meter freestyle. The year before, she'd taken part in a sponsored swim in her local river, covering three miles and raising over a thousand dollars for charity. It had always been easy for her. It had always been a pleasure.

Now it was neither.

She slapped at the water instead of slicing her hands through it, her breathing was labored, and she kept her head above the surface, afraid of what she'd see or what would see her if she turned her face beneath. The dock was close, but with every stroke she took it seemed further away than ever. The water was cold, but felt warm and slick as blood. It tasted clean and pure, but she smelled only entrails and death.

Swim, she thought, trying to give herself a regular rhythm. *Swim... swim... swim...*

She didn't know if zombies could swim. She didn't even think these *were* zombies, not really, not according to the pop-culture use of the word. They seemed to walk and work with intelligence, their only aim to trap and kill her and the others, and she'd seen no evidence of eating... no blood on their jaws. They wanted to kill in the most painful ways, and make them suffer, and she let out a sob as her hand struck a wooden post of the dock.

She was the last one left alive, which meant that she had suffered the most. And when they finally held her down and slashed her throat or plunged a blade into her eye, it would be the memories of her dead friends that would accompany her into death.

She hung on for a few seconds, trying to regain her strength. But her muscles were knotted and ice-cold, cramps throbbed in her calves, and the longer she hung here the less chanced she'd have of ever hauling herself out.

So she started climbing. She gasped in effort as she pulled herself from the lake, then screamed in frustration as she fell back in. She clung onto the post but it was coated in slime and moss, and her nails scored fresh trails as she was pulled below the surface. Kicking, coughing water, she pushed back up and tried again. Every time she went back under she expected to see Father Buckner advancing on her, walking across the lake's bed and grinning, the scythe in his hand ready to part her skin as he had done to Holden—

But she wouldn't think of Holden. Not yet. She *couldn't*.

At last she pulled herself far enough up to reach onto the dock's surface and curl her fingers in between boards. She waited there for a while, catching her breath and listening for the sounds of anything breaking surface close by, and then with one final massive effort she tugged, raised a leg, and then rolled onto her back.

Dana coughed up water and gasped as she stared at the stars. Beyond exhausted, beyond terrified, she spread her hands on the wood and relished its solidity. She was afraid to close her eyes in case she saw things she didn't want to see in there, sights that would haunt her for the rest of her life, however long that might be. And there would be such sights.

She breathed in and tasted Holden's mysterious, lightly spiced breath; glanced at the treeline to her left and saw Curt's eyes peering over the trees, blood on his temple and cheek, confident smile on his face as he revved the dirt-bike; moved her hands across the rough, dry wood and felt the warmth of Jules's blood on her skin. And Marty, dragged off and killed; sweet innocent Marty who'd had a crush on her which she had never truly acknowledged. She had enough memories for a million nightmares. If she could only keep them at bay a little while longer, she might have a chance to get away from here.

Through the woods, she thought. *As far and fast as I can. Or back to the tunnel, see if I can climb up and over the mountain or down and across the ravine.* Or... or... and what she'd said to Holden echoed back to her now, about how there would always be something in their way. Or someone. The puppeteers would see to that.

But by not giving in and drowning to steal Buckner's bloody victory from him, she had decided to fight those fucking puppeteers. And she would continue to fight them, every step of the way.

Her breathing became more regular, her determination grew. She saw a point of light moving slowly above her and thought perhaps it was a satellite. Her paranoia rich and hot, she gave it the finger.

Something smashed into the wooden dock right beside her head. The impact thumped into her skull, the noise shocking, her hair flicking up, a breath of displaced air giving her ear an intimate caress. She sat up and turned onto her hands and knees, ready to leap aside, and saw Matthew looming over her. The crowbar was still sticking through his face.

"Come on then, fucker!" she shouted, and found that she was hardly surprised. But terrified, she realized that she'd wet herself with fear. And that made her fury grow into something blazingly hot. "Come on, come on, come *on*!"

He came.

TEN

Sitterson worked the room.

He could see the glances he was getting and they made him smile, but only slightly. If he beamed they'd see him reveling in his success. He wanted to be more aloof than that. Just a *little* more. That way they'd all find him more interesting, and there were a few women in here he'd never tried it on with yet. He always liked to end these events with a blow job at least, and up to now he had an unbroken record.

Today, buoyed by his vague celebrity status after the close call and his rapid thinking, he'd set himself a much higher target. And there she was, Lin, standing over by the opened mahogany panels and actually leaning against the last closed one, as if she was ready to pull the lever herself. She chatted with a male colleague without smiling. There was another drink in her hand. And by the end of the day, Sitterson wanted her writhing beneath him with her tight hair released over a plump, fresh pillow.

"Oh, yeah," he said softly, taking another drink of tequila and glancing around the room. People from other departments had trickled in, most of them bearing drinks, food, and a readiness to celebrate their success. The atmosphere was relaxed and jovial, but Sitterson had been here long enough to sense the air of underlying hysterical relief that most people still exuded. Laughter was a little too loud and free, drinks were drunk just a little too quickly, and there was a sexual tension in the air that would undoubtedly be drawn upon before the day was over.

He remembered the evening after his first time. He'd started in Story, and following their first scenario the party had been hard and fast, like this one, and so had the woman he'd met from Admin. She'd been giving him head in a restroom, sucking like he was the last man alive, when someone from Control walked in on them. Sitterson had frozen, expecting reprimands and instant dismissal. But the woman had just smiled softly and backed out, and the Admin girl had barely missed a stroke.

There was something animal and desperate about that act, which he sensed in the air here and now, and he knew that what they did took them all back to basics. The present existed only because of what they had done today.

It was live or die, and what better way to celebrate surviving than with sex.

On the big screens the Virgin was fighting for her life

with the Matthew Buckner zombie. Sitterson watched for a moment, then looked away, across the crowd. No one else seemed particularly interested, but he knew it was something far deeper than that. It didn't *matter* now whether the Virgin lived or died, and everyone in this room dealt with stuff that mattered. They no longer had control over her fate, nor did they need to.

Hadley might well be rooting for her, and perhaps some of the others too—hell, even Sitterson thought she was cute—but his internal defense mechanism was raised again. He saw her crying and screaming, he saw the monstrous zombie trying to kill her.

But now, it was all just a movie.

Truman was still watching. Of course. Eyes wide, mouth slightly open as he attached import to the girl's life. But he'd learn soon enough.

Hadley was talking with a guy from Story and a woman from Accounts. Sitterson strolled over to hear their conversation.

"I wish I could do what you guys do," the Accounts woman said. "It's masterful."

"It was good," Hadley nodded. "It was solid."

"Are you kidding?" the Story guy gushed. "Classic *denouement*. When the van hit the lake?" He raised his hands as if to say, *What could be better?* He was reveling in the woman's adulation.

"Hell, *I* screamed!" Accounts said.

"Right?" Story acknowledged.

"The zombie, the water rushing in..."

"That's *primal* terror," Story said, as if he had

invented the concept. Sitterson thought he was being a dick; he hadn't come up with the whole scenario on his own, after all. In fact Sitterson himself had created the van-in-the-lake idea years ago, during his own time in Story.

But for now, he'd let the dick have his glory.

"Woulda been cooler with a merman," Hadley said, sounding almost wistful. He smiled at Sitterson, who laughed softly and shook his head as he strolled away.

Nodding to some people, shaking the hands of others, he edged his way toward one of their military liaisons, a big major with a clichéd moustache and hands the size of small dogs. He was talking with a werewolf wrangler—redundant during this show, unfortunately, but Sitterson had seen his sterling work before—and Ronald the intern.

From the corner of his eye he caught sight of the Virgin being pummeled by the zombie. *It doesn't matter*, he thought. It would be over soon. Nonetheless, he wished regulations allowed him to turn off the screens.

"Do you know if we made the overtime bonus on this one?" the liaison asked.

"Accounting's right over there," the wrangler said. "Ask them."

"I don't need to ask them," the major said, "I already know the answer."

"'We're accountants, and we're full of hate?'" the wrangler mimicked.

"Exactly," the major said, and he smiled.

His moustache's alive, Sitterson thought, amazed.

It must have a life of its own. It flexed and twitched while the soldier seemed utterly motionless.

"I'm an intern," Ronald said sadly. "I don't qualify for overtime."

"No big deal, Ronald," Sitterson said. The major looked at him respectfully—moustache almost saluting—and the werewolf guy nodded a greeting.

"No big deal?" Ronald asked.

"Sure. We've all been noticed today. You can take that to the bank." Sitterson walked away smiling. Today had been stressful, but the outcome was good for all of them.

As he walked past a fellow from Chem, Sitterson chuckled at the guy's efforts to get into his pretty co-worker's pants.

"Don't worry about my eyes," he was saying. "That's why we have eye washes, right? And they say baking soda is good for your complexion. Anyway... it's funny that you like the ballet, because I happened to get two tickets to..."

The pretty woman just turned and walked away.

"...your favorite..."

His voice trailed off, he looked around, embarrassed, and Sitterson made a point of pausing and smiling in his direction. The Chem guy rubbed his eyes and wandered away toward the drinks table.

And then Sitterson saw the Demolition team standing by one of the control desks. They were laughing too loudly, the desk was scattered with empty bottles, and he saw something a little too self-congratulatory about the way they slapped each other's backs and hugged.

He downed the rest of his tequila, smacked his lips, and sauntered over to them.

"You!" he called. "Yoouuuu! Knuckleheads almost gave me a heart attack with that tunnel!"

"That wasn't our fault," one of them answered, and it was the guy he'd dealt with in the Demolition control room. The woman was there, too, pouting a little now as she half-hid behind her wine glass.

"I'm just giving you a hard time," Sitterson said. He raised an eyebrow at the woman. "C'mere you, let's have a hug."

She snorted, glanced around at the others, and finished her full glass in one long swig. He could see that she was already drunk, glassy-eyed, and unsteady on her feet.

"No," the guy said. "*Seriously*. That wasn't on us." Something about his voice hit home a little too hard. Sitterson was enjoying ragging on them, but—

"There was an unauthorized power re-route from upstairs," the woman said, blinking in surprise at her empty glass.

Sitterson frowned. Then he went cold.

"What do you mean, *upstairs*?"

And then a shrill, loud, ringing sound shattered the atmosphere of the place, all within a split second. They all knew what it was, though they had never heard it for real. Perhaps it haunted some of their dreams, and played the theme of their nightmares.

Sitterson closed his eyes, trying to hold onto that air of success for just one more second, and then looked at the phone.

It was a single telephone, sitting in an alcove at the back of Control, close to where the mahogany covers had shielded the levers and their apparatus from view. Red, an old-fashioned analogue phone with a silver metal dial, its shrill ringing came from a bell within the solid plastic casing.

The alcove echoed its call, and between each of the rings the jaunty lilt of dance music still filled the room.

Sitterson locked eyes with Hadley. They both saw each other's fear. And then Hadley walked quickly across the room to answer the call.

"Turn that fucking music off!" he snapped. As his hand rested on the receiver the music snapped off.

He took a deep breath and picked it up.

We could run, Sitterson thought. But of course that was an utterly stupid idea. If something they'd begun was not yet finished, it was their duty to ensure that it was put right.

And there would be nowhere to run.

"Hello," Hadley said. All eyes on him. He listened for a few seconds. Then, "That's impossible! Everything was within guidelines and the Virgin is the only—" He winced. "No, no, of course I'm not doubting you. It's just—"

Hadley's face fell and he looked over the heads of the assembled observers, back at the large viewing screens.

What are we going to see? Sitterson wondered.

The drink in his hand felt warm and sickly, and he noticed others putting down their bottles and plastic cups. Maybe they all sensed the work they still had left to do.

And then Hadley said something which Sitterson had guessed anyway, and there was no longer cause for celebration.

"Which one?"

He turned to follow his friend's gaze.

Suddenly he was rooting for the Virgin like never before.

◇ ◇ ◇

She jumped aside one more time as Matthew swung the broken bear trap. It was easy enough to dodge—however hard he swung it, she had at least a second to judge its passage and eventual impact point—but doing so was rapidly tiring her out. And each time she concentrated on the swinging trap, Matthew's other hand lashed out and caught her across the shoulder, chest, cheek.

Several times now she'd almost backed up and jumped into the lake again, but she knew if she did that she'd die for sure. If she didn't drown from exhaustion, Father Buckner would grab her and haul her down. He was still below the surface, she knew. Still down there somewhere, stalking the lake bottom, looking up, perhaps even seeing the blurry starlit struggle on the wooden dock.

He was waiting.

She ducked to one side and felt the trap *whoosh* down past her ear. It snagged her jeans and tore them, scoring a cut on her ankle before embedding itself in the dock. She tried to jump sideways to avoid the zombie's other hand, but it caught her across the nose this time, sending a flash of bloody hot pain through her head. Her vision swam, her whole face caught fire, and it was all she could do to retain her footing on the shattered, splintered dock.

Dana couldn't run past him because he was too big. She couldn't fight him because she had no weapons—besides, the crowbar through his face proved that fighting wasn't even an issue. And there was nowhere else to go.

Fuck you fuck you fuck you, she thought, part of it directed at the zombie but most at the unseen puppeteers she was convinced were steering him. Whether or not they watched her now, she was determined not to give them the satisfaction.

Perhaps if she rushed him, striking at an angle, shoving him off balance and then tripping him into the lake... maybe then she could run and hide before he managed to crawl out. She spat blood, readied herself...

And then Matthew kicked out and struck her knee. She screamed and went down, spiking her hands and forearms on the splintered wood.

Crying, and hating herself for doing so, she tried to crawl, direction hardly a consideration anymore. Soon he'd swing the bear trap around and bring it down on her back, or her head, and then she'd die and join the others.

A board moved beneath her, one end shattered and sticking up from a strike from the bear trap. Maybe if she levered it up, bent it away from the nail still holding it down, stood and turned before his next strike, she could—

He brought his foot down on her arm, and she screamed. She twisted to look up and back at him, and he shifted all his weight onto that one leg. Desperate to scream again, even more desperate not to, she bit her lip until blood started to flow.

At least that's a wound I *made*, she thought, and something about it gave her power.

"Fuck you," she gritted.

He started swinging the chain around his head, picking up momentum for the final strike.

Ching... ching... ching...

I won't look away, she thought. *I won't close my eyes, I won't look away, the bastards won't get that from me.*

Matthew grasped the chain's handle with both hands, let it swing behind his back, tensed, and brought it up and over his head.

This is it, Dana thought, and as she imagined kissing Holden, she smiled.

There was a loud *clunk!* and Matthew jerked to a standstill. He remained motionless for a moment, staring out over the lake in surprise, instead of down at Dana. And then he stumbled backward, off balance, and fell onto the dock.

Beyond where he lay, Dana saw Marty with his bong in his hands and Matthew's chain wrapped around it. His clothes were torn and covered in blood, and he stood arched forward as if trying to escape a pain in his back. But his breath came thick and heavy, and she saw the hatred in his eyes.

"Marty!"

"Dana, get away!"

Between them, Matthew was already getting to his feet, and Dana could see Marty's hesitation. He tugged at the chain but it was solid. And if he let go of the bong, it would return the weapon to Matthew.

But she wasn't about to leave.

She pried up the broken plank, standing and levering it from the last nail. It sprung up with a jolt, she reversed it so that the unbroken end was away from her, then she held it back over her shoulder.

"Hey, stinking shithead fuck-face!" she called. Matthew turned slowly to face her. "Yeah, that's right... I know your name." She swung the board with all her might and smashed it into his face.

The zombie fell backward from the dock and splashed into the lake.

Dana staggered past where the thing had fallen and fell into Marty, welcoming his embrace and giving one back. They both groaned and hissed from their wounds, but the contact was essential right then, a sharing of warmth and hope that drove back some of the darkness.

"Marty, I thought you were—"

"Not yet. Not quite."

"Everyone else is..."

"Yeah." He pulled back a little and there was little of the joker left. Dana felt her friend's blood on her hands, from open wounds in his back.

From behind them came a splash as Matthew stood close to the edge of the lake and started striding toward them. He still dragged the chain behind him.

"You lost your bong," Dana said ruefully.

"C'mon." Marty grabbed her hand and they ran up the shore toward the cabin.

"Where are we going?" she gasped. She didn't want to go back in there. That was the *last* place they needed to go, a warren of traps and locked doors, hidden basements and stuff meant for torture.

Anywhere but there.

But Marty didn't reply, and when they were twenty yards from the cabin the door thudded open. For a brief, mad moment Dana thought, *Jules! She's survived too, or maybe Curt, up from the ravine and not burnt nearly as badly as—*

But it was Mother Buckner who emerged onto the porch, her portly frame giving her gait a monstrous sway, and that terrible saw swinging by her side.

"This way!" Marty said, steering them around toward the rear of the building. They were still holding hands. Marty squeezed tight, and she thought perhaps he needed that contact to keep going, to help him fight the pain. Because now she'd seen the hideous puncture wounds on his back, and she wasn't sure how he was moving at all.

◇ ◇ ◇

Marty steered them for the treeline. Passing between the first of the trees he felt resistance from Dana, and pulled harder. There was no way they could slow down or change direction. Time was of the essence. Out here was chaos, and danger, and a plan the scope and depth of which he could barely comprehend.

But there was one place they might yet survive. They had to make it to the hole into which Judah had dragged him earlier, or they'd be finished.

"Marty, wait!" Dana said, pulling back harder.

Behind them, he heard a terrible scraping sound as Mother Buckner rounded the corner of the cabin, saw dragging across the ground. It would still have wet flesh between its teeth.

"Dana, *c'mon*!"

Moments later they reached the hole, a dark wound in the land where Marty had been dragged and from which he had emerged again, rebirthed and enraged. It was darker than the shadows, foreboding, but he knew it was their only hope of survival.

"We're going in *there*?" Dana gasped.

Marty glanced toward the sounds of the scraping saw and wet footsteps. Behind Mother Buckner, Matthew had emerged from the lake and was slogging toward them, hauling the bear trap behind him.

"I need you to keep the faith right now, sister," he said, gripping Dana's shoulders. She frowned, and then past the hole a shape pressed through a mass of undergrowth.

Anna Patience Buckner, her single arm swinging by her side as she walked quickly toward them. Marty saw doubt disappear from Dana's eyes as she considered their predicament.

She nodded and went for the hole.

Of all of them I thought she'd be the first to die, he thought, but he instantly regretted it. Dana had surprised him with her strength and determination; he'd seen her fighting the big zombie as he'd crept up behind it. He'd never believed that he judged by appearances, and he never would do so again.

Marty knelt by the hole and reached in, grasping around for the ring he knew was there. He found it quickly, curved his hand through and pulled, and the hatch—like a storm door, only hiding something more than just a shelter—hinged up easily. Leaves and soil slipped away from its upper surface, and the stars reflected on the smooth, clean metal underneath.

Dana held back for only a second. Around them sang the sounds of pursuit—Mother's saw, Matthew's bear-trap, Anna's inexorable footsteps. Then she nodded to Marty and slipped down through the hatch.

He followed her and slammed it closed behind them, turning the handle and hearing the satisfying *clunk* of locks engaging. Moments later he heard scratching from the other side. The ring on the topside flipped over and hit the lid, something scraped the metal, and then came a faint, chilling cry of zombie frustration. It was the kind of sound never meant for human ears, and Marty and Dana quickly backed away.

The sound of their breathing echoed from the metal walls of the small, poorly lit chamber. It was barely tall enough to crouch in, but a good twelve by twelve feet square, with another metal hatch in the middle of the floor. A faint light came from a panel in the metal ceiling that had been removed to reveal several glowing cables. Hanging down from the panel was a spaghetti of wires, some stripped and spliced, others disconnected.

"What is this place?" Dana asked.

"You better—" Marty began, but then Dana stepped on Judah's mewling face. She stumbled back from the pile of zombie parts, and Marty held her hand and guided her away. Each part was moving, twitching, throbbing with unnatural life.

"Yeah, I had to dismember that guy with a trowel," he said. "What've you been up to?"

Dana stared at him in despair. Her mouth opened but nothing came out, and he saw the terrible truth in her eyes.

"Nobody else, huh?" he asked. She shook her head, and he added, "I figured."

"You figured everything," she said.

"Not even close," he said. "But I do know some stuff. Check this out." He went to the hatch in the floor and slid it open. The faint whiff of antiseptic he'd caught the first time he'd done so came again, reminding him of hospitals and endless echoing corridors and places that people only ever wanted to visit when there was something wrong.

Dana's mouth hung open. She shook her head and looked at him, her expression saying, *What?*

"It's an elevator," he said. "Two sides metal, but two are thick glass. You can't tell unless you... dangle your head in there. Somebody sent these dead fucks up to get us. There're no controls inside, but there's maintenance overrides in there." He nodded up at the dislodged panel. "I've been playing around. I think I can make it go down."

"Do we *wanna* go down?" she asked.

"Where else we gonna go?" He glanced at the closed ceiling hatch in the corner. "Sure as fuck don't wanna go back up there."

"But down there must be..."

"Whoever's done this to us? Yeah." He moved to her side and they both knelt, arms around each other. *What has she seen?* he wondered. Curt and Holden were dead and gone, and it must have been terrible. He could ask her, but he didn't really want to know. The terror came off her in waves, but also the defiance that he himself had been feeling ever since taking Judah's head off. That brief triumph had given him power, and he felt the power thrumming in both of them.

He'd already destroyed one of the puppets. Perhaps it was time to find the puppeteers.

"Okay," she said, nodding. "Okay. We got nothing else going for us, I guess."

"Only our anger," he said.

"I thought you couldn't get angry on dope."

"Haven't had a smoke in over an hour." They grinned at each other, then Dana dropped down into the small elevator.

Marty moved to the open ceiling panel and the mass of wires that hung from it.

"Get ready," he said. "The timing on this might be pretty tight."

He wound two wires, flicked a switch, then slid across to the elevator. The hatch was already sliding shut and he fell in just in time, the metal brushing his head as he landed next to Dana... and something else fell in with him.

Dana screamed and kicked him in the shin. The elevator started to drop. Something grabbed his leg, and he looked down to see Judah's arm flexing as its fingers squeezed against Marty's leather boot.

"Ah! Fuckin' zombie arm!" He kicked and stamped, and for a moment he thought it was his movement shaking the elevator. But then he stopped, the arm trapped beneath his foot, and instead of dying away the tremors increased.

"Now what?" he shouted.

"Another earthquake," she said.

"Yeah, and you think it's not connected?"

From above them came the sound of wrenching metal, and then a loud crack as something broke. Yet the elevator continued down at a slow, steady rate, apparently unhindered.

"Something up in the room," Dana said.

"Yeah."

"Almost like they're following us, driving us toward—"

"Nah," he said, shaking his head. "I should be dead. And so should you. Whoever's been fucking with us, I've got a feeling we've stuck a monkey wrench into the works." The thought made him smile grimly.

They descended for almost half a minute, then jolted to a halt. Marty turned full-circle to see which wall would open—one of the metal sides, or one of the glass—but then they started moving again. Only this time the movement felt different, and it took a moment for him to realize why.

"Are we moving *sideways*?"

"Yeah..." Dana said, leaning against the glass wall. Marty looked around the elevator. The faint illumination came from behind an opaque screen in the ceiling, and there were similar panels spaced at regular intervals along the shaft. He looked down at Judah's arm still flexing beneath his foot.

"You're going home, dude."

Then the elevator stopped. Behind Dana, Marty made out something strange. Another elevator? They were pulling alongside of it, and then—

The enraged werewolf smashed against the glass wall of its own enclosed box, mere inches from their own. The impact was loud, and Marty saw the glass flex, distorting both its appearance and the reflected image of Dana's terrified face. She fell back into him, screaming, as the creature scrabbled and scratched at the glass. An inch of air and two glass walls was all that lay between them.

It was drooling. Its eyes were intelligent, and starving. Its teeth...

"It's a fucking *werewolf*," Marty said, but voicing the fact made it no easier to believe. "So... *no*." He shook his head, and Dana turned to him and held his cheeks.

"Marty?" There was something about her voice, something calm and in control, to which he so wanted to submit.

Far too much bad dope, he thought. *I'll wake up in the Rambler in a minute with Curt driving and Jules preening in the front seat, Dana and Holden flirting and acting coy, and I'll scream myself awake and they'll laugh at me, laugh because...*

He laughed then, high and hysterical, and the elevator started moving again. Another vaguely lit blank metal wall, and then the light from behind them changed. He and Dana turned together to see a second identical elevator revealed. This one contained a grotesque alien, straight out of the movie, all sickly suckers and flailing limbs. It leapt at the glass and stuck there, its grotesquely sexual mouth sliming and sucking as it tried to probe at them, impregnate them, and then they moved on again, descending before jerking to the side once more.

"Dana..." he said, but she was already holding him, huddled in the center of the elevator, because they both knew what was to come. They'd seen two, and wagered that there would be many, many more.

And they were right.

On Marty's side they saw a little girl in a ragged ballerina outfit. Her skirt was limp and torn, as if handed down from every little ballerina ever, and she had no face. In its place was a circular mouth, red-raw and ringed with vicious teeth. She stood on tiptoe and performed a surreal curtsey as they passed her by.

Next to her was a white-faced woman with smashed glass shards for hair and melting hands. She flickered at them in monochrome, flicking in and out of view as if seen on an old, old film.

On Dana's side was revealed a tall man in a long leather coat. His skin was completely white and hairless. Across his scalp in a neat row were spinning buzz-saws, his forearms were ringed with tightly wrapped strands of barbed wire, and his teeth were spinning drill bits. He was all metal and blades, and he grinned at Dana, holding out his hand above which a strange wooden sphere flexed and warped.

"We chose," she said softly, a note of understanding entering her voice.

"What?" Marty asked, but he was already making the connections, and they threatened to overwhelm the last dregs of sanity he had left.

I'm fine, I'm fine! he thought, but he didn't think that was quite true. If he was fine—if madness hadn't touched him—he wouldn't have been able to do all the things he'd done. He'd be up there now, dead in the woods with Jules and Curt and Holden, not still alive down here with Dana. A little bit of madness never hurt anyone, one of his dope suppliers used to say.

In this case, maybe it had saved his life.

The elevator moved back into the shaft, sideways, down, and he readied himself for the shock of what might be revealed next.

"In the cellar," Dana continued. "All that shit we were playing with. They made us choose. They made us choose how we die."

"Yeah," Marty said, remembering how nervous he'd been at the prospect of Dana reading the Latin in that little old diary. If he had stopped her, maybe Jules would have solved a kid's puzzle and brought werewolves upon them. Or Holden might have smashed a bottle and brought them girls with teeth instead faces.

Holy fucking shit.

Dana started smashing at the glass with her fists. Her blows did no damage—they'd have to make the glass incredibly strong to contain all these things, he realized—but still she pounded, kicking as well, thrashing, and he had to hold her tight to stop her from hurting herself.

And it was like that, arms wound around each other, sharing the warmth of their bodies and the pain of their wounds, that they emerged into a huge underground space like a warehouse where countless elevators shifted left and right, up and down, running on almost invisible rails and columns and passing soundlessly across junctions, swapping position constantly. In each elevator was something of shade or light, and whether dark or light, it was always horrible.

Vampires, not of the limp, fluffy-collared variety, but with pale skin and too many teeth.

Three people—two adults and a child—with horribly cracked, blistered skin, beneath which lava seemed to boil.

A gorgeous naked woman with teeth in place of a vagina.

A man with six arms, each of the hands replaced with a grafted weapon of some kind, from a knife to a shotgun.

A screaming banshee with hair flowing around its head as if in slow motion.

Six elevators contained small babies that seemed to explode again and again, scattering bladed blood-red shards. A giant rabbit with oversized teeth, a woman with a scorpion's sting curved from the small of her back, a child with three heads—vampire, zombie, werewolf—a shade of something terrible, a ghostly figure surrounded by fumes that must be toxic, a minotaur with a monstrous phallus, a woman with writhing snakes instead of pubic hair, a man with steaming pipes inserted into his chest and flames in his eyes, a dog with the head of an alligator...

The horrors were endless and almost beyond imagining, and Marty and Dana held each other tighter as their elevator was carried through the impossible space.

The creatures known and unknown seemed to

recognize the intruders for what they were. Marty didn't see them leaping or scratching at their glass walls to get at one another, but whenever he and Dana drew close they tried to attack.

We're their meat, he thought, and though it was a horrible idea it stuck. Perhaps they were kept here like this, forever hungry, and when it came time to hunt…

The basement had been filled with lots of old, random stuff. And every shred of it had been linked somehow to something down here. He had no idea what it could mean, other than some sort of monstrous entertainment. But what lengths to go to. It was beyond belief.

"As soon as we stop," he said. "We'll get out as soon as we can." Still they held each other, but they were beyond comforting. Their world had changed, not only their personal place in it, but their understanding of the wider reality.

Nothing could ever be the same again.

◇ ◇ ◇

Control had cleared quickly. He hadn't needed to shout at anyone to leave. As soon as Hadley replaced the receiver and muttered those few words, glasses and bottles were dropped, and everyone raced to try and put right whatever had gone wrong.

Sitterson could smell spilled champagne and there were potato chips crushed across the floor. Truman stood on guard by the door, upright and proper, and perhaps not really comprehending. All seemed normal.

Sitterson held back a giggle.

All seemed normal!

Lin was down in the lower area of Control, earpiece in place, tapping frantically on a keyboard and muttering to someone unheard. Sitterson and Hadley, chairs pulled closer than before, were scanning through the entire complex on their screens, moving quickly and efficiently. Hadley was checking corridors and stairwells, while on Sitterson's screens were nine constantly changing views of the interiors of the elevators. He'd seen many of these things before, but some were new even to him. Still, he refused to let curiosity overcome the prime purpose of this search.

Survival, he was thinking. *Of everything. It's* all *at stake here*.

So he checked all nine images, then tapped a button that would present nine more. How the Fool had been missed, how no one had noticed, how they'd overcome Matthew Buckner, how the *fuck* they'd managed to get down into the complex... all these were questions for later.

If there *was* a later.

"We saw them go down the access drop," he said into his microphone. "They have to be in one of these! Internal security should be able to—"

"That's not protocol," a static-filled voice said into his ear. *Static? That was unheard of. Their systems were* perfect.

"I don't care if that's not protocol!" he shouted.

"Are you fucking high?" He looked to Hadley, hand held up in a *what the fuck?* gesture.

"It's the Fool!" Hadley shouted into his own microphone. "No, you *can't* touch the girl. If he outlives her, all this goes to hell! *Take him out first*." He shrugged back at Sitterson. *Fucking amateurs!*

There were security teams sweeping the complex, cameras everywhere, the creatures were contained... things would settle, everything would work out okay. But none of this was in the Scenario. Hell, the Scenario was fucked. Sitterson only hoped…

"Hope they'll accept our apology," he whispered. Hadley heard him, but said nothing.

Lin stood and turned to look up at them.

"Clean-up says the prep team must have missed one of the kid's stashes. Whatever he's been smoking has been immunizing him to all our shit." It was a startling admission from the Chem team leader, but this wasn't a time for cover-ups. Later they'd rag her on it, if they had the opportunity. And if she wasn't executed for incompetence.

"How does that help us *right now*?" Hadley said. Then he spoke into his mic. "What? Yes. If the Fool's a confirmed kill, you can take her out too. But for fuck's sake... for *all* our sakes... make sure it's a confirmed kill on him first. Dead. Headless. Blown up. A *confirmed... fucking... kill*."

"There!" Truman snapped. He'd walked over from the door to stand behind Sitterson, and Sitterson couldn't shake the irony that it was the newbie who saw them first. But that was good, that was fine. He'd buy him a drink if this all turned out okay.

He froze the current crop of nine elevator images and spotted them instantly.

"Thirty-six-oh-six. Gotcha."

"Bring 'em down," Hadley said.

Sitterson did so. No relief yet, no sigh of satisfaction. Too much had gone wrong to assume that everything would go right from here.

Every single detail, every single second, had to count.

ELEVEN

Maybe it was the screaming and the thumping against the toughened glass that had vented her terror and calmed her a little. Or maybe she'd just seen so much that there was really no alternative other than to remain calm. Her heart still thrummed faster than usual, but she felt removed from the reality she'd always been a part of and comforted by. Talking boys with Jules, going out for a drink with friends, running each morning around her neighborhood, college, exams, worrying about how she looked and whether she needed a haircut and what shoes to wear to the party next Saturday... this was all from a world so distant to her now that she could barely comprehend it anymore.

Everything that was safe and normal had been blown away, and Dana could not imagine it ever settling down again.

I'll always know, she thought. *This will always be*

here, whether we get out or not. The puppeteers had their hooks in her now, and even if she did manage to escape she suspected the strings stretched too far for her to break.

Marty was still holding her tight. She looked over his shoulder, and knew that he looked over hers. They had each seen things that the other hadn't, but she didn't want to know. Maybe much later, if they survived, when they huddled together in dorm rooms while their new, distant friends enjoyed themselves and lived normal lives... maybe then they'd talk of what they'd seen, and try to make some kind of sense.

But not right now.

The elevator was descending again. The walls visible through the thick glass walls were now rough stone. As they jarred to a halt and a mechanical whirring noise sounded somewhere far away, Dana wondered just how the hell any of this was possible.

Comprehension hit her like a brick.

This was *not* possible.

And was it really the first time she'd allowed herself to think that?

The door slid open onto a small, metal-lined lobby. Clean, unfurnished, clinical. A guard was aiming a gun at her face. He shifted quickly until he aimed at Marty, and jammed his foot in the door. He wore a black suit, black mask and goggles, and his mouth and nose were enclosed behind very modern-looking breathing apparatus. It gave his voice an electronic taint.

"Out of the elevator!" There was a pause, a quiet

moment when everything was held suspended. Then, "Step *out* of the *elevator*!"

"Why are you trying to kill us?" Dana asked. It was a helpless, hopeless question, and she imagined him saying, *I'm only following orders*. But the guard just acted as if he hadn't heard.

"Step *out*! Just the girl!"

"Just me?" she asked. Marty's hand tightened around hers, their fingers interlocking. He squeezed as if to say, *No fucking way*. She squeezed back.

"Do it!" the guard shouted. He stepped forward, edging into the elevator, and Dana heard Marty shifting slightly behind her.

Something scrabbled across the floor, moved between her feet and grabbed the guard's foot.

Judah's arm!

The guard jumped, looked down, and shot at the arm. The explosion was staggering in the enclosed space, and Dana's hearing was blasted to little more than a faint, distant hum. But she took the moment and used it, and while the guard's gun was aimed down she shouldered into his chest and drove him back against the metal door jamb.

His head swung up and back and cracked against the metal, and he slid down slowly to lean against the elevator's side wall.

Marty snatched the gun from the guard's hand and picked up Judah's blade.

"Good work, zombie arm!" he shouted, and his voice was fading slowly back in. Dana could see from his pained smile that his hearing had been numbed by the gunshot, as well.

A steady hum was growing. She rubbed at her ears,.and it sounded as though she was doing it from the inside.

"Won't last long!" he shouted. "Come on."

The small lobby opened out to house seven other elevator doors. Dana shivered as she thought about what might have entered or exited those doors, but they were all closed and silent for now, and the panels above them remained unlit. There was a small, abandoned guard's station just along from the elevators, and past that a corridor led off to a right-angled turn.

From beyond there, Dana was sure she could hear several sets of heavy footsteps approaching.

Marty pointed that way, then to his ears. She nodded. There was no escape route, other than back into the elevator in which they'd descended... or into a new one. *But where the hell might* they *all lead?* she wondered.

Before they could decide which way to go or what to do, a voice came from a speaker built into the wall above the elevators. It was clear and calm, surprisingly intimate. And it started to explain.

"I am The Director," it said, "and this has gone terribly wrong. I know you can hear me. I want you to listen."

Marty pressed his finger to his lips, shaking his head slowly. *Don't speak, don't answer*. Maybe this was just another trick. But the voice was soothing in a strange way, and if it could offer any reason why this had happened, there was no way she couldn't listen.

"You won't get out of this complex alive," The Director said. Dana swallowed, chilled by the calmness in her words, but the idea did not surprise her. She'd been thinking it herself. "What I want you to understand," she continued, "is that you mustn't try. Because your deaths will avert countless others."

The heavy footsteps had ceased now, and she could hear the furtive shuffling of people approaching along the corridor. They'd be close soon. Close enough to shoot. But the voice had her pinned like a butterfly to the air, and Marty seemed the same. Their hands tightly linked, they continued to listen.

"You've seen horrible things: an army of nightmare creatures. And they are real. But they are nothing compared to... to the alternative." That was the first kink in her voice.

She's afraid, Dana thought, *and she's trying not to show it*. And that was almost as terrifying as everything else she had seen.

Marty nudged her and pointed along the corridor, where shadows shifted slowly against the wall. Someone was just around the corner.

"You've been chosen to be sacrificed for the greater good," The Director continued, voice firm and confident once again. "Look, it's an *honor.* So forgive us... and let us get on with it."

Marty handed Dana Judah's blade and hefted the gun, then headed to the empty guard station. She followed close behind. They had maybe seconds in which to act, and much as all she wanted to do was shout—*Screw you, Come and get us!*—she knew that Marty was thinking straight.

Did they really think that *asking* them to lay down and die would make them go any easier?

As Dana reached back to close the door behind her, there was a shattering burst of machine-gun fire. Bullets struck the door and pushed it closed, and when the handle clicked up she turned the latch, locking it.

Screaming, shouting, she fell back against Marty, and they huddled together behind the metal door. The top half was glass, but it must have been of the same toughened construction as was used in the elevators. Bullets ricocheted off of it, leaving little more than tiny white impact stars where they struck.

"They're fucking shooting at us!" Marty shouted. Dana couldn't think of any suitable response, so she raised her middle finger at the door.

Fuck them.

Marty lifted himself a little, looked through the glass and ducked back down again. A fresh salvo of bullets thudded into the door, the sound horrendous, and he had to cup his hands around her ear to make himself heard.

"Five of them, big guns, mean—"

The shooting stopped suddenly, and he screamed his next word into the shocking silence.

"—motherfuckers!"

"Right on," Dana said. She glanced around the guard room, wondering whether there was anything they could use to help themselves, or if there was another way out. And then she saw the control panel at the back.

It quite obviously controlled all of the eight elevators outside. There were eight monitors, and beneath each were at least three dozen switches. The images switched every three seconds, and each one showed a monster in its elevator pod. A couple she had seen before, but most of those she saw were new.

"Sweet Jesus, how many are there?" she muttered. And the evidence here suggested that their numbers were almost beyond comprehension. Beside the buttons were dials, and above and below them small banks of switches.

At the far end of the panel was a small red button on its own. A wire grille covered it, presumably to prevent it being pushed accidentally by someone settling down a mug of coffee or a book. And the single, etched word above it read, "Purge."

Dana nudged Marty, but he'd already seen. He was pale beneath the blood that smeared much of his face, and his eyes had grown more serious than she'd ever seen. *He needs a joint*, she thought. She experienced a sharp, intense pang for the brief time she and her four friends had spent together happy. It hadn't lasted nearly long enough.

"An army of nightmares, huh?" she said. She stood and moved to the console, her appearance above the door's metal lower half prompting a renewed round of shooting. She watched the guards for a couple of seconds through the scarred glass, wondered how long it would last before shattering, and then raised her middle finger at them.

This time, they saw.

"Let's get this party started," she said. She plucked away the wire guard, hovered her hand over the Purge button and glanced at Marty. He said nothing. She hit the button.

From outside the shooting ceased, and they heard the gentle hum of elevator doors opening.

Dana darted to the window and Marty crouched beside her. The five guards were no longer looking or aiming their way. Instead, they were crouched in the lobby pointing their guns toward the elevators and whatever might emerge from them.

She moved to the viewing panel, and waved to Marty to join her. There was a pause during which she had time to see the hundreds of spent bullets and casings scattered across the floor, and to think, *They really make this glass to last*.

And then she saw movement at one of the elevator openings.

A blue tentacle probed out, a hundred tiny toothed mouths opening and closing along its length, and the guards opened fire.

In a flash the elevators disgorged their inhabitants. A werewolf, a strange alien creature with a dozen sharpened limbs, mutants, a robot with flaming hands, and others that moved too quickly for her to see... they streamed through the hail of bullets and struck the guards, taking them apart in sprays of blood and flesh, burning them, melting them with acid jetting from mouths or other body parts. In seconds the lobby became a bloody mess, and the bullet scars on their viewing window were splashed with blood and scraps of meat.

"Holy shit," Marty said, ducking down and pulling Dana with him. She tugged back, wanting to see—sick fascination, wonder, perhaps a need to feed her nightmares—but relented soon enough. Moments later they heard limbs slapping and scrabbling across metal, and then silence fell.

"Do you think…?" she whispered. Marty shrugged, so Dana rose again until she could just peer over the top of the sill. She was just in time to hear the elevators ping again in unison and seen the doors slip open. The things that came out this time were slower, more lumbering than the first wave, and they soon settled down to a warm meal.

Sitting back down beside Marty, she closed her eyes and concentrated to hold down the vomit.

"Dana?" he whispered.

"Zombies. And other things. Eating what's left."

"Well, at least they clean up after themselves."

"What are we gonna do?"

"Get out of here," he said, leaning close to her. "Somehow. Sometime. But not while those elevators are opening every few seconds to let out..."

"So let's sit and wait for a while," she said. "Maybe they won't know we're here."

"Maybe."

They held hands and waited in silence, listening to the sounds of growling and grumbling, and things being dragged across the floor. Occasionally the growls rose into angry shrieks as whatever was out there fought over a tasty morsel, but mostly the feast was performed in silence. Dana supposed there was plenty enough for all of them.

At regular intervals the elevator doors opened and disgorged something else into the complex. They heard footsteps, the hard clack of claws, slimy sliding things, the flutter of leathery wings, and the ghostly howl of creatures that should never be.

Perhaps ten minutes after the first guards met their ends, they heard the pounding of footsteps and a scream of terror as several more arrived. Dana closed her eyes and tried not to hear, but the elevators pinged, the doors hummed open, and it all started again.

Wet things struck the door.

People screamed.

Dana and Marty hugged, thinking perhaps it would never end, and they'd die in here of starvation and terror as the elevators pinged, and things continued to stalk from the nightmares where they should have remained.

◇ ◇ ◇

"There's still a chance," Hadley said. "Really. Still a chance. Maybe we'll get lucky and..."

But he trailed off, and Sitterson heard his own hopelessness echoed in his friend's voice. As they worked feverishly at their control panels—trying to contact people beyond their reach, searching for reasons why this was happening—images flickered at random across the viewing screens.

And the images they saw were of chaos and death. Sitterson had just seen a lab worker with whom he'd sometimes enjoyed drinking taken down by a mutant, thrashing as the stick-thin red thing held his arms and vomited onto his face and head. After an instant of motionless shock the man had started writhing and kicking as wisps of smoke rose from his eyes, mouth, and nose, and his head began to melt.

The mutant had sat back for a while, and then it commenced feeding.

Another camera in a corridor deeper in the complex showed a group of workers—lab technicians and administrative staff—fleeing in panic, moments before a horde of flying, scuttling, running monsters came after them. Sitterson tapped keys to track their progress from corridor to hallway to balcony, before the monsters fell on them at last. He watched only until he was certain that none would escape, and then he moved away to give them privacy in their deaths.

A lab worker was knocked from a high balcony in the rotunda, plummeting to his death. Sitterson switched cameras…

A female guard ran screaming from a strange, floating witch-like woman, her long gray hair trailing behind her like exhaust fumes, her spindly fingers catching the woman's hair and tripping her back. The guard shot a whole magazine into the witch's face with no effect. The witch grabbed her head and lifted her from the ground, opening an unnaturally wide mouth that closed around the woman's face and sucked the life from her.

As the woman visibly deflated in her black uniform, the witch's hair darkened from silvery-gray to dark gray, strands thickening and becoming more lustrous. She cast the shriveled corpse aside and floated away in her search for more.

Sitterson flipped through image after image, skipping past various levels and rooms, hallways and lobbies throughout the complex. One stairwell camera showed a long, steady line of zombies descending the flights, and he tapped a few keys to see where they were going. He wished he hadn't. A group of people had taken refuge at the base of the stairwell, barricading the doors against the horrors from outside but not considering the fact that they could descend, as well.

The zombies marched down to feed, and the people died badly.

A vampire resembling the classic Nosferatu ripped the throat from a screaming woman, splashing the security camera lens with blood.

"Kevin," said Hadley.

"Where?"

"Corridor three-B."

"Who's Kevin?" Truman said from by the door, but

they ignored him. If he watched, he'd see soon enough.

Sitterson brought it up onto one of the big screens.

Kevin.

He remembered seeing this man before, knew what he could do, but even so he was briefly taken in by his appearance—quite, calm, normal-looking, he walked amongst the chaos seemingly unperturbed by the terrible things he saw. All around him people were being killed, eaten, torn apart, melted, shriveled, exploded, digested or crushed, and his gentle smile never seemed to change.

But then an injured guard caught his attention. He stopped, knelt by the man's side, and exsanguinated the man in a matter of seconds.

"Elevator lobby," Hadley said. "Got, some unblooded coming through."

"Unblooded?" Truman asked.

"Things that haven't been used yet," Sitterson explained. "They'll be even more bloodthirsty than the rest." Hadley had brought up a view of the elevator lobby, where the walls were painted red and piles of body parts were scattered across the floor. There were still zombies chewing on bones and rifling through heaps of intestines.

The elevators opened and a man with spinning saws in his head emerged. From another open door, a woman with fire smoldering in her mouth and dripping from her nose. And more, and more, and Sitterson couldn't understand how any of this was happening.

There were *safeguards*.

Truman started talking into his intercom, his voice quivering in panic. He'd drawn and checked his sidearm, and Sitterson almost laughed at that.

Hasn't he even been watching?

"Lead Officer Truman to Sec Command, requesting immediate reinforcement. Code Black. Repeat: Code Black. Where the hell are you guys?"

"Why aren't the defenses working?" Sitterson said, working his control panel. "Where's the fucking gas?"

"I think something chewed through the connections, in the utility shaft," Hadley said.

"Something which?"

"Something *scary*!"

The light flickered and went out. The screens went dead. Sitterson heard a faint cry from Lin down in the control area, and then footsteps as she made her way up to them.

Something hit the door hard enough to buckle its three-inch metal lining.

It's all going to hell, he thought.

◇ ◇ ◇

"We can't just stay here and—" Dana whispered, and then something smashed through the window behind them and stuck against the wall above the control panel. Glass showered over her head and shoulders. She let out a startled cry and jumped up, Marty by her side.

The thing unfurled its leathery wings and turned its

head around on a long neck to look their way. A huge bat, with an almost childlike face... a small dragon, with smoke curling from one nostril… she guessed it really didn't matter which.

The dragonbat growled fire.

"Shit!" Dana hissed. She flicked the lock's latch and opened the door, backing away from danger even knowing that there might be worse behind her. Marty came with her, gun raised and pointing at the dragonbat thing, and she wondered if he'd even ever fired a pistol.

They slid along the wall away from the guard's station and scanned the scene around them. The noises were clearer now that they were out of the booth—growling, chewing, wet crunches as skulls were cracked, sucking, drooling, and dripping. The guards were dead and the monsters were eating.

One thing looked their way—it had four eyes and a mouth like something from beneath the sea—and Dana froze. But it dipped its head back to emptying a guard's holed skull of brain matter and fluid.

Dana hadn't dared draw a breath since leaving the guard's booth. And she might have remained frozen there, dinner-in-waiting, if Marty hadn't grabbed her hand and dragged her toward the corridor that led from the lobby. Things shifted and ate, and just as she thought, *Why aren't they interested in us?* a huge, boil-covered monstrosity stood before them and roared.

Boils burst across its body and misted the air, and Marty shot it once in the eye.

It staggered back against the wall and slid down, dead.

Dana caught her breath now and ran, Marty by her side. She heard his own heavy breathing, and tried to ignore all the terrible, impossible things around them. They stepped over a body with its guts and organs removed, almost slipped in something wet and warm, and then they were in the corridor leading away from the lobby. Bullet holes pocked the walls here and the entire hallway was a mess of blood and dead bodies. A guard sat against the wall, his eyes wide open and no apparent injury on his body. But Dana has never seen anyone more dead.

As they reached the turn in the corridor Marty said, "When we get around we run as fast—" But he was cut off by a terrible, piercing screech.

Dana couldn't help looking back, and she saw the dragonbat winging at them from the guard's station, fire gushing from its mouth and clawed wings ripping at the air.

They took the corner at speed, running straight into a man in a long white lab smock and with a terrible cut to his scalp. He glared at them but didn't seem to see, and as he pushed past them the dragonbat struck him in the chest.

The impact was immense. It powered him against the opposite wall, cracking plaster and splintering wooden studs, casting them both through to the space hidden beyond. The fracture was illuminated by a burst of flame, and the man's screams quickly boiled away.

The dragonbat rocketed from the hole again, meat and stringy stuff hanging from its mouth. Marty leaned across Dana to protect her and raised the gun, but the creature ricocheted from the walls and disappeared down the corridor, leaving scorch-marks wherever it touched.

They stood, and Dana couldn't help herself; she took three steps to the hole in the wall and looked inside.

The man lay dead beyond the fracture, a cauterized hole in his stomach where his guts had once resided, hands curled in like dead spiders. His mouth was open in a silent scream, and smoke drifted up past his shattered teeth. But it was something else that caught Dana's attention.

"Now what the hell is this...?" she muttered.

The corridor beyond was hacked through solid rock, vague tool-marks visible in the walls as if it had been carved long before machines had been available. The floor was uneven and home to dark puddles, and the curved ceiling was fissured and shadowy. Age seeped from the walls and hung in the air, and she felt as if she were breathing lost times.

"Whatever it is, I think it's our only way," Marty said. "Look." From the direction of the elevator lobby, several lurching creatures were coming their way, all teeth and claws. And from the corridor, a flowing fireball burnt its way toward them. Walls warped and cracked beneath its heat, and already Dana could feel the skin on her face stretching in anticipation of its touch.

Without hesitation she grabbed Marty's hand and stepped through the hole, pulling him after her.

◇ ◇ ◇

Something was hammering at the door, and Sitterson knew it would soon be inside. Hinges squealed. Metal bent.

Emergency power flicked on, and the lighting was low-level, most of the power being fed into life support. *Ha!* That phrase had flashed across Sitterson's main computer screen and he'd choked on laughter. *Life support!*

Truman stood his ground, gun in one hand and his microphone in the other, and Sitterson had to admire the guy's persistence as he tried to call in reinforcements. *Didn't he see the fucking screens?* he thought. But in a way he was jealous of Truman's defense mechanism. Holding onto routine, and order, and procedure... they were insulating him against the terrible truth. That things had fallen apart, and their true descent had only just begun.

The three large screens flashed to life again, and carnage appeared intermittently across them, images changing every few seconds and virtually all of them displaying something ghastly...

A clown skipped and leapt toward a barricade behind which several guards hunkered down, firing again and again into the advancing thing. Bullet after bullet struck it, but its baggy clown's trousers and tentlike shirt seemed to absorb the projectiles. When a few rounds took it in the face its head flipped back, but then its make-up seemed to flow as the holes disappeared and its gleeful, horrendous grin reappeared. It carried a large curved blade in one hand, but the image flashed away before Sitterson saw the blade put to use.

"The door's going to give!" Truman said.

"Go get me a coffee!" Hadley called, his laughter high and desperate.

A unicorn gored a scientist against a wall, its horn probing through his stomach and chest, grinding, tearing, and his spurting blood painted its gorgeous flowing mane red.

"We're fucked," Lin said. There was a time not too long ago when Sitterson had intended doing just that to her, yes. He considered going to her and holding her now, but that would have seemed just foolish.

A werewolf fell on a woman, dragging her down beneath a camera's eye and standing again with blood and flesh across its face and the woman's tattered scalp in one giant paw.

"Top hinge has gone," Truman said.

"How many magazines you got?" Sitterson asked.

"The regulation three."

Of course. The regulation three. Not like Truman to hide a few more around his person, was it? A grenade, perhaps? A secret nuke?

A group of goblins drove one of the complex's golf carts along a narrow corridor, running people down and reversing over them, aiming for their heads, bursting them, then stirring their extended fingers in the resultant mess before driving on, cackling gleefully and giving the camera the slimy finger.

"Hey!" Hadley said, pointing at the main screen. Anna Patience Buckner emerged from an elevator into the bloodstained lobby.

"Well, why should she miss out on the party?" Sitterson muttered. The mystery of how she'd found her way down from the surface really did not matter now.

The door bent inward, and smoke started pouring into Control.

"Time to go," Sitterson said quietly. He nudged Lin and pointed at the carpet beneath his desk, which he pulled up to reveal a code-locked trapdoor.

"But—" she said, nodding at Truman.

"He'll buy us time," Sitterson said. Hadley joined them, a submachine gun nursed in the crook of his arm.

"Where did you—?" Lin began.

"Personal life insurance." His voice was high-pitched and uncertain.

"Just make sure I have time to open this fucking thing," Sitterson said. "Oh look, the scarecrows are here."

Truman was firing into the face of a straw man who was climbing through a wrenched gap between door and frame. The bullets passed through the scarecrow's head without any effect, and he lashed out with long bladed fingers, catching the soldier across the forearm. Truman cursed and stepped back, firing again at the creature's chest. More climbed in after him, four in all, and as the soldier changed magazines one of them bit into his left bicep.

He screeched and tore his arm away, losing a good weight of muscles and flesh in the process.

Hadley let rip with the machine gun. A scarecrow danced and jittered as the bullets ripped through him, writhing like a marionette… then laughed and advanced on the shooter.

"Our monsters have a fucking sense of humor?" he shouted. "Since when? I didn't know about this!" He fired some more, concentrating on the scarecrow's legs and amputating one at the thigh. It fell over and started to crawl.

"I need ten more seconds!" Sitterson said.

"Running out of time!" Hadley snapped back.

"It's on emergency lockdown! I'm bypassing..."

"Come on, come on!" Lin said, pressing herself against his side, breasts squashed against his arm. He glanced at her and saw that her hair band had come loose, hair spilling over her right shoulder.

"Jesus Christ," he said, "you're *gorgeous*!"

"Oh," Hadley said from somewhere behind him. "Right. Grenade."

Sitterson glanced back at the melee by the broken main door. Truman had dropped his gun and was batting at the scarecrows as they sliced and bit him, and in his right hand he held a small black object. He bit away the pin and held it up.

"Son of a bitch," Sitterson mumbled, "that's against regulations."

The grenade exploded.

He sprawled across the trapdoor, Lin spilling from his back and crying out as she struck the console.

Burning straw started to drift down around them and Lin looked past him at his desk.

"Hadley!" she shouted.

"What?" Sitterson snapped.

"Blast... blew him over..." She stood, shaking her head as blood leaked from her left ear. Burning straw landed in her hair and she waved it absently away.

Sitterson stood and leaned over his ruined console, resting his hand in something that had once been part of Truman. Down in the main control area, smoke drifted as the main door fell open, and Hadley was crawling slowly for the stairs back up to Control.

But something followed him. Something dark, swimming through the smoke as if passing through water, a fin breaking the surface, black hair visible here and there, black eyes, its wet black mouth opening wide, and Sitterson knew what was to come. If it hadn't been so ridiculous he might even have laughed.

The merman closed on Hadley and turned him over, placing a huge webbed hand around his throat.

"Oh, come *on*!" Hadley said, and the creature bit off his face.

Hadley's gone, Sitterson thought, falling to his knees and turning back to the trapdoor. "Steve's *gone*."

"So will we be if—" Lin said, and then the trapdoor gave an electronic buzz and its red-lit panel showed green.

"Got it!" he swung the heavy trapdoor open and turned to Lin with a grin, about to say, *Ladies first*.

A tentacle appeared from the gloom and wrapped around her throat, constricting so quickly and powerfully that her tongue protruded, eyes bulged, and she spat blood as she was whipped back out of view. Sitterson fell sideways into the hole, hands around his head to lessen the impact.

He landed in a small chamber and stood quickly, reaching up to close the trapdoor, expecting something to fall on him at any moment and go about destroying him. *We were so close*, he thought, and he actually felt tears welling as he swung the trapdoor shut and locked it from within.

Maybe he was the last one left. Control was gone, the whole complex was infested, but the Virgin and the Fool might yet be alive.

"I can stop all this," he whispered. The chance was minimal but it was still there. And he had nothing left to do.

To his right, a ladder led through a hole in the floor. It would take him down into the deep corridors, into places he had been watching on the screens as they crawled with monsters and impossibilities. But he had no alternative. He had to find the Fool and kill him, before he himself was killed.

He lifted the pendant from within his shirt and kissed it. Perhaps they would view this as their greatest entertainment, and he would be lauded. But he shook his head as such foolishness. Nothing about *him* mattered. Whatever the outcome, things had changed beyond redemption. Even if he did manage to reverse the situation, there would be a whole new set of rules and demands after this.

He began his descent, sliding down four long, staggered ladders before landing in a tunnel. To his left it disappeared into the gloom, and somewhere down there he saw shadows flexing and heard things feeding. So he took off his shoes and turned right, padding softly to a corner and sweeping quickly around, thinking what he would do when he saw—

The Virgin. He ran right into her, and she set a fire in his stomach. He looked down at her hands. They were wrapped around the hilt of Judah's blade.

"I..." she said. "I'm sorry..."

Behind her, the Fool stood aghast. They were both covered in blood, their own and others, and the boy was badly wounded. Sitterson couldn't help feeling some measure of respect for their bravery.

But this had never been about bravery.

"Please... kill him..." he said to the girl, nodding at Marty as he felt his knees giving way. "*Please!*" The pain possessed him, stealing his sight and smell and leaving him only with hearing as the darkness came for him. He fell, the blade still protruding from his stomach.

Could have been worse, he thought. The kids' panicked breathing faded away, even though he was sure they still stood over him.

Yeah... I could have died a whole lot worse.

TWELVE

He grabbed the pendant around his neck before he died.

Dana bent to the dead man and turned his hand so she could see it. A weird, five-pronged thing, it stirred something in her that she couldn't quite understand.

"Come on!" Marty said.

Dana looked down at the knife still in the guy's stomach. She'd done that. However accidental, it was her hands on the knife when it had gone in. She closed her eyes but felt no shame.

I should, she thought. *I should feel—*

"Hey! We have to find a way out before everything else finds a way in." Marty touched her arm but she couldn't take her eyes from the dead man's face. He looked almost relieved.

Dead puppeteer, she thought.

"Dana!"

She looked up at him and nodded, and they started

again along the tunnel. They passed a ladder that led up, but there were sounds coming from there that they had no wish to put a name to. Further along the tunnel lay the remains of a dead woman. Parts of her had been eaten and then apparently regurgitated, and in the six globs of chewed material small shapes squirmed, busy gathering bloody flesh to their infantile mouths.

The route curved down and to the left, sometimes with rough steps carved into the floor. Other times they had to hold each other to prevent themselves from slipping on the slick, smooth rock. They were far from the metal-lined corridors now, but there was still a string of bare bulbs dangling from the rough stone ceiling.

We're going deeper, that's all, Dana thought, and she felt the weight of the world around her. There was no sense that they were escaping the complex they had entered, only that it was changing. They no longer heard the sounds of monsters running and people dying, but in some ways what replaced that was worse.

The air around them was a held breath.

The ground shook again, a single violent shrug. Dana slipped and fell on her side, bringing Marty down with her. He landed on his back and cried out, and she noticed just how much he was still bleeding. He looked pale.

"None of us deserved this," she said, and Marty only shrugged.

"Only the good die young."

"Are you good Marty?"

"Yeah," he said, frowning slightly, then nodding

firmer. "Yeah, I think so. And so are you."

"You don't know me."

"I know you well enough." His face softened, and she could almost have loved him then. "Come on," he said. "Let's see what we can find."

They went deeper, and at the end of the rocky tunnel was a heavy wooden door.

We don't want to go through there, Dana thought, but Marty started trying to turn the handle. It moved a little both ways, but he groaned as his wounds pained him.

"Here," he said, handing her the gun. She took it. It was warm from his grip. She hated guns and had never held one before, but she remembered the mutant he'd shot, and knew that they'd be dead without it.

"Let me," she said, but Marty grunted with effort.

"Nah. Got it." The handle slipped and something in the door rumbled and clicked, and Marty tugged it open.

A breath of air washed out over them, warm and damp and stinking of something she could not identify. *Something living*, she thought, but that wasn't quite right. It had the scent of potential; of something not quite living, whether that meant newly dead or yet to be born. She shook her head. Weird thoughts.

And Marty took her hand and led her inside.

They passed through another tunnel and descended a dozen deep steps, emerging into a stone chamber thirty feet across and seemingly without a ceiling.

Darkness hung heavy above them, and the chamber was lit by five large flaming torches fixed equidistant around the walls.

Dana gasped.

"This is somewhere we should never see," she whispered.

"Yeah," Marty said. "I feel the same. But check the freaky stonework." Below each torch was a large stone slab, free-standing, maybe twelve feet square and inlaid with intricate carvings. The etchings of four slabs glittered with reflected light, and Dana identified at least part of the scent that troubled her: blood. They paused in the center of the chamber and she turned a full circle, and as she saw each carved stone a sickening dread settled deeper over her.

"Oh, and..." Marty said, nodding down. "Look familiar?"

It did. Inlaid into the floor in different colored stone was a representation of the five-armed pendant. The guy she'd stabbed had made an effort to grab that before he died, and she'd seen the tension on his face as he willed himself to remain alive long enough to hold it in his hand. It had eased him into death, that pendant, and now they were standing at the place on the floor where the five arms merged.

Each arm pointed at one carved slab, and each slab was lit by a burning torch. But Dana knew that this chamber was more than just a place for display.

It was much more important than that.

"Oh, suddenly I feel a bit seasick," Marty said,

glancing over his shoulder. "Look, back where we came in."

At the bottom of the stone staircase they'd crossed a small bridge that spanned a space maybe four feet across, and that space circled the rest of the chamber. Even behind the upright slabs there seemed to be no connection between the floor and the walls.

"I'm liking this less and less," Dana said, edging over and peering down into the void. The flaming torches lit the rough rock wall a little way down, but beyond that was deep, heavy darkness. It looked solid, almost as if she could fall in and it would ease her fall, holding her suspended like a cartoon cloud in a kid's imagination.

She closed her eyes, swayed, and stumbled a few steps back.

"Deep?" Marty asked.

"Can't see the bottom," she said. "But there seemed to be something..."

"Don't tell me," he said.

"Something *moving* down there."

"Okay. That's it. I officially want to cut this vacation short."

"I don't think we ever could have, even if we'd wanted to." She turned a slow circle again.

"No way out," Marty said.

"Look at these. Five of them."

"Weird. What are they?"

"Us," Dana said. "I should've seen it like you did. All of this: the old guy at the gas station, the out-of-control behavior, the monsters... this is part of a ritual."

"A ritual sacrifice? Great! You tie someone to a stone, get a fancy dagger and a bunch a robes. It's not that complicated!"

"No, it's simple. They don't just wanna see us killed. They want to see us *punished*."

"Punished for what?" Marty asked, and then there was movement on the stairs. Dana gasped and raised the gun, wondering what monstrosity they'd see coming through… demon or zombie, alien or mutant.

"For being young?" the woman said. She was tall and elegant, calm and reserved. She might have been beautiful, but Dana sensed a pressure of responsibility on her shoulders that seemed to crush her sense of self. She was like a mannequin given life, her beauty a suggestion rather than something she carried well.

"Who're you?" Marty asked.

"The Director," Dana said, answering for her. "It's you we heard over the speakers."

The Director nodded affirmation, then continued. "It's different for every culture. And it changes over the years, but it's very specific. There must be at least five."

She pointed to one of the slabs, the blood-filled carving showing a woman standing erect, holding open her robe to reveal her nakedness. "The Whore."

"That word..." Dana muttered, remembering the way the spooky gas station guy had muttered it when he looked at Jules.

"She is corrupted, and she dies first." She pointed to the other slabs one by one, naming them. "The Athlete. The Scholar. The Fool. All suffer and die, at the hands of the horror they have raised. Leaving the last, to live or die as fate decides." She pointed at the last slab, and this one looked different, the etching there not so defined.

Unmarked by blood, Dana realized.

"The Virgin."

"Me?" Dana snorted. "Virgin?"

"Dude, she's a home-wrecker!" Marty said.

"We work with what we have," the Director said, shrugging. "It's symbolism that's important, never truth."

"What happens if you don't pull it off?" Marty asked. He'd twigged it, but Dana knew that he'd had more of an idea than any of them. His humor was his own defense mechanism, the same as Jules used her overt sexuality, and Curt hid behind his machismo. Or used to.

"They awaken," the Director whispered. And she looked utterly, insanely terrified.

"Who does? What's beneath us?"

"The gods. The sleeping gods, giants that live in the earth, that used to rule it. They fought for a billion years and now they sleep. In every country, for every culture, there is a god to appease. As long as one sleeps, they all do. But the other rituals have all failed." She shook her head, frowning. "All at once, all the failure... never like this before."

There was another huge rumble. The floor bucked beneath them, and two of the huge slabs seemed to rock on their foundations. Dust filled the air, grit pattered down from the shadows above them. Dana wondered how high the ceiling was, then doubted there was a ceiling at all.

"The sun will rise in eight minutes," the Director said, her voice firm once more. She turned to Marty, the Fool. "If you live to see it, the world will end."

"Right," he said. "That's harsh."

"Marty—" Dana said.

"But maybe that's the way it ought to be," he said. "Maybe it's time for a change."

"We're not talking about *change*," the Director spat. "We're talking about the agonizing death of every human soul on the planet. Including you. You can die with them, or you can die *for* them."

"Gosh, they're both so enticing..." he said, rubbing his chin, and it took a moment for him to notice what Dana had done.

Maybe this is all one final trick on their part, Dana thought. *But can I really take that chance?*

She aimed the gun at Marty's face and squeezed her finger against the trigger.

◇ ◇ ◇

"Wow," Marty said. Those guards had been blasting at him for all they were worth, but this was so much worse. This was *Dana* aiming a gun at him. He stared at its tiny black mouth and wondered if he'd see movement there before his eyes were ruptured, skull shattered and brain spread to the darkness. He looked past the gun to her face, disturbed to see how determined she appeared.

"Marty," she said, "the *whole world*."

"Is in your hands," The Director said to her. Right then Marty wanted to strangle the tall, pompous, self-righteous bitch.

Dana glanced at The Director, shaken, and Marty saw the weight of the world crushing down on her slender shoulders. She sure was foxy; he'd always thought so. And though he was sure she knew what he thought, he'd just never had the balls to tell her. Look at her, after all—gorgeous.

And he *was* the Fool.

"There is no other way," The Director said to the girl. "You have to be strong."

And then Marty caught movement from the corner of his eye. A shadow, crossing the small bridge onto the strangely carved platform, barely seen, but it resolved into something solid when the scent hit his nose. *Wet dog*, he thought, and from the smell it must have been wet with blood.

"Yeah, Dana," Marty said. "You feeling strong?"

"I'm sorry."

"So am I," he said softly.

As she leveled the gun again and her face tensed with concentration, the werewolf leapt at her. The gun went spinning and the creature crushed Dana to the floor, claws slashing, teeth snapping at her face as she ducked her head left and right.

Dana kicked and bucked, and the creature shifted its weight and balance to remain pinning her to the ground.

Fighting to the last, Marty thought, then he saw The Director going for the gun.

He jumped, sliding across the stone floor toward the dropped weapon.

Dana screamed, the werewolf howled. Good. If she was screaming, it meant she was still alive.

As his fingers brushed the gun's grip, The Director landed on his back, jarring his chin against the floor and sending spikes of pain up through his jaw and into his brain. He tasted blood and the grit of a broken tooth.

The woman clawed at his back, trying to pull herself over him to the gun, but Marty punched up and back over his shoulder. His fist hit her jaw and he heard a gentle crack. She moaned. But she never stopped pulling and kicking, and in seconds she'd be at the gun that lay just beyond his reach.

One chance, he thought. *The Fool has to fool her*. He went completely limp, resting his face against the cold stone and letting out a deep breath. The Director paused in surprise… and Marty pushed up with all his might, spilling her from his back and flipping over so that he landed atop her. Her head thunked against the stone and breath puffed from her, and he stood and fell onto the gun.

He turned and knelt, aiming at the flailing mess, knowing that if he took too long to aim it might mean the difference between Dana living or dying. He fired three shots and the werewolf reared up on its hid legs, its chest red with blood. It turned to him and he fired again, hitting it in the face. It screeched and ran from the chamber, a howl retreating into the tunnel beyond.

Dana rolled over, eyes wide and white in the bloody mask of her face. She held her hands up, as if afraid to touch any part of herself, and her breath came in rapid, short gasps.

"Dana..." Marty breathed, and The Director tackled him from behind. He flipped up and back, the gun flying from his hand, and he struck the floor hard enough to wind him. He was aware of a terrible space, and depths that he hated to imagine, and as blood dripped from his face into the abyss he was sure he heard an excited intake of breath.

Movement in the chamber again…

The Director fell on him, fists pummeling at his face, long nails raking his skin. He punched back and raised one knee, trying to shove her aside. Then she was going for the gun again.

More movement... the rustle of clothing... but he couldn't look...

He heaved her up and to the side, turning with her and using the momentum to sit astride her, his arm pressing down hard on her throat. Her eyes swelled and her tongue protruded, and she tried shaking her head. *She's pleading!* he thought. And for just a second he considered everything this woman had said, and what Dana had been prepared to do.

Footsteps... slow, methodical, soft...

He eased back slightly.

"Marty!" Dana said.

He turned to look at his dying friend, but instead he saw Anne Patience Buckner standing right behind him. Her little girl's rotting face held no emotion, and as she swung the hatchet instinct took over. He fell to the side and brought The Director up on top of him again, and the hatchet struck the back of her skull.

Bone broke. Metal scraped. Her eyes went wide, mouth hanging open, and a line of blood ran across her lowered face.

The ground shook again, thudding as if echoing with the memories of huge impacts far below. Anna Patience was trying to tug the hatchet from The Director's head, making the woman seem to nod up and down as if in response to some internal dialogue.

Marty heaved backward and kicked The Director out over the gap. The zombie girl, unwilling to let go of her precious hatchet, went with her, and Marty rolled onto his stomach to watch them fall. The torchlight lit them for a couple of seconds as they spun together, bouncing from the rough wall and falling quickly, soundlessly into the darkness.

He watched for a moment more, listening for the sound of them hitting bottom. But nothing came. Perhaps the noise was swallowed by the receding grumble of the latest tremor. Or maybe they were still falling.

Then he stood unsteadily and limped over to where Dana lay bleeding. He sat by her side, brushing bloody tears from her cheek. She smiled. Her chest and stomach had been shredded by the werewolf, and there was a bite mark on her throat that must have been one move away from ripping it open. But she was still alert, and she grabbed onto his hand.

"Hey," he said.

"You know… I don't think… Curt even has a cousin."

"Huh. How are you?"

"Going away…" she said softly, but her grip never lessened.

"I'm sorry."

"I'm so sorry I almost shot you… I probably wouldn't have…"

"Hey," he whispered, "shh, no… I totally get it." With one hand he felt around in his shirt pocket and brought out three ready-rolled joints. He chose the least damaged one and put it in his mouth. Then he found a book of matches from another pocket and lit one, inhaling. It had never tasted so sweet. Perhaps if he smoked enough if would make all this go away. But somehow he doubted that.

"I'm sorry I let you get attacked by a werewolf and then ended the world," he said. He took another long smoke and held the joint out to Dana. She took it with a shaking, blood-spattered hand.

"Nahh, you were right," she said. "Humanity…?" She blew out the smoke in a cynical puff, waving the joint at the air in a single dismissal of all they had known. "It's time to give someone else a chance."

"Giant evil gods."

"Wish I coulda seen 'em." And she actually managed a smile, even as the light in her eyes—the sparkling light, the joy of life that for Marty had set her above all the rest—started to fade.

"I know!" he said, trying to hold back his tears. The last thing he wanted her to see was him crying. "*That* would be a fun weekend." He took the joint before she dropped it and lay down beside her.

The chamber shook, the stone slabs cracked, dust filled the air from above, and then something else crashed down and exploded across the slab: a battered suitcase, its innards consisting of old 8 mm film reels. They rolled in ever-decreasing circles and then came to a stop.

"Oh," Marty said.

And something was rising. Thumps came from far below, distant at first, and then closer and closer, and to Marty they sounded for all the world like something climbing the walls of that bottomless hole.

Taking another drag on his joint he turned away from Dana, because he didn't want to see her die.

They still held onto each other, and always would. They waited for the end.

◇ ◇ ◇

No human eye bore witness to the cabin exploding apart, nor the giant, gnarled hand that emerged from its splintered heart, nor the arm that powered it a hundred feet into the air, fingers flexing and scratching at the night.

But that would change soon enough.

ABOUT THE AUTHOR

TIM LEBBON is a *New York Times* bestselling writer from South Wales. He's had over twenty novels published to date, as well as dozens of novellas and hundreds of short stories. Recent books include *The Secret Journeys of Jack London: The Wild* (co-authored with Christopher Golden), *Echo City*, *The Island*, *The Map of Moments* (with Christopher Golden), and *Bar None*. He has won four British Fantasy Awards, a Bram Stoker Award, and a Scribe Award, and has been a finalist for International Horror Guild, Shirley Jackson, and World Fantasy Awards. Fox 2000 recently acquired film rights to *The Secret Journeys of Jack London*, and Tim and Christopher Golden have delivered the screenplay. Several more of his novels and novellas are currently in development, and he is also working on TV and movie proposals, solo and in collaboration. Find out more about Tim at his website: www.timlebbon.net